Even before Adino turned to walk away, his eyes told me what was happening: he was leaving, for good. I followed him, my heart pounding, thinking he would turn around and come back any minute. But he didn't. And when I realized it was for real—that he was, indeed, leaving me—I ran down the driveway after him.

"No! No!"

He kept going, walking farther and farther away from me. I sank to the ground, unbelieving. Adino was leaving. And everything I'd hoped for and wanted was leaving with him. I had driven away the truest love I'd ever known.

I looked to the sky and cried silently to God. *Help me. . . .* When I lowered my eyes to look after Adino, I caught my breath.

He had stopped. He stood still, watching me. I looked up into his face. . . . And I began to hope that there might be a tiny fragment of love remaining between us that could be salvaged.

Above all else, I knew now that this was what I wanted.

CHILDREN of DARKNESS

A TRUE STORY BY

RUTH GORDON

LIVING BOOKS
Tyndale House Publishers, Inc.
Wheaton, Illinois

Bible verses are quoted from *The Holy Bible,* New
International Version, copyright 1978 by New
York International Bible Society, unless otherwise
noted.

First printing, April 1988

Library of Congress Catalog Card Number 87-51345
ISBN 0-8423-0363-4
Copyright 1988 by Ruth Gordon
Printed in the United States of America

In loving memory of my father

Foreword

It is a universally acknowledged proverb that experience is the best teacher. Ruth Gordon is well taught because she has so much personal experience with the cult about which she writes. Having been an enthusiastic devotee of the Children of God for five years, she is eminently qualified to speak a message of truth and compassion to the church concerning this cult.

I believe her book will serve to warn Christians of the dangers and expose the alluring factors of cult groups in general and the Children of God in particular.

Most books about cults are filled with lengthy sections of theological and social analysis. They are exposés of the leading concepts in the cult belief system. What makes this book so gripping is that it is a story—a real-life chronicle of one person's spiritual pilgrimage leading up to when she was ensnared by the cult, her experiences inside the cult community, and her marvelous deliverance from the cult.

Many people become involved in cults. It is not that they are enamored with the philosophy or "world- and life-view" of the cult. Rather it is the personal and relational dynamics of the cult's appeal and the psycho-spiritual factors that make so many vulnerable to being caught up in such a movement.

This book reveals these factors masterfully. Ruth Gordon's narrative of her personal experience is powerful because it rips the cloak of deception from the cult, leaving its naked hideousness to be seen by all. It does more than inform you about cults in general or the Children of God in particular. It moves you vicariously through the experiences of being a cultist and than snatches you from the clammy clutches of hell leaving you wounded but wiser for your journey.

Enter here, pilgrim—watch and learn. Be warned and warn others.

Rev. Ronald E. Steel
Briarwood Presbyterian Church
Birmingham, Alabama

Acknowledgments

There are many to whom I am grateful for their
loving and prayerful support, especially during
the last two years in which I have struggled physically, emotionally, and spiritually while compil-
ing this manuscript. I especially want to express
my thanks to:

Missionaries to Brazil, Dr. Russ and Pat Shedd
and Rev. Bill and Mary Fawcett and their families, who nurtured and accepted us when we
were so bedraggled and lost, and who were the
first to expose us to the authentic and unadulterated truth of the Holy Scriptures;

In the U.S., Randy and Phyllis Page, Dr. Ray and
Ann Burwick, Mark and Shirley Gibberman, and
their families for their unrelenting prayers. Also,
my friends James Brown, Rev. Ron Steel, Cathy
Cook, and many many others at Briarwood
church, for their day-to-day forbearance;

My children, Isaac, Aurora, Nicky, and Jeremy,
for putting up with their mommy when she was
under stress and for relinquishing a lot of time
with her;

My husband and best friend, for undergirding
me with his quiet and steadfast strength, his ten-

derness and understanding, and his sacrificial love and commitment of purpose in serving Christ;

Tyndale House, for including me in their family. In particular, Wendell, for hearing me out, Ken, for his patience and flexibility, Scotty and Carol, for the many unseen hours they slaved over the original manuscript, and dear Karen, who made sense out of it all.

Last and most important, my thanks and praise to the Author and Finisher of my faith.

Prologue

It's just a laundromat, I keep telling myself. *It's a place to wash clothes—as normal and American and inconspicuous as anyplace you could think of. And I'm as normal, American, and inconspicuous as the people around me. I am . . . I know it.*

I look around and realize it's been almost a decade since I've been in a laundromat. I feel as though people are staring, their gazes boring holes into me. Maybe I'm wrong. Probably am.

I long for someone to talk to, but everyone is busy with their children or doing their laundry. Nobody seems to notice, or care, how desperately lonely I am.

Forget worrying, I tell myself as I start separating clothes. *No one's looking. They all seem to be keeping to themselves.* I look up and see that it's true, no one is watching me. I'll be ready, though, if someone should want to talk. As I look down at the machine under my hands, I feel displaced. How could it all have happened? For six years—almost my entire adult life—I lived under a cloak of darkness. That's what makes me different from everyone here. I'll never be able to change the fact that I was a member of a cult. *But, God, please help me understand how I can find peace.* I know there isn't anything I can do to change what has happened, but I can't help wondering if there was any way I could have known where my strange journey would take me.

The metal of the washer is warm under my hands. It seems alive. The vibrations shoot through me and I begin to feel nervous again. My eyes dart from the window to the door to the people around me, then back down to the machine. The noise of the washer mingles with the roar of the dryers in the background, crowding out my unpleasant thoughts for a short time, and I find sweet but temporary relief from anxiety.

Soon I will have to go back to the apartment and face reality. But what is reality? It's hard to tell anymore. My senses have become dulled by depression; I spend hours in front of the TV trying to help the days go by without having to think or feel. I seem to be walking on a ragged edge and I don't know how much longer I can last.

Lord, I'm so tired of crying ... so tired of being tired. Once again the questions race through my mind: How did I get myself into this awful state? What's going to happen to me and my family? How do I keep going?

Yet I must hang on a little longer, for the children's sake. After all, it's not their fault. I sigh and remember that Mark will be home soon, and that I will find comfort in his arms. Mark, my husband and my friend—the only person on earth who truly understands.

CHAPTER

One

I knew little about Haight-Ashbury, only that the songs on the radio that summer had called us there. I was fifteen then, the summer of '65, and the whole hippie scene had begun only a short time before. Still, when we arrived the streets were brimming with flower children. The beatnik era was giving way to the hippie movement, and the area by the Bay was a mecca for this new generation. There were musicians playing in the parks and on street corners, and the strains of folk anthems drifted from coffeehouses throughout the night. It was all happening there, and I saw something new and different every day. I'd watched some of these things taking place in southern California. When I had begun high school the year before, the new sights and sounds were everywhere. Jug bands and folksingers converged on the parks, in streets, and on the college campuses in town. Suddenly the tone of life was different.

The music of that era spoke of our searches and our deepest longings—of revolt against indifference and the status quo. The folk music of the movement had gained momentum—not the more traditional music of the Kingston Trio, but songs of questioning and protest by young rebels like Bob Dylan and Joan Baez. Songs such as "If You're Going to San Francisco" were a call over the airwaves for the restless to strike out, to seek answers to their frustration and confusion, and to find themselves. And for various reasons, countless thousands of young people did go forth, many making their way to California. Perhaps no other generation has been so influenced, so moved to action, by music.

I myself played the guitar and even managed to attract a few modest crowds on the library lawn in downtown Santa Barbara and at the University Student Center (UCSB). The folk songs of Donovan, Joan Baez (whom I tried to emulate), and Peter, Paul, and Mary seemed to voice the yearnings and turmoil that had grown within me throughout my youth. Because of this these songs became a channel for me to express the anguish of my adolescence.

Music had always been a part of my life. I can't remember a day of my childhood that I didn't hear my older brother playing the piano in the morning. Both of my parents encouraged my involvement in music in elementary school. This included singing in the glee club and learning to play the violin and the piano. But the day that music turned my life around was my twelfth birthday when Mom and Dad gave me a guitar and a book on how to play it in "seven easy steps." I can't remember ever enjoying a birthday gift more. I fingered the strings in ignorance and wonder.

The first piece I learned was the two-chord classic, "Molly Malone." I practiced the song until my fingers reached the chords without effort. A couple of days later Mom realized the sounds she heard coming from my room were the sounds of a guitar being played, and she asked me to perform for a group of her friends.

I remember sitting before them in the living room, nervous but excited. I began playing the song exactly as I'd practiced it, yet the sounds that came from those strings seemed altogether different when it was played in front of others. It was beautiful. As they applauded I thought, *This is great. I love it!*

"Patty, play another one!" someone requested.

"That's the only one I know," I admitted.

But it wasn't for long. That small bit of encouragement proved to be just the motivation I needed. My self-esteem was low at that young age. Though I was very thin, I had been called "Fatty Patty" for years. Soon I learned that when I performed I could get the recognition and admiration I craved. Moreover, I was able to sing about things I never would have had the courage to express any other way. Singing and playing the guitar gave me something to hold on to and gained for me an acceptance I felt I would not have had otherwise.

Like most young teenagers, I listened to rock music. But I loved the folk songs because I could play them. Occasionally I had jam sessions with friends who played guitars, recorders, and flutes. I began to discover the gift of music I had been given. While I never attained the vocal quality of my "mentors" (Joan Baez and the others), that didn't matter to me because I knew I could communicate through music. In fact, it became a bridge for me as I made the crucial passage from junior high to high school—a passage that was indeed traumatic because of the situation in my home.

My father was a melancholy person by nature. I think that was as rooted in his spirit as it was in his temperament, a result of being bombarded constantly by the frustrations that followed many of the struggles and failures in his life. My parents started their family at a great financial disadvantage. My father had to leave my mother and my oldest brother in Brooklyn, New York, when he came to Santa Barbara to work in a shipyard. After a short time he was promised a partnership in another business, so he moved his young family to the West Coast. But the partnership fell through for some reason, and he struggled constantly with finances after that—a struggle that only worsened with the addition of my other brothers and myself to the family.

Because of these financial pressures our home life was often stressful during my younger years.

Also, for as long as I can remember, there had always been tension between my mother and me. I was closer to my father; I might even have been his favorite, though I wasn't conscious of it as a child. But he gave me quite a lot of attention and called me his "little princess." Because of this, I became an unwitting point of conflict between my parents.

At the age of five, I was diagnosed as having a defective heart valve. Each year after that until I was ten, Mom and I made a pilgrimage to a specialist in Los Angeles for a checkup. The trips were always fun, and Mom made sure I had plenty of coloring books and candy to keep me occupied and content on the long bus ride. I was never aware of the seriousness of my illness, and I looked forward to the trips as some special treat all my own. In 1960 I underwent surgery, which corrected the problem, but I developed a heart murmur as a result of the operation.

The worst aspect of my illness was the fact that I was restricted from many activities—an extreme hardship for any child that age. Mom usually was the one who enforced these limitations, and I resented her terribly for it. I had no idea that she did it for my own good, because I needed more rest than other children. I just felt that I was receiving some kind of undeserved punishment. Eventually the conflicts over my restrictions ended up deepening the tensions between Mom and me. This sparked in me a pattern of rebellion that worsened over the years, and I would often find myself in contests of will with Mom. Because of my poor attitude, we continued to fight well into my teenage years.

Since things were tense at home, I sought security through friends in school and at church, where I was involved in a variety of youth activities (church camp, Vacation Bible School, choir, etc.). During that time, I began to develop a knowledge and awareness of God. But spiritual matters were not talked about in our home. I realized that I had never heard a prayer except maybe "grace" at holiday meals. My parents, like many of their contemporaries, were silent and very private about most things, including God.

That attitude of silence set the tone for the whole household. It was sort of an unspoken rule that we should not discuss certain subjects. I accepted it as normal simply because I knew no other way. Besides, it seemed there was already enough tension at home. I was hesitant to bring up any matters that might stir controversy.

I prayed almost every night during those years. I believed God was real; every summer I heard testimonies at church camp about how he had changed people's lives, and I was always touched. I would ask Christ to come into my heart and forgive me of my sins and change my life.

But going home was like waking up from a dream. My life there wasn't the way I wanted it to be. At the first sign of conflict, I always reverted back to the way I had been before camp—I became angry and yelled. Then I struggled with defeat, feeling I hadn't changed at all. I had a hungry little spirit crying out to be fed, to be nurtured, to grow—but it withered before it ever had a change to thrive. I felt the pressures at home were too severe for me to live the kind of changed life I wanted and needed. As a result, I led a double life. I believed that Jesus was present in my life, but only when I was around other Christians.

My life grew even more complicated the summer before my first year of high school, when Dad bought our first house way across town. At first I was excited about the news; it meant a nicer place to live with more room. But I encountered difficult adjustments that proved even harder than I'd expected. Because of the distance of the move, I was uprooted from my church and lost the security I had known in being within walking distance from my friends.

When I started high school in the new part of town I had no friends at all, let alone any Christian friends. At my old junior high I had already survived the peer pressure of being new, but now I was faced with having to start that awful struggle all over again. It was in the midst of this conflict that I began to notice the jug bands—washboard, string bass, the whole thing. These bands were playing the folk songs I knew and identified with. Through these bands I began to meet the kids who were evolving into what the country soon would call hippies.

It was also around this time that I first smoked marijuana. A boy I'd wanted to date for a long time finally asked me out, and I was so overwhelmed that I probably was more vulnerable than I would have been otherwise. But smoking marijuana ("grass") that first time made me feel really good. It took away my feelings of insecurity; everything seemed to blend together in harmony, and I was happy and peaceful. Soon the only time I was happy was when I was high.

Eventually some of my new hippie friends and I began experimenting with other drugs. One night after taking PCP (a horse tranquilizer) we drove to the mountains to "trip out." But the drug had a terrifying effect on me; it made me feel as though I had suffered brain damage. Everything seemed to be in slow motion, and the sounds around me were blurred yet intense. It took great effort to blink or swallow. I remember praying, as the car went curving up the hill that night, "Oh God, help me. Help me not to stay this way permanently." Fortunately, the effects of the drug wore off in a few hours.

Because of my less-than-desirable activities, I eventually became a habitual liar, so my parents never knew what I was doing. Their first exposure to my drinking came one night when I was out on a double date with my boyfriend. We had driven to the town bird refuge where I had my first taste of wine. It tasted so sweet that I guzzled an entire bottle from the case in the trunk. In a matter of minutes I was out cold. Each of the other kids took turns walking me around, trying to revive me, and finally my boyfriend took me into a gas station restroom and held me up in front of the mirror.

"Look at yourself!" he said, trying to shame me

sober. My mascara had run in black streaks down my cheeks and the wine had spilled all over my rumpled dress. But it was no use. I was past the point of being able to do anything.

The next thing I remember was my boyfriend leaving me slumped in a heap on the floor just inside the front door of my home. Mom had waited up for me. When she realized I was drunk she went into a rage. She lifted me by the arms and dragged me into her bedroom, leaving me at the foot of my father's bed. He awoke, startled, when she shouted, "Look at this! Just look!"

I lay helpless. My twin brother had been asleep in his room and was awakened by the commotion. All through those turbulent years he had worried about me, though I wasn't aware of it at the time. I thought of him merely as a "goody-two-shoes" who never got into trouble, so we weren't very close. But that night he ran into my parents' room in my defense.

"Leave her alone!" he yelled, and he picked me up and carried me into my room where I slept through most of the next day. My mother despised my boyfriend for what "he had done to me" and forbade me to ever see him again. As a result, my whole dating life was done on the sly.

Shortly before this time Dad developed diabetes, and he began to have heart trouble as a result of it. In order to avoid stress, which aggravated his condition, he rented a room in a boarding-house as a refuge from the constant bickering at home.

It was never necessary to explain Dad's absences

to my friends because I avoided inviting anyone over to my house. My relationship with my mother rapidly deteriorated, and my life at home, it seemed, was only a matter of eating, sleeping, and arguing. I got to the point where I literally pushed my mother around if I got angry enough. I talked back, lied, and got into her things.

The summer I was fifteen I ran away from home because of yet another disagreement between Mom and me. One evening while I was in the bathroom getting ready to go out with a girl-friend, Mom walked into my room to talk to me. My cigarette pouch was lying on the bed. She opened it and found a small plastic sandwich bag full of marijuana and a twenty dollar bill (which I had stolen from my father while he was asleep).

When I came out of the bathroom and saw that the pouch wasn't on the bed, I panicked. I scanned the room, then hurried outside and found Mom watering the lawn. "Where's my cig-arette pouch?" I shrieked.

"I've got it, Patty," she said, gritting her teeth. And I knew then that she'd found the dope.

"I want it now, Mom."

"I'm keeping it," she retorted, "and I am going to show it to your father when he gets home."

I was horrified, and she sensed it. Telling Dad would be the worst thing that could happen. I wasn't worried so much about punishment; I simply didn't want him to be disappointed or hurt by something I had done. He had suffered enough as it was.

Mom and I fell into the worst screaming battle

we'd ever had. Finally, I ran to my room, frantically grabbed my guitar and a few clothes, and then my friend and I ran out of the house. I was still screaming at Mom as I bolted out the door and across the yard. Blades of grass stuck to my feet as I climbed into my friend's car, trembling with anger and fear.

We drove to my friend's house, and I was still too upset to think straight. I couldn't stop thinking of Dad and how he would react to the news of my drug involvement. My friend offered to help, but I knew I couldn't stay with her, just as I knew I couldn't go home. So we walked around town the rest of the day as I tried to gather my thoughts. I simply did not know where to turn.

We stopped to talk to a couple of boys whom my friend knew. They were students at the junior college. When one of them mentioned that they were hitchhiking up to Haight-Ashbury in San Francisco that evening, I saw my chance to escape.

I hitchhiked up the coast with the two guys, sleeping alongside the highway as we waited to get rides. This was the first real adventure of my life. Barefoot, with a guitar strapped over my back, I felt free from everything—and it seemed so good. My sense of adventure and excitement overcame any fears I might have had about personal safety.

The two boys and I stayed together most of the time we were in Haight. We spent the nights in broken-down houses or storefronts or old houses called "crash pads," which several people rented to stay in while they "came down" from drug trips. Street people always knew someone who had a crash pad. Often, I played my guitar on the streets to make money for food; it was the first time I literally sang for my supper. When I couldn't make money that way, I resorted to panhandling, the practice of walking up to strangers and asking them for spare change.

Everyone seemed to have their own brand of answers to everything. Peace and love were spoken of freely, and I wanted to know just what those terms meant because no one wanted them as badly as I did. Though I had acquired some measure of freedom by running away, when we left to go back to Santa Barbara a few weeks later I was no less confused about my life than when we had arrived in Haight.

There was one thing, however, that I was certain about: having tasted the sweetness of independence, I was determined that I would not go back home to live. I stayed with one of my two hitchhiking companions for a couple of weeks, then I moved in with the other fellow for about the same length of time. I drifted aimlessly, trying to establish a life by myself, and determined that nothing would ever tie me down again.

One day I decided to call my mother to tell her that I was in town and she shouldn't worry about me, but she shouldn't expect me to come home. I was filled with the rebelliousness that had run wild in me for two months. I went to a phone booth and called, delivering my declaration of independence to my mom when she answered.

When I finished, she was momentarily silent; then she delivered her own bit of news.

"Patty, when I told your father about the drugs, he notified the police. There's an APB [All Points Bulletin] out for your arrest."

Suddenly I felt weighed down again. I had thought that the trouble would have blown over by now. But with those few words from my mother, it all came flooding back. Worst of all, I felt my father had betrayed me.

Mom warned me that if I didn't turn myself in voluntarily, I would be arrested and sent to Juvenile Hall, the home for delinquents. That was the last place I wanted to go. Home may have seemed like a prison at times, but it was certainly better than Juvenile Hall.

I turned myself in and was sentenced to a year's probation. Also, because my parents said they couldn't handle me, I was placed in the home of a Quaker woman. To my surprise, we hit it off from the beginning. I thought of her as a bit radical in her own right; she wore her long, silver hair in a braided ponytail and dressed differently than other people her age. I was spellbound by her tales of travel, especially about the years she had spent in Guatemala.

Still, though we got along, the Quaker woman and I lived in two different worlds. I had won her trust, but that was mainly because she was oblivious to my continuing involvement with drugs. On the surface everything seemed OK, but I actually spent that year of probation going out to get drunk, getting high, peddling grass on a small scale, and meeting with my hippie friends.

The person who was the strongest influence in my life at this time was a young man named Steve Williams. I had met him while hitchhiking. We spent most of the summer together, and we became romantically and physically involved.

Soon school started—it was my senior year—but I continued in the same pattern of rebellion. The only difference was that now I was experimenting with a greater variety of drugs and using them more frequently.

Then my world fell apart: I found out I was pregnant. The thought of abortion never entered my mind (thank God), but I was shattered. What was I to do now? How would I cope? I hated to admit it, but I needed to talk with Mom. Reluctantly, I dialed her number, anticipating the worst possible reaction: rejection.

I was crying and trembling as I waited for her to answer the phone. When I heard her voice, I couldn't speak for a second, then I finally got the words out: "Mom, I'm pregnant." There was a moment's silence, then, instead of the rebukes and accusations I'd expected, she calmly tried to comfort me. For the first time I started to realize that she really did love me after all.

The next six months are a blur in my memory. One of the few things I recall clearly is the day, when I was about four months pregnant, that the high school authorities advised me to withdraw from school because my pregnancy was beginning to show. A few weeks later, I dropped out. I just couldn't fit in anymore, and I wasn't ready for what pregnancy involved. It all happened so fast. I just wanted to pretend it wasn't real. But then I was sent to an "unwed mothers'" class sponsored by the YMCA, and as I listened to the instructor I knew there was no way I could deny the reality of the child within me.

Steve and I hadn't kept in touch since school started. In fact, when I tried to locate him and tell him I was pregnant, I discovered that he had moved to a different state to live with the aunt who had raised him! But when I contacted him and told him the news, he came back to California.

We were married late that summer, though Steve never really asked me to marry him. My brother arranged our wedding, and on the day of the ceremony I went to a friend's house to get ready. Mom and I had fought that morning and my face was red and puffy from crying—a great way to start what was supposed to be the "most wonderful day of my life." When I was dressed, I sent for a taxi and rode to the church alone. I hardly knew anyone there except my family. Only a few of my friends had come. I walked down the aisle, miniskirt-clad and pregnant, and there stood my husband-to-be. He looked even worse than I did. He had hepatitis, his eyes were yellow from jaundice, and he was stoned on acid.

I was five months pregnant with Steve's child on the day of our wedding—but as I looked at him during the ceremony I realized he was as much a stranger to me as the baby being formed in my womb.

After the wedding was over, we borrowed a friend's car and drove it to the mountains while we smoked pot and got high. My last memory of my wedding day is of Steve and me smoking a hookah pipe in the hotel room until we were stoned out of our minds.

CHAPTER
Two

Soon Steve and I moved to be near his aunt. Steve went first to find an apartment and make preparations. Mom's wedding gift to us was money for our first month's rent, and the place Steve found was mediocre—a one-bedroom apartment with plain, ugly, standard furniture. The move was a little scary because I had never lived anywhere but Santa Barbara, and when I moved I left behind everything and every friend I had ever known. Still, while the circumstances prompting the move weren't ideal, the optimist in me said this was another adventure.

At first it was fun playing house (which is what our teenage marriage amounted to in those first couple of weeks), and I began to exhibit many of my mother's homemaking traits. She'd never worked outside our home and consequently had spent a lot of time with us children as we grew up. She taught us to be responsible for various chores, though I frequently got in trouble as a teenager for not doing mine. Now, however, I gladly accepted the cleaning and cooking responsibilities in my first home.

Steve was nineteen when we married and I was seventeen. We both were children even by today's standards; we certainly were children by measure of maturity. I probably had matured in a few ways, having survived on my own for a while at fifteen and experiencing the hormonal changes of pregnancy. But Steve, like many young fathers, ran from the responsibility. He didn't work for almost the whole first year of our marriage. In fact, he contracted hepatitis right before the wedding and couldn't get a job, so we lived off welfare checks during the first few months.

It's hard now to remember the good times, but we did have some moments of happiness. And I suppose we thought we loved each other. But as almost anyone could have predicted, our first year together was, overall, horrible. Steve and I fought about everything; when we weren't fighting, we were getting stoned. It was not the kind of bonding process to build a relationship on.

Because I was pregnant, I didn't take hard drugs. But I did smoke some grass and dropped acid a few times to help dull the loneliness and the fear I felt when I was left alone. Miraculously, when Laurel was born shortly after I turned eighteen, she was normal. Steve was gone the day I went into labor, but his aunt came to drive me to the hospital. I don't remember much about the delivery except that I was numb from the waist down. I hadn't known what to expect—certainly not a big, cold hospital—but I was overjoyed when my baby girl was born. The scene, however, was nothing glorious; apart from the attending doctors and nurses, I was completely alone the entire time. I was relieved the next day when my mom arrived.

She had flown up to help take care of her first grandchild and namesake (Laurel, though I would call her Laurie). I truly hated to see Mom leave a few days later because, just as I'd expected, Steve began to leave me alone in the apartment with the baby most of the time. I had been scared when I was by myself before, but now, with Laurie to take care of, I was even more frightened. How was I supposed to deal with all of this?

Eventually an even worse fear came to pass, one that deep down I had expected but wouldn't allow myself to consider. I was holding Laurie one day in the living room when Steve walked in the front door. He just stood there.

"Hi," I said uncertainly.

He stood for a few more minutes, watching me and Laurie. When he finally spoke I could hardly believe his words: "I'm leaving." He turned slightly, then paused and spoke quietly over his shoulder. "Aunt Cora has agreed to take care of Laurie—"

"What are you talking about?" I interrupted him frantically. "What about me? What am I supposed to do now? How will I live?" He just shook his head in silence and walked out of the room. I stood there stunned, realizing I was completely on my own and wondering how I'd survive.

Broke, without friends or family—or even so much as a driver's license—I was forced to hock my wedding ring and beloved guitar. I used the money to stay in a cheap boardinghouse for one week while I scanned the classified ads for a job.

Steve's aunt did take Laurie, though she seemed to have only contempt for me. She considered me the tramp who had ruined her nephew's life, and she made it clear that while Laurie was welcome in her home, I definitely was not.

That first week after Steve left I found a job as a live-in housekeeper. Shortly thereafter I started training as a waitress, and soon saved up enough money—fifty dollars—to buy a run-down old '55 Chevy. Even though the car had bad wheel bearings and used a quart of oil a day, I used it to drive the long distance to see Laurie as often as possible. I hated having to rely on Steve's aunt, but I seemed to have no alternative.

I was working the eleven-to-seven shift at Sambo's one night when one of the waitresses whispered, "Your husband is in the back and he wants to talk to you!"

I almost dropped the plate I was carrying. Carefully setting it down, I turned and walked to the back door where Steve was waiting.

"Hi," he said.

"What are you doing here?"

He looked down. "I've been thinking things

over, and I was hoping you'd be willing to get back together . . . to try and make our marriage work."

I could hardly believe what I was hearing. I knew I had to be cautious, though. For all I knew, Steve was just lonely. We had been through this fight-and-make-up routine so many times that my trust in him was minimal. He couldn't keep a job and he had often left me to go on drug-dealing sprees. All I wanted was some stability, someone to share the responsibility of a family, and I doubted I would find that in Steve.

After talking for a while, he finally convinced me that he loved me and that we should try working things out. We stayed a few weeks in a tiny crackerbox row house, then rented a small home in a better neighborhood, which we painted and fixed up while we made plans to bring Laurie back to live with us. By that time she was about eight months old, but we wanted to wait until things were back to normal before we went to get her.

Although we both worked hard at our marriage, between Steve's day job and my night job we hardly saw each other. The sincerity behind our reconciliation eventually disappeared. I couldn't stand not having Laurie with me and Steve was gone most of the time—sometimes to parties, and sometimes to be with other women —while I was at work. Loneliness once again became my constant companion.

My need for a friend compelled me to go to the local pound to look for a pet. In the first row of cages I saw a muddy, but cute sheepdog with big brown eyes that begged for attention.

"Mister, how much is that dog?" I asked the attendant.

"Nine dollars."

A steal! She was mine.

I named her Simba, which means "lion." I showered her with commands and affection, and in response she seemed almost human. She even followed me to my waitressing jobs and sat outside the door until I finished working.

One night at Sambo's I struck up a conversation with a guy who had become a regular customer of mine. His name was Dave. He seemed different from the other men who came in; he was self-assured, and displayed a maturity I was unaccustomed to. He had soft, blond features, was a stocky, outdoors type, and was interesting to talk to. Before he left one night he asked me if I would go to the zoo with him sometime. That seemed harmless enough, and I craved the care and attention he seemed to be offering, so I said yes.

We went the next day, and then I hesitantly accepted an invitation to dinner at his trailer. It all seemed so innocent to me then. Besides, Dave wasn't a kid like Steve; he seemed responsible and sincere—and those traits were appealing.

Dave and I saw a lot of each other after that, and I realized that I couldn't live with Steve any longer. My marriage was virtually over, and both Steve and I knew it. I rented a room and went to the house to get Simba and my things and to tell

Steve I was moving out. He didn't argue or try to talk me out of leaving. We had both known it was coming to this.

During this second separation, I didn't even consider the possibility of taking back Laurie. That is, not until a couple of young mothers who lived in my apartment complex offered to help. I had told them that Laurie was with my husband's aunt, because I couldn't afford a babysitter, and that Aunt Cora seemed to be growing more and more possessive of my daughter. They expressed concern over my plight and said they'd baby-sit free of charge. I was overwhelmed by their generosity.

One of the young girls drove me to Aunt Cora's house, and I walked to the door with my heart pounding. Steve's aunt came to the door, wearing her usual forced, polite grin. It was never difficult to see that she was unhappy at my being there. I always felt like an outsider when I was in her house, as if I were imposing upon her just by wanting to hold my daughter for a while.

She opened the sliding glass door, and I said "Hi," doing my best to look cheerful. But I could tell she sensed that something was up. She eyed me suspiciously.

"I came to take Laurie for a walk," I said casually.

"She's asleep right now," she said, the cold smile still in place.

"Could you wake her, please?"

"I don't think I should. It's her nap time."

"I drove all the way over here. Besides I'm her mother."

She finally saw it would do no good to argue with me, and she went to wake the baby. When she came back into the room holding Laurie, she stopped for a moment as if she were going to say something. She didn't, though, and handed the baby to me with reluctance.

When I had Laurie in my arms, I turned toward the door. Suddenly I felt Aunt Cora grab Laurie's legs from behind. "What are you doing?" I said.

"You're not going anywhere."

Apprehension filled me, but I tried not to panic. "I told you, I'm just going for a walk."

The words had no effect on her. She began to pull harder, and Laurie started to cry. The pretense was over now.

"She's my baby!" I shouted, holding tighter. I was afraid to pull Laurie away for fear of hurting her. Aunt Cora was clutching and pulling without mercy, and Laurie cried louder. I held tightly, screaming at the woman to let go. She wouldn't.

Finally, I knew I had no choice. I let my baby go.

I ran out of the door and to the car, and my friend drove straight to the police station. We explained what had happened to an officer, and he accompanied us back to the house. He knocked, but there was no answer. Again he knocked; no response.

I heard creaking inside. She was tiptoeing around with the baby.

"She's in there!" I pleaded. "Listen!"

The officer knocked again, and we waited a

few more minutes. "I'm sorry," he said finally.

"She's in there with my baby," I said. "You've got to make her give me my baby. She's mine."

"I can't," he said. "If she won't open up, there's nothing I can do without a warrant."

I turned to my friend, and her face was blank. I'd never felt so helpless. We went to the car and drove back to my empty apartment. A few weeks later I received divorce papers in the mail.

Laurie was placed in the custody of the court during the divorce proceedings. When the time came for the judge to rule on custody, I was sharing a house with another girl. I had moved around a lot, from place to place and job to job, struggling with the increasing instability of my emotions. I felt so alone.

Family court started off badly for me when Steve showed up with his aunt, friends, and an older sister. I was all alone. Steve's lawyer began his case by telling the judge that I was an unfit mother because I took drugs and smoked pot around the baby. I couldn't believe my ears. Steve had been the one to leave so many times to go drug-dealing! I was furious, but I couldn't get a word in.

The final straw was when Steve's aunt said that when I was at her house I, in anger, had almost dropped the baby, but that she had caught her. At that I jumped up and protested loudly. "You liar! How can you dare lie in court that way!"

(Thinking back, I can see that my sense of morals and justice was very distorted. I had broken the law by driving without a license and had taken drugs, but I couldn't fathom someone lying in court to gain custody of a child.)

After the initial proceedings, my caseworker took me aside and suggested I consider giving up Laurie for adoption. If I did that, she said, she would make sure Laurie would be placed with a good family, and I wouldn't have to worry about Steve or his aunt getting her. I think the counselor saw my weakened emotional condition and understood that I was in no position to give my baby the kind of home life she should have. She told me to think about that option—and that it might be a way for me to give Laurie a better chance for a happy, normal future.

Dave encouraged me to give up the baby, too. Whatever his motives might really have been, I felt he was merely echoing the question my counselor had asked me: "What kind of life could you give Laurie?"

That question resounded in my head. I began to realize that the best thing for Laurie *was* a stable home and family life, but I had neither the strength nor the resolve to provide it for her. I wasn't able to say, "I'm going to raise my daughter myself, no matter what," and to make the necessary sacrifices. I didn't know what was the right decision, and my only sources of counsel were telling me to give Laurie to someone else to raise. No one suggested I keep her, and I was too confused and uncertain to decide that for myself.

I couldn't even handle my own life; how could I expect to raise a child alone? Besides, I had been away from her for a long time—she was eleven months old. So, finally, I took the advice I was given and agreed to give Laurie up for adoption. Though I had hardened myself somewhat to cope with the separation, it was still terribly traumatic when I finally signed the adoption papers. I tried not to think about the fact that I was trusting a woman I barely knew to make sure the agency picked out the right family for my baby girl.

Throughout all of this, I had relied on Dave for emotional support. He had become a vital part of my life. Then, several days after the court proceedings were over, Dave announced he was moving to Oregon—he had bought a business and a house there—and he asked me to go with him. I thought this was a dream come true. I had just been divorced, given up my child, and was alone again; life didn't seem like much of an adventure anymore. So I was more than willing to be cared for by this fatherly boyfriend. It was as though I was being rescued by a knight on a white horse. In reality, though, I was running again—trying to escape the guilt of my failed marriage and the memory of my beautiful baby girl who would celebrate her first birthday with someone else.

The house Dave bought in Oregon sat on a large piece of land in the country. It was a small, one-bedroom place with a tiny kitchen, a small bathroom, and a potbellied stove. To keep myself occupied and carry my share of expenses, I got a job as a waitress in a nearby town. I took the bus downtown every day, and when I came home I cooked and cleaned and enjoyed being with Dave. He made few demands on me, and after a few weeks he even bought me a beautiful, used, red-and-white Ford so I wouldn't have to take the bus to work. My life finally seemed to be headed in the right direction.

I hoped to marry Dave. I even met his parents, a wealthy couple who lived nearby in a retirement community, but the introduction was awkward. I could tell they thought I wasn't good enough for Dave, and that angered me. But as long as I had Dave's love, I didn't need anyone else's approval.

Eventually, though, Dave's work demands and involvement with his friends resulted in my being left home alone a lot. So I bought another guitar and often passed the time Dave was gone by playing the folk songs I loved so much. And I practiced a style of music that, early in our relationship, Dave had introduced me to: the blues. I listened to all his B. B. King records, at first just to please him, then because I enjoyed them. I soon discovered that the blues, like the folk music, expressed what I felt inside.

Since the very beginning of our relationship we had planned a month-long camping trip to Mexico. We selected a date in January for our departure, and for weeks prior to that we bought equipment and maps and packed duffel bags and bedrolls, all in celebratory anticipation. On the eve of the trip, our sofa was covered with last-minute necessities: canteens, sunglasses, pillows, and clothes.

Dave had gone to have a farewell drink with his parents, and while I was waiting for him to get back I put some blues records on the stereo and got stoned. Finally, I decided that I would go alone to get a beer at a nearby bar.

I started smoking another joint, and, as everything around me seemed to slow down, I drew water for a steaming, hot bubble bath. Soon I was looking at my own silly face, grinning back at me in the bathroom mirror. But I thought I looked graceful as the brush went streaking through my hair, and my arms felt weightless as I put on my makeup and got dressed.

The marijuana had made me lose all perspective of time, so I was startled when about eleven o'clock the front door opened, and Dave stumbled in, red-faced and drunk. For a moment, neither of us spoke—we just stood there, facing each other in our separate realms of stupor, like punch-drunk prizefighters.

He took a long look at me. "Where do you think you're going?"

"Oh, hi," I said. "I'm just going to go out and get a beer."

"At this late hour?"

"Yes." I couldn't understand his strange behavior. "I'll be back in an hour. It's just a few minutes away."

"We've gotta leave at four. You'll never get up in time."

"Dave, I'm just going to have a beer and come right back." I was starting to get angry; he'd never acted this way before. "You're always telling me I need to go out on my own more."

He didn't take his eyes from me. "You'd better not leave."

I hadn't gone to all the effort to get bathed and dressed up just to stay home now. So I shut him out, wanting nothing more to do with him at that point. "Well, I'm going for a beer whether you like it or not," I said, and hoisted my purse on my shoulder.

He hadn't budged, but his face got mean. "If you go, I'm leaving," he threatened.

I winced inside—he knew that was my sore spot. But tonight I wasn't threatened that easily, partly because I was high and partly because of the long, elaborate ritual I'd just gone through to get dressed.

"That's OK, go," I said calmly. "I'll be back in an hour."

And I was. It took me fifteen minutes to get to the bar, half an hour to down a beer, and fifteen minutes to get back. I had hoped Dave would stay put long enough to perhaps crash on the bed. When I pulled into the drive, however, the jeep was gone. "Oh, shoot," I muttered. "That guy is so stubborn."

As I got out of my car, I wondered what time we'd actually push off the next day. Then, when I walked in the door, I noticed that some of the things on the sofa were missing. The kitchen light was on, and a lengthy note lay on the breadboard.

I walked over, picked it up, and read:

Dear Pat,
    I guess we expected too much of each
other. It's better this way. . . .

There was more, but those words were all I
needed to panic. *What? What does that mean? Is
that all?*

I ran through the house calling Dave's name,
but he wasn't there. I called his dog, but only
Simba came. I called his office, but no one was
there. I called every bar I could think of, but no
one had seen Dave. I called his parents, but
they hadn't heard from him. Neither had his
former girlfriend.

I ran back to the living room, and suddenly remembered his final words to me: "If you go, I'm
leaving." I stopped dead in my tracks.

Dave had gone to Mexico—alone. He'd left me.
My knees buckled, and I began to cry. If I'd known
what he'd meant, I never would have gone out. I'd
have gotten angry, like always, sulked, and gone to
bed. But that would have been it. If only we had
fought about it. I couldn't cope with the fact that it
had all been a misunderstanding.

I sank onto the floor and sobbed.

"Oh, Dave . . ."

We'd been so happy. How could I have been
ready for this?

I cried even harder, and began to tremble violently. It was all gone, everything in my life, and I
was flooded with confusion. My marriage had

ended in disaster, and now Dave was gone; he was really gone!

I was crying so hard I was getting sick, but I couldn't move. I could only lie there, my head heavy and my body drained of life. Finally, I began to crawl, pulling myself by my arms. I dragged myself to the bedroom, but I couldn't lift myself onto the bed. I curled up on the rug shivering and crying, my head throbbing. I tried to sleep, but I couldn't. I could only lie there, conscious of nothing, drifting in and out of delirium but never sleeping. And that's where I stayed until the sun began to stream through the window.

I had regained some strength just lying there, and as soon as I knew people would be waking up, I dragged myself to the phone and, barely able to speak, called everyone again. The response was the same; no one had seen Dave. I called the office one last time, but he hadn't left word there either.

It was over.

I crawled into the living room and sat cross-legged on the floor, rocking and crying hysterically. The effects of the beer and marijuana had long worn off. Finally, I sat silent and still, sapped of all strength. Half the day went by, but I had no concept of time. I felt as if I were dying.

I was utterly destroyed. All sense of life seemed to have left me except the constant ache. I wanted to kill myself. At least that would end the relentless agony. I had nothing left but misery.

There is no life for me, I thought. But because I was afraid of suicide—and of hell—I knew I couldn't take my own life as I so desperately wanted to.

"O God," I cried, "I want to die. Why am I alive? I just want to die. . . ."

I wept and rocked and wept some more. Suddenly, as a ray of late morning light crossed the floor before me, I looked up and saw that the front door had cracked open. At first I couldn't see who was there. He was speaking, but I couldn't grasp the meaning of the words.

Finally I recognized him. It was one of Dave's drinking buddies. My appearance must have shocked him; I looked delirious, sitting there in wrinkled clothes and my eyes all swollen. He came over and lifted me off the floor, and then he said something about trusting the Lord. He mentioned a "Christian" commune downtown where several ex-drug addicts had been miraculously changed by God.

"God?" I cried. "God?" I clutched his shirt in hopeful hysteria, as he helped me to his pickup truck. He kept talking about God. I couldn't understand why this usually obnoxious beer-drinking man was saying these religious-sounding words to me. But his voice was comforting and it sounded true.

"Listen to me, Pat," he said. "These people were on drugs until Jesus Christ changed their lives."

I couldn't believe what I was hearing. "Are you sure?" I asked. By now I was on my knees on the seat of his pickup, clutching his leg in desperation. "Is it true? Are you sure?"

I began to cry, then suddenly laughed hysterically, totally out of control. *There couldn't possibly be other people like me,* I thought. *Nobody's been through what I've been through.*

We stopped in a small residential neighborhood, in front of a big, old, two-story house. "Where are we? Is this it?" I asked. Dave's buddy helped me up the walk and knocked on the door. I was so weak and exhausted that he had to hold me up.

The door opened and a girl in a long dress, with long, dark hair appeared. She smiled at him and then at me, and said, "Hi! We love you. Jesus loves you."

I had never heard those words said that way. It was as if heaven had opened to me, and, when Dave's friend helped me through the door, it was as if I had walked into a celestial city.

The girl hugged me and I melted inside. I began to weep uncontrollably. A thin fellow in a T-shirt, beads, and jeans came running down the stairs, laughing and saying, "Praise the Lord!" I couldn't remember having heard anyone say that before, but at that moment I knew exactly what it meant. There were posters on the walls with Bible quotations, and though it was all confusing, these people looked just like the hippies I'd known. And that was the perfect answer for me: I was like these people in appearance—*and they knew God.*

It was true! What Dave's friend had said was true!

He told them my name because I was so over-whelmed I couldn't speak. Everything they said sounded new to me, yet somehow familiar. I turned and looked outside and saw that Dave's friend was now standing by his truck, talking to the long-haired girl. He waved to me as the door closed between us. I never saw him again.

CHAPTER

Three

I was still standing by the door wondering what was happening to me when someone gently took me by the arm. I looked into the face of the bearded young man who had run down the stairs.

"I'm Timothy," he said, smiling. "Come with me. It's almost time for supper."

The kitchen was a big, warmly inviting room. About ten young men and women were sitting down on long benches surrounding a crudely built wooden table. Light from the setting sun came through the window, flooding the room with a soft, yellow glow. Two girls with long hair were setting places at the table.

"Sit here," one of the girls said, indicating a place near the end of one of the benches. I gazed at the people around me for the longest time. There was something different about their eyes—they seemed to reflect so much life and love.

The girls served each person fragrant home-made bread and homemade vegetable soup ladled out of a big kettle. While we ate, different people began to tell me about their lives. I stared in wide-eyed wonder because every one of them talked about God in such a special, personal way.

"You know, Pat," said one young man, "when I was looking for answers, I thought Jesus was just some character in a made-up fable. But he wasn't. He was there with me all along. I never found any answers until I met him."

A pretty young girl turned to me. "I didn't think anybody loved me," she said, "that anybody *could* love me—until Jesus came into my life. Nothing compares to his kind of love."

"I thought my life was over when I lost my mother," said a shy-looking girl in a long dress. "All my friends were there for me, but I still felt so alone. I don't think I could have survived without Jesus."

I was dumbfounded that these people admitted their weaknesses, longings, and loneliness—everything I had experienced.

Two or three more people chimed in. They were all different from anyone I had ever met. Their conversation was different because it was full of good things, not the hopelessness I was accustomed to. Their voices were filled with peace and contentment, and everything they said verified the calmness that had overcome me when I first walked into their house.

As I listened, I acknowledged in my heart

that what I was hearing was true. All of a sudden, I knew: this was the answer—Jesus was *everything!*

Suddenly I blurted out, "*I* want it!" They all looked at me for a moment, as if they were waiting for me to say something else.

I just sat there, smiling, and looking from face to face in innocent anticipation. But they all just kept waiting.

Finally, I explained with a shout: "I want Jesus to change my life *too!*"

The kitchen was filled with the sound of their voices praising God, and everyone began to hug me, telling me again and again they loved me and that Jesus loved me. "Praise the Lord! Hallelujah!"

When we all sat down around the table once more, everyone smiling, a young man with the sweetest expression I'd ever seen led me in prayer. The others continued praising God.

While we prayed, everything within me gave thanks to God. I had never spoken truer words in my life than those I spoke at that moment. The focus of my whole existence had become tiny and narrow when I was in Dave's house. I had been so dead mentally and spiritually the day that Dave's friend came over. When he spoke to me about God I had no defenses or resistance left—I had reached the point where I was ready to hear the voice of the Lord.

One of the young men at the table asked me if I wanted to be baptized that night. "Sure," I said, only vaguely aware of what that meant. But I wanted everything—all God had to offer. I didn't understand the significance of baptism, but I did know that it was something Christians did for God.

I followed a girl upstairs, and she gave me some old clothes to wear. Everyone was waiting in the living room as we descended the stairs, and a big guy with a Bible in his hand took charge.

The sun had gone down long ago, and when we walked outside the winter air was bitterly cold. We all piled into two cars, and I sat in the back-seat of one, between Timothy and the girl who lent me her clothes. My head was buzzing from all the excitement.

There I sat, riding in a car between two people I didn't know. Yet I felt very comfortable.

When we stopped at a small clearing beside the Columbia River, I noticed patches of snow dotting the ground. "OK, let's go," Timothy said, smiling as he reached for my hand. The frozen grass crunched under our feet as we walked toward the riverbank. I shivered from the cold, but the night sky was beautiful. The moon hid behind the clouds, outlining them in silver.

The man who was in charge opened the Bible and read about the meaning of baptism. When he finished, he waded out into the water, and Timothy and I walked out behind him. I shivered in the freezing river, but I didn't mind. I realized I was relinquishing the rights to my life, that the old Patty was dying—in fact, had already died—and that I was being born into a new life.

When I reached the leader he put one arm

around the small of my back, and the other on my forehead.

"In the name of the Father, and of the Son—"

He dipped me slowly into the rushing Columbia River, and during those few seconds I was under, I knew that something good was waiting for me. I opened my eyes as I was lifted up, and I saw that the clouds parted directly above me to reveal a bright white moon. I felt as though God had smiled down on me at that moment, approving and acknowledging me with this beautiful, mysterious demonstration—his little lost daughter had finally entered his fold. Completion had taken place.

Someone threw a blanket around me, and as we walked back to the car I realized that the emptiness within me had been filled; my loneliness was gone, and I knew I would be satisfied with this new love forever.

I awoke the next morning to a powerful throbbing sound. I looked up from the sofa where I'd slept, but I saw only a young man padding around the living room in his socks. I realized that the throbbing in my head was due to my being ill and having a fever. Easing my head back down on the pillow, I went back to sleep.

When I opened my eyes again, I found the long-haired girl who had met me at the door sitting beside me. The light in the room had changed, so I knew it was midday. She urged me to take a few sips of hot tea with lemon and honey, but I was so sick I couldn't sit up.

"How are you feeling?" she asked me. I tried to

speak but couldn't because my throat was sore and swollen. She lifted my head to give me a sip of tea, but the heat of the concoction aggravated the pain in my throat. I knew I should try to drink some, though.

I was feverish and dizzy, and all that day people drifted in and out of my consciousness.

For three or four days I lay on the sofa, covered with blankets and barely able to move. Yet the people there showed me only kindness as they nursed me through my illness.

When I finally began to recover, the bearded young man named Timothy sat on the floor beside the sofa. He was thin, with thick, dark shoulder-length hair. His eyes were a piercing blue, and he had an irresistible smile, complete with dimples.

"Praise the Lord," he said, smiling. I had heard that expression used many times during the past few days, and had noted how it was used as a greeting and response.

"Hi," I said.

"Feel any better today?"

I nodded from beneath the blankets.

"How would you like to live with us?" he asked.

Those words—full of acceptance—were like another dose of the hot milk and molasses they had fed me while I was sick. I was overwhelmed. I didn't have to try to change or play a part. I could wear my jeans and go barefoot and continue playing my guitar. God had answered my prayer of desperation and carved out a place for me.

The next day I bundled up to drive back to

Dave's and get my things. When I pulled into the drive and walked in the front door and through the house, everything looked strangely different. It seemed eerie, as though I didn't belong there—as if my life there had occurred years before, and was now only a faint memory. I left without looking back.

During the first few days in my new home, Timothy took me under his wing. He showed me Bible passages that he thought were important for me to know, taught me about matters of faith, and was willing to listen whenever I, in wide-eyed wonder, discovered something new about God.

The first time I went to the church with the group, I made a point to go barefooted. The rebel in me was still strong, and the church, I had been told, was "straight"—full of the kind of Christians I had known before. I still preferred being different from the rest of society. This first trip to church would be a sort of testing ground to see how the people would react to me. To my surprise, I felt genuinely accepted when we walked in. Soon my attitude began to change about the congregation—and about the church in general.

One of those first afternoons at the commune, I pulled a cigarette out of my purse. As I started to light it, one of the girls said in a kind voice, "I'm sorry, Pat—we don't smoke here."

"What?" I didn't know what she was talking about.

"We believe the body is the temple of the Holy Spirit. So we don't smoke."

"Oh. OK." I was so embarrassed I wanted to crawl under a rock. She wasn't at all pious about it, but even so I felt ignorant and unspiritual. After that episode, I was too ashamed to smoke in our yard or on the porch. So I went on occasional drives around the block to smoke. Eventually, though I realized that I was estranging myself from my fellow commune members by continuing the habit. I also sensed that while they couldn't see me, God was viewing all my actions. Because of this, within the next three days I had stopped altogether. I knew it had to be God working in me to make such an easy transition from my habit of chain-smoking two packs a day for five years to not smoking at all.

Across the street from our house was another two-story commune called Maranatha House. Our members knew most of their members, and they looked much the way we did—long hair, beards, jeans. But they led a much stricter lifestyle ("legalistic," or living by the letter of the law). I didn't understand much of what they did or why they did it, but like many who are young in the faith, I considered their actions a sign of spiritual maturity.

One evening at dinner, about ten days after I had moved to the house, Timothy announced that he had been in prayer and had decided to leave for Denver to help start a commune there. He would be joining a couple of guys from our commune and from Maranatha House, who, months before, had moved to Denver to make the initial preparations. They had just sent word they were ready for others to come. Timothy said that Isabel, a girl we all knew from Maranatha House, would accompany him on the trip to help establish the new ministry.

I was appalled by the news. Not only had Timothy been my spiritual shepherd, but he was the only person in the house to whom I was close. I would feel awkward if I was left behind with the others. After dinner I followed him out to the porch. When I thought the time was right, I asked if I could go with him.

He stopped and looked at me, considering the proposal. "Pray about it, Pat," he said. "Pray about it, and I will, too. The Lord will tell us if it's right."

Pray about it? I'd never thought to pray. And that was just the opportunity I needed to begin my prayer life. "Lord," I said that night before bed, "I want to go with Timothy so badly. Please let me go, and let him know it's right. Thank you."

A couple of days later, in the midst of making arrangements to move, Timothy called me aside and said if I still felt it was God's will, that I could go.

"What?" I said.

He paused for a moment, with a peculiar look. "Don't you want to go?"

"Oh, yes. Yes, I do." I was shocked, but delighted. *Hey,* I thought, *God really does answer prayers.*

We packed during the next couple of days, and I left almost all of my belongings with the commune—mostly in gratitude for everything they'd done to help me.

I met Isabel the day we were to leave when she brought her things over. I found myself a little intimidated by her. She wore a long dress, parted her long, blonde hair in the middle, and had serious eyes. I thought she looked like a prophetess.

When the time came to leave, we loaded Simba into the backseat along with my cats, an orange Persian and an ugly, multicolored mix, both of whom sat in a box on the floor. All the members of the commune gathered in the front yard to pray together, then we hugged and said our final good-byes.

Timothy had convinced me to sell my car and buy a less expensive one so we could use the leftover money for food and emergencies on the trip. I had reservations about doing this because my car had always been trouble free. But I agreed after Timothy insisted it was the unselfish thing to do.

So the first leg of our journey carried us to the used car lot where we made the trade-down. But we hadn't even driven a mile off the lot when the rickety old car came to a dead stop—right in the middle of a busy four-lane thoroughfare.

"What happened?" I said in a panic. *Could it be that God didn't want us to go?* "What's wrong with the car?"

Timothy looked ahead with consternation and kept trying to start the engine.

"Oh no," I moaned. "What are we going to do now?" I felt the tears form.

"We just need to trust the Lord," Isabel said. "Let's pray."

I quieted a little. Isabel sat with head bowed in the front seat, while Timothy, the anger beginning to show, kept twisting the key and stomping at the gas pedal without results. Finally we admitted we were getting nowhere, and Timothy went to call a tow truck.

Three days later, after repairs, we had another send-off. This time everything seemed to be in good working order. And no matter how far we traveled, whether I was awake or drifting off to sleep, I had an ever-present sense of God.

Along the way, Isabel and Timothy had spoken of the "brothers and sisters" and "other bodies of believers." I was anxious and curious to see these people, as well as everything else they talked about. I couldn't imagine so many other people having had an experience like mine. Who had kept this secret from me for so long? And why didn't the world know about these people and what they shared?

As the morning began to break, we passed several hippies along the road. My heart broke as I realized that what I had found—the peace and love I had found in Jesus—was what they were searching desperately for. I wanted to share it with them.

Suddenly the car made a loud noise and Timothy, who had been sleeping in the backseat, woke up. Isabel pulled onto the shoulder of the road. We scanned the highway behind us and saw a long, brown object about a hundred yards back that looked suspiciously like a renegade car part—our muffler. Timothy got out and retrieved it.

We made it safely to Salt Lake City with the muffler in the trunk and stopped at a cheap-looking service station for repairs. As we waited, Timothy and I sat on a bench and talked about the meaning of being a "new creature" in Christ.

He told me he used to be a real acidhead. "They used to call me Spaceman because I was always tripping," he said. "I dropped acid every chance I got. When I met Jesus, I didn't want to even think about all that. So I changed my name."

"Really?" This genuinely surprised me about him. "Why change your name?"

"Well, I did it to put my old life behind me."

Hmmm, I thought. *I'm a new creature, too, and I want to start everything new.* I pulled my Bible out of my bag and proceeded to study about the different women in the Bible, searching for someone I could identify with, whose name I could share.

As the morning turned to afternoon, I learned about Esther and Sarah, and finally I turned to the Book of Ruth. That story came to life as I began to see parallels between Ruth's experience and mine. The verbal interchange in Ruth 2:10 actually occurs between Ruth and Boaz, yet I sensed that through that passage God was speaking directly to me about my relationship with him: "At this, she bowed down with her face to the ground. She exclaimed, 'Why have I found such favor in your eyes, that you notice me, a foreigner?'"

That verse embodied the gratitude I had toward God for saving me and the bewilderment at how I could ever have come to find grace in his sight after alienating myself from him for so long. Furthermore, the latter part of verse eleven seemed to be the Lord's approval of my coming on the trip and a confirmation that he was with me all along, watching over me: "You left your father and mother and your homeland and came to live with a people you did not know before."

And finally, verses twelve and thirteen signified the interaction of my faith with God's Word at that very moment: "'May the Lord repay you for what you have done. May you be richly rewarded by the Lord, the God of Israel, under whose wings you have come to take refuge.'

"'May I continue to find favor in your eyes, my lord,' she said. 'You have given me comfort and have spoken kindly to your servant.'"

God knew my every thought and desire. I had been uprooted from the West Coast, I reasoned, to seek his will for my new life in him. And I had finally found rest under his watchful eye.

In all honesty, I didn't like the name Ruth, and I was disappointed that was the name the Lord chose for me. But I believed he did choose it, and I decided from that day forward to be Ruth . . . and to be his completely.

CHAPTER
Four

The late afternoon sun gave Interstate 70 a golden glow as we weaved through the Rockies on our way to Denver. We had been given a break on the cost of the car's repairs by the mechanic in Salt Lake City, but even with that we were nearly broke. We drove on, fearful of further mechanical failures but ever mindful of the promise of a new life waiting for us.

The Rockies were beautiful. After the flat barrenness of Utah the huge mountains seemed to rise like a giant. They looked much more majestic than the mountains I'd seen on the West Coast because they provided a dramatic, visual contrast to the deserts of the western states. Once we started to climb through the Rockies, the temperature dropped abruptly and we were surrounded by the fresh scent of the pines and evergreens.

Timothy and Isabel already had begun to call me Ruth. I was sure the change in names would be easy because the people at the Denver commune would know me by my new name only. I couldn't wait to meet the other Christians, and for them to meet me—as Ruth.

The sun was setting as the road began its descent toward Denver. My heart welled with anticipation and gratitude to God for this wonderful experience he'd given me.

"From what they told me," Timothy commented as he reached to turn on the headlights, "the house is big like the one in Portland." Suddenly, without warning, a huge bird came into view in front of our car. Timothy tried to swerve, but it all happened too fast. We heard a loud *thump,* and I screamed. Timothy pulled the car onto the shoulder.

"Oh no," I moaned from between Simba and the cats, and I began to cry.

"Ruth, it's OK," Timothy said.

Isabel turned calmly from the front seat and strained to see what we'd hit. "I think it was a pheasant," she said. She got out with Timothy to inspect the bird, which now lay on the side of the road. I watched them in the rearview mirror, and soon Isabel walked back to the car to get a brown grocery bag. "Please come help, Ruth," she said.

God, give me strength, I prayed. *They need me to help bury it.* I followed Isabel, my eyes to the ground, to where Timothy knelt beside the bird. When I looked up, he was plucking its feathers.

"It's a blessing from the Lord, Ruth," he said. "He's provided for us again. Give us a hand."

"Can you hold the bag for us?" Isabel asked.

"What?" I was still crying.

"It's a gift," Timothy said. "We can take it for a celebration feast at the new commune."

The grocery bag with the limp bird was set between Timothy and Isabel in the front seat while I clutched Simba in the back and kept an eye on the curious cats. We made it to Denver without further incident and found the new commune easily. Two of the men Timothy knew, James and Phillip, ran out to greet us with hugs. They took the animals to the backyard while Isabel and I moved our things into the small, added-on room upstairs where two bare mattresses had been placed on the floor. I dropped my belongings and looked out the big picture window at the last of the pink and orange sunlight reflecting on the clouds. Colorado was simply gorgeous.

"Let's go downstairs, Ruth," Isabel said. "We've got to get the pheasant started."

"Oh yes," I said. I felt like such a tagalong with Isabel. She prayed about *everything* and always seemed to know exactly what to do. She appeared to be so humble, mature, serious, sacrificing —everything I wanted to be. As we prepared the meal, she advised me on the biblical responsibilities of women.

"We need to let the men eat first," she said. "That's one way of obeying God's Word, by showing submissiveness toward the men in the body of Christ."

I nodded in agreement, listening intently.

"We'll stay in the kitchen until they're finished," she went on, "then we'll eat what's left."

But I felt unspiritual because I was so hungry that the thought of waiting wasn't a pleasant one.

When the pheasant was finally in the oven, James and Phillip showed us the rest of the house. In the middle of the huge dining room was a table with sawed-off legs; pillows lined the floor. "We break our bread together here," Phillip said.

That night, in an elaborate ritual full of spiritual meaning and celebration, Isabel served the stuffed pheasant to the fellows. I stood by in the kitchen, the guilt building as my stomach growled in protest. Finally, when the dinner was over, Isabel brought in the remains of the bird. It looked like a skeleton, but we picked at the bones and ate what was left of some molasses bread Isabel had brought.

I learned how to make molasses bread the next day—at 5:00 A.M. I was also introduced to Postum, the noncaffeine breakfast beverage that was popular among health-minded Christians.

Life at the Denver commune was similar to the way we had lived in Portland. Eventually, under Isabel's subtle, unspoken supervision, I adopted her strict mores. I wore only long dresses, and I never used makeup. During our commune meetings and Bible studies, Isabel and I never spoke unless directly addressed, and we wore scarves to cover our heads, following Paul's instructions to the women of the Corinthian church. We groped for every specific directive in the New Testament and applied each one in the strictest legalistic sense to show our obedience to the Lord. (He must have chuckled at our pious observances like an adult watching children play dress-up.)

Sometimes on weekends we piled into a car and drove several miles to Boulder, where we went into the mountains to pray. We also held midnight baptisms, similar to mine in the Columbia River, where we trudged across snowy fields and broke through ice-covered lakes to perform the services.

Both James and Phillip had jobs, and they provided a meager income to the commune. But we barely had enough to live on. Still, I didn't mind doing without because I did so for good reason: I was among people who lived the sacrificial life that Christ talked about, a life centered on faith.

One afternoon I crossed the street on my way to the neighborhood grocery store. I whistled for Simba, who had been sitting in the yard beside the house, and she jumped up and ran to catch up with me.

Suddenly, I saw a car come speeding down the street. "No!" I shouted. The car's brakes screeched and Simba stopped at the sound, right in the middle of the street. I heard the terrifying sound of relentless steel hitting warm life. Simba fell, and the car halted over her.

I burst into hysterical tears as I ran to the street. I knelt in front of the car and dragged Simba from underneath it. She was silent as I held her, crying out to God for help. I don't even remember seeing the driver of the car, but a neighbor who lived down the street ran over and took Simba from me. He carried her to his pickup truck and drove us to the animal hospital.

We followed a doctor to the emergency room, where I clutched the arm of the young man who had driven us there.

"You'll have to leave her with us," the doctor told me.

"What's going to happen?" I cried.

"I'm not sure. She may lose this leg, though. I'm sorry, but we'll do our best. Please, you'll just have to leave her with us."

O God, I thought. *Why did it happen?*

On the long drive home, I went from being angry with myself for having been careless to becoming angry with God for the first time. I couldn't understand how he could allow Simba to suffer so much. I had a familiar, overwhelming urge to run from everything.

I turned to the neighbor. "Do you know where I can get some grass?"

"Sure," he said, puzzled. He knew I was one of the Jesus freaks from down the street, and that they didn't use drugs of any kind. But he drove me to his house and we went inside.

There were several people at his house, most of them on drugs. I joined them, but with a very heavy heart. Why was I doing this to myself? To God? After all he had done for me . . . didn't he deserve better from me than this?

The conversation drifted toward the subject of religion, and I recall angrily refuting the blasphemous statements made against Christ. Depressed and hating myself for what I had done, I wandered back to the house to find everyone preparing for Communion. Oh no! I had forgotten it was Good Friday.

I dreaded facing everyone. I was sure they'd all be able to tell I was high. The dining room was lit by three short candles at the center of the table. On one end, a bottle of wine stood next to a large goblet and a loaf of unleavened bread Isabel had baked.

I stood in the hallway until everyone was seated on the floor around the table. Finally I walked in and sat at the nearer end of the table. I lowered my eyes as Timothy, who sat at the opposite end, began to speak.

"The Lord took the bread and said, 'This is my body which is given for you: this do in remembrance of me.'"

He took a piece from the unsliced loaf and passed it to Isabel. She broke off a piece and passed the loaf to the next person, who did the same. When everyone had a piece of bread Timothy nodded, and we all ate it together. As I chewed, I focused on the floor in front of my knees.

Timothy lifted the goblet. "And he quoted, 'This cup is the new testament in my blood, which is shed for you.'"

He sipped the wine slowly, then passed the goblet to Isabel, who cupped it gently in her hands. In the glow of the candles she looked so serenely beautiful.

When she turned to me with the goblet, I couldn't look her in the eye. My hands trembled as I took the cup, and I sipped the wine and passed it on.

Timothy continued, "And the Lord said, 'I appoint unto you a kingdom, as my Father hath appointed unto me; that ye may eat and drink at my table in my kingdom.' And the Lord also said, 'Simon Peter, behold, Satan hath desired to have you, that he may sift you as wheat. But I have prayed for thee, that thy faith fail not."

At those words I began to cry. I lowered my head, feeling the tears spill down my face. I thought of Jesus' broken body, and the tears increased. I felt everyone's arms around me as I spoke.

"I'm so . . . sorry . . . ," I said in a choked voice.

Each one held me as I continued to cry. I sensed their forgiveness and God's, but was unable to forgive myself for failing my first test of faith.

The next morning several of us went to pick up Simba. "It's a miracle," the doctor said. "After cleaning her wounds we discovered we could save her leg after all."

Simba's leg was put in a cast, and after that she had only a slight limp, which could be detected only when she ran. I considered it an undeserved healing from the Lord—one he'd given in spite of my weak faith.

I never touched drugs again. More important, however, my faith increased. *If only I could have held out and trusted God to take care of it,* I thought. I realized that no matter what kind of circumstances arose, my relationship with Jesus was secure.

Timothy continued to teach me songs on the guitar and we often played together at churches and coffeehouses in the area. Timothy was a good musician and songwriter, and my admiration for him grew. His gentle, caring manner appealed to me, and I began to marvel at what life could be like with a husband who lived to serve God.

One night Timothy shocked me with the announcement that he was returning to Oregon. He had been praying about going to Bible school, he told everyone at dinner, and now he thought it was time to go. I struggled to finish eating, trying not to reveal my disappointment.

After dinner, I approached him on the front porch when he was alone, as I had in Portland.

"Timothy."

"Hello, Ruth." His expression told me he had sensed my growing attachment to him.

"Take me with you."

"I can't," he said. "I feel the Lord calling me closer to him through this, Ruth. I have to make this trip alone."

"Timothy, you should go to Bible school if that's what the Lord wants. Taking me won't keep you from that."

"No, Ruth," he said, "*no*. I need to go alone."

We said good-bye to him a few days later. I didn't cry, but I felt hollow the rest of that day. In the weeks following his departure the commune attracted a few more members. We continued to go to the mountains, witness, pray, baptize, and celebrate life together. Living for Jesus was the life I had always wanted. I relied on the group's activities for the growth of my personal faith, which was still young, but it seemed as though I had known the Lord forever.

One day one of the newer brothers, Phillip, got a letter from his cousin in Albuquerque, informing him that his uncle was very ill. Phillip told us he thought he should hitchhike to see him. As I was always eager to move on (especially after Timothy's departure), I volunteered to go with him. As the group discussed it, I reminded everyone that Jesus sent out the disciples in pairs. My use of a biblical directive in that instance won everyone's hearty approval— including that of Isabel, who no doubt was pleased with my progress.

The group had heard of a large Christian commune in Phoenix, Arizona, called God's Place, and they were anxious to know about its people and ministry. We decided that Phillip and I would go there after leaving his uncle's home. There was only one thing that concerned me. Until now, I had taken Simba wherever I went, but she hadn't fully recovered from her accident. I was heartbroken that she couldn't go, but one of the brothers offered to drive her to Phoenix as soon as she was better.

The sun was shining brightly the day we left, though the Colorado air was cool. I wore some women's combat boots that I'd purchased for the trip and a backpack full of my belongings. Phillip was similarly outfitted. We didn't have a penny between us, but neither of us worried about it.

I knew this trip was only the beginning of another great adventure. Phillip and I hitchhiked through northeastern New Mexico and shared our faith with the strangers who picked us up or offered us a handout. All the while we praised God for his protection and provision.

Phillip stayed in Albuquerque with his uncle, who was feeling much better, and I caught a bus to Phoenix. I went to sleep during the ride and awoke to see the rose-colored sun peeking over the Arizona desert. It was one of the most beautiful sights I'd ever seen, and I thanked the Lord just for allowing me to witness it.

The God's Place commune in Phoenix was a magnificent sight—a three-level log cabin surrounded by acres and acres of grassy grounds. It housed about fifteen young Christian hippies and doubled as a coffeehouse. The people there had the same enthusiasm for the Lord I had seen in the other communes.

At night young people from the area came to hear music and the gospel, and the wonders of their transformed lives continually amazed me. I learned new songs and more about the Bible and the growing movement of young Jesus people across the nation.

After a couple of weeks, Phillip arrived driving a white Ford Econoline van. He said he was going to Augusta, Maine, to visit his brother. He asked if I wanted to go along. "Of course I want to go!" I enthusiastically responded.

Five of us made the trip, and I saw beauty I'd never imagined! The green, rolling countryside of Pennsylvania, the monuments and landmarks of Virginia, the quaint, English-looking houses all along the East Coast. In almost every city and town along the way we saw the graffiti that linked us to our traveling brothers and sisters in Christ, "One Way," referring to the one way to heaven, to eternal life: Jesus. Every time I saw those two words I felt the security and awe of knowing that God was moving through his people everywhere.

When we got back to Phoenix, Simba was waiting for me. A week later I overheard a young man named Bill saying he planned to hitchhike to Dallas to see his family and friends. Bill's girlfriend at the commune had just broken off their engagement, and he wanted a change of scenery. He was a soft-spoken fellow, and I could tell he was upset over the situation and could use some company on the trip.

"Two by two," I said to him. "The Lord sent them out two by two." He smiled, and I knew Simba and I would be going with him.

I said good-bye to my new friends and thanked everyone at the commune for welcoming me there. We left the next morning, catching a ride with a trucker. When we reached Dallas and stepped down from the cab of the semi, I felt the thickness of the heavy, humid air as it filled my lungs.

"Thank you!" I gasped over the roar of the engine as the trucker drove away.

Bill and I tiredly walked toward the neighborhood where he'd grown up, with Simba close behind. We caught a few rides and finally found our destination: a friend's white house with black trim in a quiet neighborhood. The sun was barely up so it was still too early to knock. We spread out on the porch to catch some sleep. Simba put her head on my feet.

Minutes later the front door opened and a woman stood in her bathrobe. She had long, raven-colored hair that was pulled into a ponytail at the nape of her neck. She was smiling even before she recognized Bill, and when she did her exclamation was joyous. "Oh, *Bill*-y!"

Bill stood up to receive her affectionate embrace, and he introduced me.

"Julie, this is Ruth. She's a sister from God's Place. She just came to meet the Christians down here and see what's going on."

Julie Reese was beautiful. She looked about thirty-five, had striking blue eyes, and an accent that implied an East Coast background. "Oh, Ruth," she said, "you're going to stay with us, aren't you?"

"Thank you." I smiled, surprised at her quick invitation. I had never met anyone with such a genuine, caring warmth.

Julie's husband, Jason, worked at a local newspaper. The Reeses were involved in the burgeoning charismatic movement among Catholics. They had a girl and two boys, ranging in age from three to eleven. With three children, and Jason working long hours to support them, they had no apparent reason to take in a transient hippie and her sheepdog. But they did, without reservation.

Bill left to go to his parents' house. Little did I know, I would not see him again for a very long time.

I didn't see much of Jason during my first few weeks with the family, but I could tell he thought I was special. He loved it when I played my guitar and sang, and he even arranged some singing engagements for me at various Catholic schools, retreats, and churches. I still enjoyed the attention I got by being different from others. Instead of dressing up to go to church, I wore a red-and-white western shirt, jeans, a big red felt hat, a gray cape, combat boots, and my guitar slung over my shoulder. Jesus had met my spiritual needs when I was a hippie, and I was determined that no one was going to make me change my appearance.

I always shared my testimony when I sang, and after one of my first engagements, a little old woman walked up to me with a joyous look on her face. She put some money into my hand and walked away. I needed money at the time, and I realized that the gift God had given me was something special. I knew he had spoken to those people through the music, and they had heard him.

The Reeses were generous and I had few worries. It never crossed my mind to get a job. My life-style seemed normal to me; I was discovering a world that intrigued me and that was what life seemed to be all about. It was one big exploration, and I loved every minute of it.

In just a short time Julie and I became close

friends. She was like a mentor to me, nurturing my young faith and encouraging me in my musical gifts. I spent most days talking with her about the Bible and listening to her tell how the Lord was working through his people in Dallas. Whenever I could, I went to the Christ for the Nations Institute to hear well-known speakers and Christian leaders.

I also attended a Bible study and praise gathering on Wednesday nights, made up mostly of young charismatics. Julie and I often sat up all night talking about the subject of the study or other spiritual things.

One morning I awoke to hear Julie talking frantically on the telephone. I put on my bathrobe and hurried into the kitchen. She had hung up, but her hand was still on the phone as if she were contemplating calling someone else.

"What is it?" I asked.

"Ruth! I just found out Billy's joined some extremist religious group."

"What?"

"They're supposed to be Christians, but he hasn't written or called his parents in weeks. Ruth, I don't think these people are what they say they are. Billy's at some camp that they started in west Texas, but I can't get through to talk to him—they always say he's busy. I'm not sure what to do."

I contacted two of Bill's friends, Dan and Robert, and we hurriedly made plans to go to this camp and try to find out what was going on there.

We went to a tiny community located several

miles out of Dallas. Just outside of the town was a sprawling ranch-like facility surrounded by high chain-link fences and barbed wire. It was called the Texas Soul Clinic, and it was the home base of a radical group of young Christians who called themselves the Children of God.

Small cabins dotted the landscape within the fenced-in enclosure, and there were a few larger buildings up ahead near the main entrance. We drove slowly toward the gate where two longhaired young men with walkie-talkies stood. As they approached the car, I sat in the backseat with my arm around Simba, gazing about the place.

Dan announced that we'd come to see Bill. One of the young men stepped away from the car and said something into the walkie-talkie. After pausing, he waved us through.

We followed the road past a large ranch house to a small cabin, where a young woman waved to us from the porch. We parked and got out, and I told Simba to stay in the car.

The woman led us into what she called a "greeting room." Its walls were covered with news clippings and photographs of the Children of God's exploits. Most were ministry-related, a few described their arrests for having disrupted services in other churches. Interspersed with the clippings were small posters with Bible quotations.

Two female members sat in the room with us. They seemed uneasy at our presence. We were there for a long time before Bill walked in, escorted by another young man.

"Billy!" I said excitedly.

"Bill, how are you?" Robert asked.

Around Bill's neck hung a miniature ox yoke on a thin leather band and a long string with a clothespin holding several pieces of paper. Though I hadn't known Bill very well, he now seemed like a total stranger. He looked a little spaced-out and acted as if he didn't want to see us.

"Can we speak with him alone?" we asked.

"Oh no." His escort shook his head and said nothing more.

There was an awkward silence. We sat down and tried to get Bill to talk about his decision to join the commune, but he seemed vague and distracted. I asked about the yoke around his neck.

"It's a symbol of the yoke of Babylon," interjected the young man beside him. "Like the one Jeremiah wore."

"Why the clothespin?" I asked.

"I'm memorizing God's Word," Bill replied vaguely. His expression never changed. Suddenly he stood up. "I've gotta go," he said.

"Billy, wait—"

"No, I can't stay. I've gotta go." The young man rose to go with him.

We all stood up. "Bill, let us hear from you," Robert called to Bill.

"We love you, Bill," Dan said. Then we looked at each other in confusion and helplessness.

One of the young women stood up. "Would you like to stay and have lunch with us?"

"Yes, we'd like that."

The woman gave us a tour of the facility. I was horrified. The only bathrooms were a long row of outhouses. A stack of newspapers sat in front of each one. Young women walked around in thin blouses held together only by string. Almost everyone we saw wore wrinkled or ragged jeans.

When we came to the large dining hall, we saw it had rows and rows of long tables—probably twenty or so. The woman led us to one of the front tables. Soon after we sat down, the rest of the 300-plus adults and children filed in. It took perhaps fifteen minutes for them to come in, and the room grew louder and louder.

Just in front of us was a high stool and a microphone hooked into a public address system. A bearded man with a guitar climbed onto the stool, watching as the room filled. After a while, he leaned into the microphone and shouted, "Revolution!"

That startled us, but not as much as the loud, fierce shout that followed:

"For Jesus!"

We were overwhelmed by the volume of the response.

"Holy Ghost!" he shouted again.

"Power!" they screamed, fists clenched tightly.

"Power to the Lord!"

"Power to the people of the Lord!"

A final roar echoed throughout the hall and then everyone sat down to eat. The bearded man strummed a few chords on his guitar, and in one corner of the room several members began dancing in circles.

I smiled in nervousness at the passersby, and one after another, they stopped to talk to us. We made small talk, asking about their communal life and ministry, but I longed to get out of there.

The food was unappetizing—leftover bread, aging fruit, and a starchy entree. The bearded man made some announcements, and someone else led everyone in prayer. Finally we ate.

After lunch we were led to another cabin, where we waited for the car. Against one wall a short, dark-haired, weasel-faced fellow in an embroidered shirt and jeans was leaning back in his chair. He said his name was Caleb, and that he was an artist. "You say you're Christians?" he asked.

I looked at him in surprise. "Yes."

"Then what are you doing out in the system?" His eyes were piercing, and he went into a stream of obscenities, railing against us and "the system."

"You say you love the Lord," he said at one point, "but you're part of the system. You're part of America, the Great Whore that God has called his people away from. He's called us to revolt against the world system and establish his kingdom of righteousness."

I didn't know what to say to this intimidating, vulgar man. He seemed to have the entire Bible memorized, but his words held nothing of the purity I believed God wanted from us.

He went on. "The Bible says, 'He who forsaketh

not all that he hath cannot be my disciple! He who loves his father and mother more than me is not worthy of me.'" And he went into another stream of swearing.

"But I do love the Lord!" I said, breaking in.

"How can you?" he shot back at me. "America is the center of the world system, and you're a systemite. You can't serve both mammon and God."

I was helpless. I had no Scripture memorized with which to respond to his accusations. I knew what God had done for me and that his presence was real in my life. But this foul-mouthed young man spouted more Scripture and opened his Bible to certain passages, demanding, "What about this? How can you deny this?" I was dumbfounded.

I felt relieved when it was time to go. But gnawing within me all the way home was the frustration of not knowing how to defend my faith.

CHAPTER
Five

I prayed with the Reeses daily for Bill's return, but after what I'd seen at the Texas Soul Clinic I didn't know exactly how to pray. Although the experience there had been disturbing, I didn't know if Bill was actually in danger. I had felt uncomfortable the entire time, but the Children of God seemed to know a lot about the Bible and salvation. I was very confused because they were young people like me, whose lives appeared to have been dramatically changed by God. The news clippings and photographs on their walls had told how they converted drug addicts. Yet I couldn't understand why they were so vulgar.

Several weeks after the trip to the Children of God compound, I got a letter postmarked from Oregon. My heart raced. It was from Timothy! I hadn't heard from him since he'd left Denver. I tore open the envelope and started reading. When I finished, I was in shock. I couldn't believe what he had written. I reread one sentence over and over: *I've been praying for a wife,* he wrote, *and every time I prayed you came to mind.*

My heart had been broken when he left Colorado, and after all this time I was still infatuated with my memories of him. Now I didn't have to force myself not to think about him anymore. I felt like the luckiest girl in the world.

"Thank you, Lord!" I shouted. I was so overwhelmed and surprised by the proposal that I thought, *God must be rewarding me for my patience.* In the letter, Timothy asked me to pray about the decision, but I had just one answer in my head. We would make the perfect pair—two Christians eager to serve the Lord, worshiping him together with our music, and loving each other with his perfect love.

I wrote back immediately with my official yes, and Timothy began hitchhiking down to Dallas to get me. We would hitchhike back to Portland for the wedding, stopping along the way in Santa Barbara to see my parents and in Santa Clara to see his mother.

When he arrived, all the memories of our times together came flooding back through his blue eyes. "Ruth," was all he said when I opened the front door—and I melted. We picked up where we left off, and it seemed as if we'd never been apart.

He stayed at the Reese's for two weeks before we started the trip back. During that time we learned new songs together and took our guitars to play for the hippies at a beautiful park nearby.

As Timothy talked eagerly to them about Jesus and the Bible, I began to look up to him even more as my spiritual leader. My spirit stirred and the Word of God came alive whenever we talked about God and his plans for our lives. I felt honored to be considered a worthy mate for him.

Finally the time came to leave. I squeezed what I needed into our two backpacks, and with faithful Simba tagging along we set out for California.

I was so full of joy of the Lord and of love for someone who genuinely cared about me that I looked forward to seeing my family. Timothy and I sang on the road between rides, and we witnessed to most of the people who picked us up. I saw the sun rise over the Arizona desert again, and I said good-bye to it. I was beginning a new life. The summer months had opened up a new world to me, and now it was time to harvest one of the greatest blessings of my life with the Lord. I was going back to Oregon, where it all began, to be married.

I had seen neither Santa Barbara nor my family for two years. It was early October when we arrived. Mom was happy to hear all that had happened, but she seemed skeptical. She thought I was just on another one of my tangents. Barry, my brother, reacted the same way, and I felt hurt and disappointed. I wanted so badly for them to know that what I had experienced was real, that I was a different person.

When I visited Dad at his rented room, he seemed sadder than I had ever remembered.

When I told him that I was a Christian now and living for the Lord, he too reacted coldly. He replied that he didn't believe in Jesus Christ. My deep emotional attachment to Dad didn't diminish. I wanted him to know that I was happy and straightened out, but I also wanted him to know the joy I'd found in the Lord.

Everyone in my family seemed to think Timothy was nice, but I'm sure they were skeptical in that regard, too. They knew what I'd been through with Steve, and Timothy was a bearded, long-haired young musician. Not at all promising as a husband for their vulnerable daughter.

When I said good-bye to everyone, I didn't know when or if I'd ever see them again. Timothy and I went on to Santa Clara, just south of San Francisco Bay. His mother was very polite and accommodating, but she didn't seem interested in either of us. She was divorced and acted a little peculiar toward me, but I couldn't tell if it was disapproval or indifference.

I hadn't expected that kind of reception, but nobody was going to rain on my parade. The disappointment withered quickly next to the anticipation of my new, upcoming marriage.

Timothy and I were wed in a riverside ceremony conducted by the pastor of a church in Portland. Timothy was not employed so we had to start our lives out in a rented room at a rundown boardinghouse. It was here that we spent our wedding night. We didn't have a honeymoon because the next morning I had to start a waitressing job that would support us while Timothy looked for employment. But I didn't mind. I was so happy to be married to him.

I was even happy to be waitressing again. It was a job well-suited to my friendly and efficient nature. Best of all, I loved people. I never felt that my waitressing was a case of me supporting my husband.

Apparently my being the one who was working didn't bother Timothy. He was always looking for work himself, but the only jobs he found were low-paying and temporary. As a result, he never had any money. When he wasn't job-hunting, he traded things for cash. I soon learned that he was a born horse trader and that no belongings of ours were safe. His deals brought in just enough money to put a little bread on the table—but that was all.

We still sang together on weekends at a church coffeehouse and that kept us reasonably content. But I had to change jobs constantly to try to make more money, and the financial problems resulted in increasing tension in our relationship.

Not far into the marriage I discovered that Timothy habitually berated himself for making mistakes or slipping up in his faith. "I'm rotten to the core!" he would yell, pounding his fists in frustration. For days after some minor spiritual failure he would act as though his world had come to an end. I slowly realized he was far from the mature spiritual leader I had once thought him to be.

Early that winter we moved to a small cabin in the mountains in Washington. I was grateful for the change of scenery, because our marriage needed it. Timothy hadn't worked for the four months we'd been married, and I had grown impatient with his lack of initiative. He seemed to have become totally indifferent to finding a job. He just kept trading everything.

One stormy afternoon, Timothy returned to the cabin after spending all day looking for work. He burst in with excitement, and I thought he had gotten a job. Instead, he announced with boyish delight that he'd traded his guitar for a fiddle, and he held it up proudly for me to see.

My heart raced. How was I to conceal the disdain I felt for this immature act? This was the final straw. "Timothy! How could you do this?" I raged. "Why didn't you ask me first?" He stared at me, clenched his fists in frustration, and stormed out of the cabin.

I began to cry and recognized that terrifying, dark feeling of being left again. "O God," I cried, "give me an answer. I need an answer." In despair, I stared out the window watching the river below. Later I wandered back to the bed and sat down. Just then I happened to glance up at a plaque on the wall: "He that dwelleth in the secret place of the Most High, shall abide under the shadow of the Almighty forever" (Psalm 91:1).

A faint melody began to form in my thoughts, and I quickly grabbed my guitar and a pencil and paper to jot down the words and chords to the music I was hearing in my heart—my first song as a Christian.

Jesus was a meek man,
He came to the sick at heart
To mend them, and to give them
Eternal Life.

And Jesus called the little children
To come unto him as little lambs,
And he cared for them . . .

He that dwelleth in the secret place
Of the Most High, shall abide
Under the shadow of the Almighty
Forever and ever.

As I sang my song I felt God had given me a beautiful experience out of the tumult that had taken place—and I was grateful.

Unfortunately, things didn't get better. The scene of us arguing and Timothy storming out was repeated several times during the next months. In a short while, everything seemed to be gone from our marriage—our dreams, our talks, our love. We moved back to the city, and my life took on a predictable pattern: I went to work, came home, fixed dinner, ate, went for walks with Simba, and went to bed. Timothy didn't talk about his trades anymore. He just sulked around the house.

Four houses, three cars, and five months later we were hitchhiking back to Dallas, hoping something there would save our marriage. After all, the Reeses were in Dallas, and Timothy and I had been happy with them before striking out for Oregon. Maybe we could recapture that happiness.

We arrived in Dallas with only sixty dollars, so we stayed the first night with the Reeses. Julie and I stayed up all night as we had before, but this time my heart poured out grief. She consoled me but confessed that she never thought Timothy was right for me. I wondered how she could have seen through him and I couldn't.

We found an inexpensive apartment to live in and set about trying to save our marriage. But it was too late. After only a few weeks Timothy told me he couldn't deal with our situation anymore. He said he was going to the mountains to pray, to try and determine God's will for him . . . and he didn't know when he'd be coming back. He went into our bedroom and started packing.

I couldn't handle watching him sort through our things, and I knew I wouldn't be able to stay and see him walk out the door. So I got up and called Julie.

Fifteen minutes later I heard her car drive up. Timothy was still packing as I hurried out, and when I got into the car I burst into tears. It was over.

For the rest of the weekend I stayed with Julie trying to recover from the initial shock of Timothy's abandonment. I couldn't bring myself to go back to the apartment. But after a few days I realized I had to get on with my life, and so I returned home with a slight hope that perhaps the whole dreadful experience had been a bad dream. Maybe Timothy was back.

When I arrived it became apparent that he had

not returned. I dropped to my knees in renewed despondency and began to weep. I was so utterly alone.

"God, what did I do wrong?" I asked him tearfully. "What is left?"

I didn't know what to think about my life. Everything I had been given was gone except for my beloved Simba. Every bit of faith had crumbled. How could God use me now? What could he do that would bring blessing again? Nothing, I thought. Nothing he could do would raise me out of this.

Early one morning several days later, when visiting the Reeses, I sat praying in the dark on the floor of their living room. The curtains were drawn, and a thin beam of light shone on the carpet beside me. My spirit had withered, and I desperately hungered for love.

I opened my Bible and my eyes immediately fell upon a series of verses from Isaiah 54. All at once the words leaped from the page, and I felt as though God was speaking to me almost audibly:

> "Do not be afraid; you will not suffer shame. Do not fear disgrace; you will not be humiliated. You will forget the shame of your youth and remember no more the reproach of your widowhood.
>
> "For your Maker is your husband—the Lord Almighty is his name—the Holy One of Israel is your Redeemer; he is called the God of all the earth.
>
> "The Lord will call you back as if you

were a wife deserted and distressed in spirit—a wife who married young, only to be rejected," says your God.

"For a brief moment I abandoned you, but with deep compassion I will bring you back. . . .

"Though the mountains be shaken and the hills be removed, yet my unfailing love for you will not be shaken nor my covenant of peace be removed," says the Lord, who has compassion on you. (Isa. 54:4-7, 10)

Hearing his voice so clearly, I again experienced the peace that passes all human understanding. He had found me again when I didn't have the strength to find him.

I spent the rest of the summer trying to put the pieces of my life back together. My grief began to subside, and the Reeses were even more generous than before, kind and patient with me in my brokenness.

I clung to that Scripture passage from Isaiah with all the faith my spirit could muster. I told myself I would always remember the power of the Lord's love for me as revealed through that passage. In addition, I had begun to read a book given me by a friend. It came to be a turning point for me and I will never forget it: *Hinds' Feet on High Places* by Hannah Hurnard. The story is an allegory about a little girl named Much Afraid— and I saw myself in that girl. She was crippled and rejected; she experienced terrible trials, all symbolic of her spiritual condition. I could not put the book down.

I read it in my every waking moment—on the bus to work, walking down the street, lying in bed at night. I soaked up strength from it the way a sponge soaks up water. I began to get excited about my relationship with Jesus again, happy that God saw fit (as the theme of the book suggested) to strip me of everything in order to prove to me that he was all I needed.

I was freed from a lot of guilt and accepted that I was not totally at fault for the slow destruction of my marriage. In reading the Hurnard book and studying Scripture, I realized that neither Timothy nor I had been spiritually mature enough to be married.

When I received no word from him after six weeks, I sensed it was over for good. Then, in the course of recovering from my hurt, I developed a hardness toward men. I think it was a subconscious attempt to avoid further hurt. I began to build walls of anger around myself. Soon my bitterness released that old monster that had lain dormant since my conversion: rebellion.

Finally I knew it was time to move on, so I moved into a duplex with my ever-faithful Simba and three cats. The International House of Pancakes (IHOP) down the street had just hired me for their graveyard shift. Meanwhile, Julie convinced me to go meet a group of young people with whom she thought I'd fit in— Christian musicians who attended a small college nearby.

As I spent time with this new group of people, an idea began to form in my mind. After the slow summer of rebuilding my emotional life, I wanted growth. The past few months had seemed so fruitless. I wasn't involved in any Bible study or evangelism groups. Now I wondered if I might find the growth I needed by attending classes at the Bible college.

Although by God's grace I had regained hope after my ordeal with Timothy, my bitterness was proof that I hadn't found complete healing. The possibility of going to the college presented a fresh alternative, a structured means of gathering my thoughts about where my life might, and should, be headed.

But there was one catch. Simba would not be allowed to go on campus with me. When I found that out, there was nothing to decide as far as I was concerned. I couldn't even consider leaving Simba alone all day while I went to school. It was bad enough that she was alone during my work hours. No, it was out of the question. She was too dependent on me. And I on her.

Several days later the night shift had seemed particularly long. When the four rowdies at my last table finally left, I was glad to be off work. I looked forward to the five-block walk home with Simba. I scooped up my jacket, burst out the restaurant door into the cold air, and whistled for Simba.

She wasn't there. I looked around, concerned. She *always* waited for me just outside the door.

"Simba!" I called. Something had to be wrong—she wouldn't leave.

I whistled louder and listened for the rattle of her tags, but there was only silence. I walked behind the restaurant into the parking lot. "Simba?" She always came when I called—always. I felt the panic starting to rise inside me. I ran to the near-empty street.

"Simba!"

I stood motionless, waiting to hear the jingle. Still no sound. I returned to the parking lot, fighting the fear. I wanted to hurry home to see if she was there, but I was afraid to leave the restaurant in case she came back.

Several times I started walking toward home, only to stop and go back to the parking lot. Finally I could wait no longer and I started for home again, calling her name every half block or so.

"Simba!"

My mind raced as I scoured the neighborhood on the way home. When I turned the corner of my block, I ran toward the house, hoping to see her sitting on the porch. But as I got closer, I saw she wasn't there.

"Simba!"

There was no answer.

I stopped and could no longer hold down the panic. I clutched my head in anguish. Simba had been with me through it all. She was the one true friend who had offered me faithful love through everything, who went everywhere with me and always waited for me. And now she was gone—and I knew it was forever. I felt as if my heart had been cut out. All I could think of was that God had finally taken away the last thing I loved.

I threw my fist into the air and shrieked, "Why did you do this to me!" I was barely conscious of the few lights that came on in houses along the block as I walked slowly up to the porch and sat down, unable to go another step.

Simba wasn't coming home.

After more than an hour of the night's stillness, I slowly went inside. Once there, though, I couldn't stop looking out the window, hoping to see a bustling white ball of fur come running up to the house. I began to cry softly, and finally I curled up on the bed. But I tried not to sleep; I didn't want to risk not hearing the rattling of tags.

I awoke the next day about noon with an unexpected feeling of peace and acceptance about the loss of Simba. *Maybe God took her away because I loved her too much,* I thought morbidly. *Or maybe it was so that nothing would prevent me from attending the Bible college.* Whatever the reason, I knew my life would be different from now on.

I checked the requirements for enrollment at the college. Because I had not graduated from high school I was told I could only enter as an auditing student without receiving any college credit. That was fine with me. My classes were in the afternoons, so I could still work night shifts at IHOP. It was my first attempt to give what we hippies had always called "organized religion" a chance.

The college had some small buildings on a campus only a few miles from the park near where I lived. Many warm afternoons I sat with friends on the lawn singing the new Christian folk-style songs that were springing from the newly forming generation of Christians. I remember the night we first played "One in the Spirit," which had only recently been written. About a dozen of us sat in the circle as I and a few others played our guitars. I was deeply moved watching the faces around me turned heavenward with eyes closed, singing praises to God and exulting in his presence among us.

I was quite taken with the pastor of the college, who led the Sunday morning chapel services. He was a distinguished man, a natural leader with an ability to make Scripture come alive. His gift for teaching was one of the reasons many young people enrolled at the college.

After only a few weeks of classes, however, I became disenchanted. My worship class, in which we studied the history and nature of worship, was interesting. But my basic theology class seemed to depersonalize God. I had never known the Lord in the well-outlined theological context set forth by my professor, and I found the apparent dissection of God complicated and presumptuous. *They're trying to explain him away in human terms,* I thought. I couldn't see him or know him by these standards.

Trying to resolve my confusion in class one day I began writing my second song, called "Let Jesus Touch You":

I asked the Lord to scrub the walls of my
  heart,
The loneliness of the world had torn my
  heart apart,
Then Jesus said, "I will give you a brand
  new start,"
Now I'm singing, bringing this message
  to you.

Peace that passes the understanding of
  the mind,
Love that's real and on your own you just
  can't find,
Let Jesus touch you,
Let Jesus touch you,
Let Jesus touch you,
In your heart.

Jesus isn't what I was brought up to think
  he was,
No one ever told me of the miracles he
  still does,
Church camps never changed me, hypocrites estranged me,
Yes, I'm sure you understand what I am
  saying to you.

After living in streets, running from
  pain, and flooded with pride,
I couldn't find peace or love no matter
  how hard I tried,
Then someone told me that Jesus' love
  was real,

And I could have it inside.
That's why I'm singing, bringing these
words of life to you. . . .

The message was simple; it revealed the young state of my faith at that time. And I left class that afternoon bewildered, thinking that perhaps Bible college wasn't for me after all. I stayed, though, mainly because of the persistence of Scott Clark, a friend I'd met there.

Scott was as straight as an arrow, always clean and orderly, like the Eagle Scout uniform he sometimes wore. We were unlikely friends, but only so far as outward appearances were concerned. I was drawn to Scott because of the genuine concern he showed for me as I struggled with these new concepts of faith. And although hardened inside, I was still gregarious and made casual friendships easily.

Scott quickly discerned the discontentment behind my happy exterior. Life was no longer an innocent experience of God's love; my seemingly perfect marriage had failed and my faith had come up short in the aftermath. The Lord had continued to show me his grace, but the simple faith I had relied upon for more than a year and a half suddenly seemed inadequate. Scott played a major role in my searching process. We talked for hours. I would pace the halls of the school, my hands dug deep into my pockets, and question matters of faith that I'd always taken for granted. He would walk alongside me, answering, encouraging, and seeing me through every crisis.

I played my guitar and sang at a coffeehouse that the college sponsored. Scott was often by my side. He was there for me—sort of a watchdog for my faith.

Scott was the prototype of the all-American boy: blond, nice-looking, trustworthy, ever helpful. But not long after we'd become friends, he revealed that he was slowly going blind. He could see fairly well when we first became friends, and the deterioration process was mercifully slow, but over the course of the term I saw the effects of his gradual loss of eyesight. He never became angry or bitter; instead, he always showed faithful, diligent love toward those around him. Though I had suffered a severe fall—a fall from faith—his example was helping to build me up again.

One Sunday morning in November I went to the chapel service on campus. I settled into a seat near the aisle, and the pastor announced that the service would feature a guest singing group. As he spoke, a parade of young hippies walked up to the front of the congregation.

"Brothers and sisters, let's offer praises to the Lord with our fellow ministers of the gospel—the Children of God!"

With a sickening realization I watched the group and was horrified. Yes, there were the same people. *Lord, what are they doing here?* Immediately I thought of Bill and looked for him, but he wasn't among them. He was only one of hundreds, maybe thousands by now.

Suddenly the auditorium was filled with energetic singing and guitar music. A number of the Children of God swirled in step to the Jewish folk dance I had seen at their compound more than a year before, randomly grabbing unwary members of the congregation. They all looked genuinely happy yet intensely serious. They looked straight at us as they sang, their eyes reflecting the fierce conviction of their music and dance. I could barely watch them. *How could they have been invited here?*

Finally the song ended, and one of their leaders stepped to the podium. He was short, with dark, wiry hair and piercing eyes. "I'm Philip," he said. "We want you to know what the Lord is doing through the Children of God."

I was angry at their presence, but I said nothing to the people around me. The group seemed to be dedicated, zealous young Christians, most of whom had been converted from drugs. Nobody in the congregation knew of the intimidation I had gone through at their camp or the hurt that the Reeses and I and Bill's parents had experienced over his involvement with this group.

Philip talked about how the Children of God rehabilitated drug-addicted hippies, brought them to Jesus, and trained them to evangelize. He made a good impression and that angered me even more.

The music started up again, and the group members held hands, kicking left and right and circling faster and faster. Suddenly I felt a tug on my arm. I looked up, and one of the Children of God members was trying to pull me out of my seat to join them. I pulled my arm away from him and looked straight ahead, angry and embarrassed.

That night, partly because of the chapel experience, I got into one of my depressed moods. Scott and I drove to an area airport just to walk around and talk things over. We were strolling the upper tier, where many people sat to watch the planes take off, when I looked down to the lower level and saw two hippies sitting on a bench with a Bible, obviously witnessing to another young man. One of the hippies was doing most of the talking. The other one looked up and saw me smiling.

"Are you guys Christians?" I inquired.

"Yes," he said.

"So are we," Scott told him with a smile.

"Hey," the hippie said, "come on down."

We walked down the stairs, but as we approached them I recognized the one doing the talking. It was Philip. My heart began to race and I wanted to turn and run.

Scott didn't know who Philip was, and before I could say anything we had sat down on the bench with them. Philip didn't pay much attention to us at first. He just kept talking to the young man. But when he said some things that weren't biblical, Scott challenged him.

Philip gave Scott a hard look. All I wanted to do was leave. Then, just as I'd expected, Philip immediately began to verbally attack Scott. He was condescending and condemning, and I grew angrier by the minute. Scott responded calmly, though, with Scripture and sound reasoning. Suddenly Philip was having to fight for his convert. He began to accuse us of not giving our all to Jesus. "You love the system," he said. "You're still a part of the world Jesus commanded us to come out of. You are wishy-washy Christians. The Word says you can't put your hand to the plow and look back—that if you're lukewarm, the Lord will spew you out of his mouth."

Neither Philip nor Scott gave an inch, and I grew increasingly anxious as Philip's exchange became more heated. Finally, I tugged Scott's arm. "Let's get out of here," I said.

"Want to go back upstairs?" Scott asked.

"No. Let's just go home."

I had enough of confrontation—and the Children of God—for one day.

About a month later I was hurrying across campus to class when I noticed everyone—students and faculty—walking toward the auditorium.

"What's going on?" I asked a girl nearby.

"They called a special assembly. Everyone's supposed to go."

I followed everyone to the large hall, which was filling rapidly.

The pastor sat between two administrators, a somber expression on his face—an uncharacteristic expression for him. When the room was packed, a portly school official ambled to the podium.

"We have a serious problem," he said, "and we need to pray."

The auditorium buzzed as everyone looked at

each other, puzzled. A second administrator stepped to the podium and led us in a lengthy prayer. The room echoed softly with sincere "amens" and "hallelujahs." As the noise died down, the portly official stepped up again.

"Our pastor," he said, "has confessed to us a grave sin."

The room fell silent in disbelief.

"The board met last night on this matter. And we," he paused briefly, "we decided that it's in the best interests of our Bible college that he step down from his position."

Everyone was shocked—what could he have done?

"We must pray for forgiveness—both his and ours," the official continued. "We all need the Lord's sovereign grace at times, and we need to seek the Lord about how we should proceed."

He turned and nodded to the pastor, who slowly unfolded himself from his seat. He awkwardly smoothed his slacks and loosened his tie. He let out a deep breath, then stepped cautiously to the microphone, and spoke in heavy tones.

"I have committed adultery—"

My blood ran cold. I stared as the pastor tried to finish his sentence over the sudden gasp of the audience. He lowered his head, then raised his hand. The looks on the faces around me revealed that most of the other students were as shocked as I was.

"I have repented and sought the Lord's forgiveness," he said softly. "Now I need yours." He looked down again, and stepped back from the podium. The portly official quickly came forward.

"It's important that we receive this in the spirit of Christ's forgiveness . . . ," he began, but I heard nothing else. As I stood and walked out, I thought, *So much for the faith in men that I've regained.* And so much, too, for organized religion. The angry rebel in me emerged full force.

CHAPTER
Six

The school temporarily closed its doors until
things "cooled down," as one administrator put it.
The coffeehouse remained open, however, and
though bewildered and disillusioned, I continued
singing there. I included a few of my own compositions in my repertoire, but mostly I sang the
new contemporary hymns and a few folk or rock
songs such as "Bridge over Troubled Water."

Scott still came to hear me sing whenever he
could, and afterwards we usually sat at the
round, wooden cable spools that were used for tables and talked. Scott's patience toward my unrelenting bitterness seemed limitless.

I didn't see much of my college friends other
than on the nights I sang at the coffeehouse. Most
of them still gathered there, but many had become disillusioned over the pastor's confession
and resignation and had disassociated themselves from the school altogether.

The gentle glow of the candles on each table in the coffeehouse offered little solace one night as I walked to the microphone. I climbed onto the high stool, picked up my guitar, and fingered the strings, humming the tune of the song "Bridge over Troubled Water." The chords came easily, and an old familiar feeling came back too. As I closed my eyes and sang, I thought of the losses I'd faced in my life that year.

Suddenly, the door burst open and a group of seven or eight hippies walked in carrying guitars. I continued singing as someone quickly whispered, "Uh-oh. It's the Children of God." I struggled to retain my composure.

They're going to make a scene, I thought, but kept on singing. I tried to think of a way to keep them from ruining the evening. I wasn't going to let them take over the coffeehouse, which was clearly what they wanted to do. I decided to take the offensive and invite them to play a song.

"Hi," I said to them when I finished. "You look like you're ready to play something for us."

Their presence had put everyone in the coffeehouse on edge. Like me, the people in the audience felt as if we were under these hippies' watchful, accusing eyes.

"Yes, we'd like that," one of the COG group enthusiastically responded to my invitation. He leaned toward his group and said something, then announced, "We'd like to do a song called 'We are Gypsies Led by Abraham.'"

I left the stool and sat down at one of the few empty tables, waiting nervously for them to sing their song and leave. They didn't all approach the front, however, just the four who had guitars. The rest of the group formed a circle around the room, holding hands and singing.

The first few chords caught my attention immediately. It was like the gypsy music my father had often played, and I was captivated. It was driving, yet haunting, and it drew me in, but I would not let myself enjoy it. I still didn't trust these people.

The group kept singing, and as I looked around the room I could tell people were moved. *These people must really be gypsies of the Lord,* I thought, *and everyone here knows it. They live the life they're singing about.* For a moment, the awful memory of the compound in west Texas escaped me.

The song ended, and my spirit stirred as the guitar players started another one. The people who had danced together now stopped and merged into the audience, witnessing to everyone there. One of them, a shy-looking young girl about my age, sat down alone.

I saw the chance to do some witnessing of my own, something I hadn't done with much conviction lately, and I walked over to her table and pulled out a chair. "Hi," I said, "my name is Ruth."

"I'm Mary," she said, somewhat excited to see me. "Praise the Lord, Ruth. I really loved your music."

As we talked, mostly about spiritual things, I noted that she had the sweetest smile. Her relationship with the Lord seemed genuine, and I liked her. I felt comfortable with her, which was surprising after my encounters with Philip and Caleb.

As we talked, the guitar players were singing something about being "Mountain Children," creating a mystical atmosphere in the room. As I listened I felt more and more drawn into the spell the music and lyrics seemed to be weaving. It was wonderful, and inviting, and I wanted to hear more. Mary's voice was soft as she told me about the Children of God's work for the Lord's kingdom. While she spoke, a stocky, good-looking young man who had been among the guitarists came to our table. He was clean-cut, had relatively short hair and didn't wear a beard like most of the other men. He wore a button-down shirt, well-pressed corduroys, and wire-rim glasses. He was friendly and, like Mary, gave me the impression that he liked me.

"What's your name?" I asked him.

"Issachar," he said. Philip, Mary, Caleb. The Children of God obviously adopted biblical names when they joined the group, just as I had done when I became a Christian.

The candlelight gave Mary's face a warm glow, and the gypsy music continued as Issachar made casual, friendly conversation. They had such good rapport with each other and with me that I thought, for the briefest second, that they were the kind of friends I'd like to have. I soon felt so at ease with them that I asked, "Why are some of the Children of God so intimidating?"

Neither showed surprise at my question. "Not

everyone's like that," Mary said. "Most of the group has mellowed out quite a bit. You know how it can be when you're young in the faith. You want everyone to know the truth about Jesus. You don't want anything to compromise your walk with him, or anyone to refute the truth about him."

We talked for a long time, not just about the Children of God, but about serving Jesus with one's whole heart and obeying him fully. I didn't bring up any of my personal problems. In fact, as we talked I'd forgotten about most of them. I just felt invigorated to be talking about God with these people.

After a while the music stopped, and soon the coffeehouse began to shut down for the night. Mary smiled at me again and said, "Ruth, it was so nice to talk to you."

"Yes," Issachar said, "I believe it was God's will that we met tonight."

Somehow I didn't want our encounter to end this way. We hadn't come to a resolution. I wanted to witness to them, and they to me—we all wanted to reach the truth. So I offered to walk them out to their car.

We stepped out into the brisk night and walked toward their van. The moon was out, and I grew thoughtful in the darkness. Suddenly Issachar turned to me and said, "Ruth, we're having a turkey dinner tonight for Christmas. You ought to come."

"What?" I laughed. "You're kidding. It's one o'clock in the morning."

"No, really." Mary laughed too. "There'll be a lot of people there. We'd love for you to come."

"Come on, Ruth," Issachar said. "I know you'd like it."

I had to get up at six that morning to go to work, but I wanted to go. Having met two nice members of the Children of God, I wanted to make sure my previous suspicions were correct before writing them off. I just couldn't justify ending it here. Besides, I was still very curious about them.

"Sure," I said, "I'll go."

"Oh, good!" Mary exclaimed.

The group had started loading their guitars into the van, and I handed them mine. As they climbed into the back of the van, I felt a strong tug on my arm. It was one of my friends from the college. He pulled me aside and said, "Ruth, what are you doing?"

"It's OK. They just invited me to have dinner."

He looked puzzled, as if to say, "At one o'clock?"

A girl from college pleaded with me. "Ruth, don't. You don't know what you're getting into. They teach strange things."

"I just want to see for myself," I said. I figured I was a big girl and I could certainly take care of myself.

"Ruth, don't go," the fellow said. "You don't know—"

"I'm not being forced to do anything," I interrupted him impatiently. "What's wrong with going for dinner?"

I looked toward the van. Someone had started singing in the back; the doors were still open, and they all were waiting for me. Mary beckoned to me.

"It'll be OK," I whispered and I started for the van. I knew they were concerned, so I turned and gave them a reassuring wave.

I climbed into the crowded van, and Issachar shut the doors behind me.

Several people were playing their guitars in fun and singing a little ditty—"We love you, Mary, we love you, Mary, we love you, Mary, yes we do, we love you, Mary, we love Mary, praise the name of the Lord." They repeated the verse several times, including each person's name. They rocked from side to side, arms around each other, smiling and laughing. I glanced at Mary, who sat across from me. She smiled as the song continued.

"We love you, Ruth, we love you, Ruth. . . ." I was caught by surprise when I heard my name. I didn't think I would be included; they hardly knew me. As I looked around, they all were smiling at me. I felt a little embarrassed but enjoyed the attention. This love, I thought, was real. I could feel it.

Ten minutes later we pulled to a stop. "This is it," Issachar said. "The Rock House."

I stepped down and saw an enormous house in a quaint old neighborhood. I thought perhaps the building may have been a rooming place at one time. The most distinguishing characteristic was the foundation of stone all around the base of the house. Hence, I assumed this was the reason for the name "Rock House."

All the lights were on, and the silhouettes of people filled the windows. "How many people live here?" I asked.

"About forty," Issachar said. "But there'll be a lot more than that tonight."

He was right. There had to be a hundred people there, and they all were downstairs singing and dancing and laughing. I had never seen so many people in such close quarters. I felt sort of strange among them and a little out of place, but Issachar stayed with me most of the time. When he wasn't around, someone else always was.

I felt uncomfortable nevertheless. A number of the young people there were ragged-looking. Some had dirty hair, some had wrinkled or dirty clothes. Girls wore the string blouses, I remembered, and no bras. Most of the people, including the young men, were wearing leather pouches similar to small purses over their shoulders.

As I watched I thought that I'd never seen a group of Christians so tightly knit. They constantly hugged each other and seemed to love each other deeply. Most of the people who approached me tried to witness to me, quoting the same Scripture verses, saying the same phrases ("I forsook my possessions, my family, and my job to serve the Lord"; "Why should I live in the 'pit' [the world] when I can be the Lord's disciple?"), and asking the same questions ("Why don't you come follow Jesus and not just live for him halfway? You can't really love him if you are part of the 'system.'").

Some of them mentioned the teachings of a

man named Moses, saying his prophecies fell into line with both Jesus' prophecies and those of the Old Testament. I didn't know the particular passages they talked about well enough to agree or disagree, but everyone else seemed to know what he was talking about.

After a while, some people started the responsive yells I'd heard at their ranch a year before: "Revolution!" *"For Jesus!"* This time, though, it didn't startle me. In fact, it was rather exciting. Everyone was called to gather in the large, rectangular living room that was lined with couches. As the guitars began playing we held hands and formed two circles—one within the other—because there were so many people. We started dancing. Once again, as I looked around, I was impressed by the size of their ministry.

Everyone in the place seemed happy—excited, yet peaceful. They sang a few more songs, then everyone formed a dinner line. I noticed that most of the people quoted Scripture verses to another member before receiving their plate.

"Why are they doing that?" I asked a girl nearby.

"We have to learn a couple of verses from the Word every day, or else we don't get our supper," she responded.

That was peculiar, I thought. The dinner, though, was not. It reminded me of home: turkey, dressing, mashed potatoes, cranberries, hot tea, rolls, and a slice of pumpkin pie. Even though I fed myself well at the apartment, I hadn't had a luscious home-cooked meal like that one in a long, long time.

After dinner, everyone suddenly quieted and an authoritative-looking girl strutted into the room and began to speak. Issachar sat next to me on the floor and said we were about to see a videotape of Dad's youngest daughter, Faithy, in Hyde Park, London.

"Who's 'Dad'?" I asked. "Everyone keeps talking about him."

"That's Moses," he said, smiling. "He's God's end-time prophet."

I was bewildered. As the video began, a loud whoop went up from the room followed by hushes, then an eerie silence. A young woman with long, blonde hair appeared, standing in the midst of a large crowd of hippies. "Praise the Lord," she began cheerily.

She gave a brief review of the "Revolution for Jesus" and its first international move to London. I didn't understand much of the rest—it was mostly insiders' talk, I figured. When the video ended, everyone in the room cheered wildly.

When Issachar drove me home, he invited me to come back to the Rock House the next evening. "Our doors are always open," he said with a smile. "There's a lot to talk about, Ruth."

There was indeed. And a lot to think about, too.

After my waitressing shift I went home and took a long nap. When I got up I fixed myself a sandwich, got dressed, and went back to the Rock House.

The place looked desolate; apparently, the

only person there was the "greeter" who came to the door. All the members were out "witnessing" he said. He told me to sit down and have a "class" with him. This was a short Bible study written by one of the leaders, named John, formerly of the Jesus People movement.

I returned again the next day—then frequently during the next few weeks. I avoided Scott, knowing he would be upset. I didn't want to have to give account to my friends from college, so I didn't go back to the coffeehouse. I split time between work and visiting the Children of God "colony."

During those two weeks I learned the Children of God's fundamental doctrines on the Holy Spirit, witnessing, and Old Testament prophecy. They probably didn't know they had a skeptic on their hands, and when they made certain references to Scripture with which I wasn't familiar, I wrote them down to check in my Bible at home. I was hoping to find blatant errors, but when I looked them up, sure enough, they were all there.

The classes intrigued me and quenched my thirst for biblical teaching, though I was still doubtful about their interpretations of passages with which I was not familiar. Most of the interpretations seemed legalistic and radical, but I had no way to disprove them. Some of them, however, seemed to make sense. So I wasn't sure what to think.

I took the study materials home and sat at my dining room table poring over the lessons. I was still uncomfortable with the teachings in general, but I couldn't figure out why. I could find nothing specifically wrong with them. After a while, I began to think that I was the one who was wrong for refusing to embrace the apparently biblical foundations of the Children of God.

I had become acquainted with several of the commune members and their leaders, and they all urged me to join. Some even came to see me at the IHOP, where I sat and talked with them during my breaks. They seemed a little pushy, but I didn't mind; I was learning to ignore that.

One day after class I was upstairs at the colony with Issachar, making casual conversation. Suddenly Issachar grew serious, then reached into his shirt pocket and unfolded a piece of paper.

"I want to read you something, Ruth," he said. "It's a very special letter. OK?"

"OK," I said, trying not to show my curiosity.

With deep emotion, he began to read a letter entitled "Mountain Men." As he read, I noticed it had been typed and photocopied. " 'Relating to an incident where some of the Children of God were arrested by police for merely witnessing to groups of kids who gathered around them during a Frontier celebration in the Rio Grande valley of Texas across the border from Mexico.' "

"What?" I asked, slightly confused.

He didn't look up. " 'I climbed many mountains,' " he read, " 'and I was almost always alone. Why? One: It's hard work. Two: Not very many people desire to climb mountains. Three: It's lonesome. Four: You have to forsake all to do it.

Five: It's apt to cost you your life. Six: Lots of scratches and bumps.'"

"Who wrote that?" I asked.

"Just listen," he said, then went on reading: "'If you're going to climb them, they have to be worth dying for, to brave wind and cold and storm, symbolic of adversities. But on the mount you feel so close to the Lord! The voice of his Spirit there is so loud it's almost thundering! The voice of the multitude is so loud in the valley, you can't hear the voice of God.'"

What he read started to make sense to me. In fact, it described the past few weeks of my life. I had experienced many things with the Children of God and had found them satisfying. After such a long, dry period, I finally had begun to grow spiritually again. This group had nurtured me.

Issachar read on. "'How many people who go back really see what they are getting into? . . . A terrible letdown! You're just sliding back into the slough—back into the morass of humanity and mire of the multitude.'"

Every word seemed to ring loudly in my mind.

"'Only pioneers climb mountains. . . . Pioneers must have Vision—vision to see what no one else can see; Faith—faith to believe things no one else believes; Initiative—initiative to be the first one to try it; Courage—the guts to see it thru!'"

The words were more water for my thirsty soul. I was drinking them up fast.

"'Only his disciples came unto him. When he went up into the mountain the only ones who had the priceless privilege of hearing the world's most famous sermon—the only ones who really heard from heaven that day were the ones who left the multitudes and took the mountain—the ones who followed Jesus all the way.'"

Issachar stopped there and folded the letter. "That was a letter from Moses to his followers, Ruth."

I was amazed. I thought it described the kind of life every Christian had to want, a life of serving the Lord. I certainly wanted it. As far as I was concerned, the man who wrote the letter had to be extraordinary.

After that, I felt I understood the Children of God better. Like the saints of the early church, they preached the gospel to the unsaved and were persecuted for it. On top of that, they were rebels. So their way of living the crucified life told me that I could be both a Christian and a rebel—in fact, they were saying that being a Christian *necessitated* being a rebel.

I went home that afternoon and started reading my lesson. It was on forsaking all to follow Christ and was based on the Book of Acts. I read about Pentecost and the countless miracles of the New Testament church, about Peter bringing three thousand to Christ with his first sermon, the angel freeing him from prison, and the healing of the crippled beggar. It was all exciting, and I couldn't help but wonder why the church wasn't like that today.

From what I had seen of the Children of God, I knew they had forsaken everything to live together as disciples and minister the gospel full-time.

I examined my own life and saw in contrast what a selfish existence I led—caring only about myself, doing my own thing. Where was the victory in Jesus? I had no vision, no goals, no motivation other than day-to-day survival. My college friends didn't even come close to accomplishing what the Children of God were accomplishing every day. Suddenly, I was struck with the fear that perhaps I hadn't been serving God at all.

I knelt and prayed, "O Lord, help me. I want to serve you, Father." I continued praying, but couldn't find peace. I turned to the lesson again, and it directed me to a passage in Luke 14:

"If anyone comes to me and does not hate his father and mother, his wife and children, his brother and sisters—yes, even his own life—he cannot be my disciple.

"And anyone who does not carry his cross and follow me cannot be my disciple.

"Suppose one of you wants to build a tower. Will he not first sit down and estimate the cost to see if he has enough money to complete it? For if he lays the foundation and is not able to finish it, everyone who sees it will ridicule him, saying, 'This fellow began to build and was not able to finish.'

"In the same way, any of you who does not give up everything he has cannot be my disciple."

That next morning I rushed over to the colony to look for Issachar. I had some exciting news and I wanted him to be the first to hear. I had to wait all day before I could talk to him because he was out taking care of some business—he was an accountant before he forsook his job and joined the COG, and now he helped the "family" with legal matters.

After dinner he showed up. I had felt some reservations and doubts while I was waiting, but when I saw him I blurted out, "Issachar, I want to forsake all and follow Jesus, too!" Everyone around us went into an uproar, and suddenly I was surrounded by people hugging me and swinging me around. I felt loved and accepted, a very welcome feeling after all the rejections I'd experienced in my life. I knew the time had come to burn my bridges behind me and move forward to a new life with God.

CHAPTER

Seven

When things calmed down, the people around me explained that joining the Children of God meant I must relinquish everything—bank account, car, whatever. I had to forsake it all by giving it to the commune. They stressed I should hold nothing back from the Lord, lest I be destroyed like Ananias and Sapphira. Issachar reminded me that this was what the first-century church had done in the Book of Acts.

I knew that joining the Children of God wouldn't be just another adventure for me, and that it would require an absolute commitment. Yet as I looked at the faces around me I knew that was exactly what I wanted and needed.

Suddenly I saw a familiar face in the crowd of disciples. "Bill? Bill, is that you?" It was indeed my friend from the commune! Nobody knew who I was talking to because he had assumed a biblical name upon entering the Children of God family (as did all new members)—and he seemed a little embarrassed by this revealing of his identity—but then he ran over and hugged me as if I'd just made the single most important decision of my life.

He was given permission to accompany me to the apartment to help me in the "forsake all" process. In the van on the way to my home I picked up my guitar and began playing one of the songs I'd learned at college. Bill quickly rebuked me. "Why do you sing all those systemite songs, Ruth?" I was mortified. No one had ever interrupted me in the middle of a song before. I learned then that I was supposed to sing only the songs of the "Revolution for Jesus," compositions written by members of the "family." I also learned very soon not to buy or read newspapers, magazines, or any other reading material from the "outside," watch television, or listen to the radio.

We arrived at the duplex and I went into the kitchen to start wrapping all my beloved Blue Willow dishes. I'd collected them for years, piece by piece. When I walked back into the living room, Issachar and Bill were putting everything that I'd worked so hard for into large boxes: my velour towel sets, matching bedsheets, drapes—everything. Nothing was sorted or taken account of. It was all just thrown with a *whoosh* into massive boxes. The tangible memories of my adult life were literally passing before my eyes. I wasn't prepared to watch my beautiful dresses and outfits manhandled so carelessly. But I found that as those belongings were being cast into the boxes, so were my worldly cares for them.

As we drove back to the commune, I knew I was beginning to understand. The Rock House would be my new home. It would be an adventure—my next step of faith with the Lord.

"You should get situated in one of the girls' dormitories," Issachar said when we got to Rock House. He took the suitcase from my hand and gave it to a long-haired girl, who smiled knowingly. "Come with me, Ruth," she said, and I followed her down a dark hallway where I'd never been allowed to visit.

The walls of the bedroom were lined with three-tiered bunk beds. *You're in the Army now,* was my first thought; my second was, *This is a part of "forsaking all."* That thought reminded me of my renewed commitment to Jesus, and I felt a surge of security well up inside.

"Let's go through your things and see what you'll need," a red-haired girl said eagerly as she unsnapped the locks on the suitcase and began sifting through my neatly folded clothes. I couldn't help thinking how out of place my nice things looked compared to theirs, and my face flushed a little.

"Oh, Ruth," said the red-haired girl ominously, staring down into my suitcase. She took a short stack of family photos from it and, upon further inspection, produced the selected few personal letters I had brought. She turned to me with a serious look. "You won't need these."

I swallowed hard.

"Really, Ruth," a tall young woman said with a nod of sympathy and a knowing look. "You won't want them."

It was killing me. *Forsaking all means all, not some. Remember Lot's wife,* I told myself, recalling the Scripture passage from one of my COG lessons on not looking back to the past.

Suddenly the red-haired girl was ripping up the photos and handing them to the next girl, who tossed the pieces into a trash can. A protest rose in my throat, but I suppressed the feeling and didn't say anything.

Nevertheless, as each personal item was disposed of, I felt saddened. All my bridges to "the system" were now burned. Except one.

Scott's car was parked in front of Julie's house. *Oh, God,* I thought, *why did he have to be here?* I had planned on asking Julie to break the news to him—that is, after I broke the news to her. Now the situation would be doubly stressful.

I wouldn't have been allowed to go back to the Reeses' house had Bill not known the family also. I told him that I at least needed to say good-bye to Julie, and, although we both knew it was against the COG's rules, he spoke to the leaders on my behalf.

The COG leaders already considered me a "problem case" because of my prior Christian indoctrination. I would have to be retrained and taught the "true" Word of God. Already I had shown resistance to some of their regulations.

First, I had refused to change my name to another biblical name because, as I explained to them, I had already done that when I first became a Christian. It was difficult for them to accept this. Also, I refused to quit my job at IHOP without giving two weeks' notice. This angered them because such a job was a part of the "system." I couldn't see my employers as enemies, however, and I cared enough about them to not leave them in a bind. Yet COG was determined to keep me one way or another, even if they had to temporarily make a few compromises.

They agreed to let Bill drive me to the Reeses', where I planned to give my Blue Willow dishes to Julie and my guitar to her thirteen-year-old daughter, Heather.

Bill waited in the car while I rang the bell. When Julie opened the door, her brown eyes widened. "Oh, Ruth," she said, and hesitated for a moment before giving me a hug. She obviously knew something had happened to me. Word probably got around somehow to both the Reeses and Scott that I had been regularly visiting the COG colony.

I walked in, at peace because my mind and heart were settled, but when I saw Scott standing across the room, I grew cold. Neither of us said anything, and I could tell he already sensed I had rejected him in some way.

"Ruth," Julie asked warily, as if she didn't want to know the answer, "where have you been? I've been trying to call you."

"I joined the Children of God," I said outright. I had to let them know up front.

Immediately their faces filled with horror.

"It's what the Lord wants me to do," I said in an effort to reassure them, but it didn't help.

"Oh, Ruth," Julie began, "you just don't know . . ." Her voice trailed off. Suddenly I began to resent them for not trusting my judgment in the matter.

"I've prayed about this," I said, "and I really feel it's the right thing for my life."

"Oh, my God," Julie groaned, and she started to cry.

Scott stepped forward angrily. "You don't know what you're doing, Ruth!" he shouted. I'd never seen him so furious. He stopped talking and tried to calm down. "You're making a big mistake," he finally said. "Think about it some more. Let's talk about it, Ruth."

I simply looked at him and he turned his gaze to the floor, his face showing his pain. Julie continued to cry. Scott made a sudden step toward me, then stopped abruptly and looked at the floor again. He stood there for a moment, unable to look at me, and finally turned and left the room.

Julie looked up with tears on her face. "Oh, how could you, Ruth?" she said. "How could you do this to us? To *yourself!*"

I realized then that they both had worried over me for the past few weeks. They didn't want to see me leave.

I wanted to console Julie, but I knew there was nothing I could say to help her understand. "I'll be back in a minute," I said calmly, and walked out to the car to get the things I'd brought.

The next morning I awoke just before daybreak to a rousing solo.

"Rise and shine and give God the glory, glory...!"

My gosh, I thought as I opened my eyes, *it's still dark outside.*

I felt someone touch me on the shoulder. "Ruth, get up," said one of the sisters. I looked up and saw all the girls getting up and scurrying around. "We've only got fifteen minutes in the bathroom before it's the guys' turn."

"OK," I moaned, trying to hide my displeasure. I had to use the bathroom, but decided to wait until all the other girls came out. But they continued to pile in, and few of them came back. Finally a tall young woman advised me to go ahead.

I peered inside, hoping my embarrassment wouldn't be noticed. I had become quite modest since my hippie days and I longed for privacy, but this was obviously going to be an unfulfilled longing.

I now understood why so many of the COG women had hairy underarms and appeared unkempt. There wasn't time for such self-conscious acts of grooming! Every hour of the day was scheduled. After we dressed and made our beds, all the disciples divided into small assigned groups for "tribe" meetings. My tribe leader led us in song with a guitar, then gave a short devotional and prayer. But all I could think about was food.

Afterward everyone assembled in the living room for breakfast, which usually consisted of either instant oatmeal, pancakes made from cake mix, or leftover donuts we got free from the generous proprietors of a local Dunkin' Donuts. After breakfast there was a short meeting of the entire household, and then it was "Jesus Job Time." Everyone had an assigned task: the older members went out to witness or solicit donations, and the new converts, or "babes"—which, I discovered, included me—stayed for cleanup and several hours of Bible classes. At the end of class each of us was given two Scripture verses to memorize daily. The passages had to be quoted from memory in exchange for supper each evening. The Scripture references were printed on cards and ranged from basic salvation verses to entire chapters and long prophesies out of the Old Testament.

After supper, everyone gathered in the living room for what was called "inspiration"—a combination of singing and dancing. During this time one of the COG leaders usually gave a brief, Scripture-based talk or read one of the prophetic letters by Moses, the COG's founder, about whom I had heard so much. These letters were commonly known among COG disciples as the Mo letters.

When it was time to read one of these letters, a hush always fell throughout the room. I realized that Issachar had taken a big chance when he read to me parts of the Mo letter called "Mountain Men." Since I hadn't been a follower then, he probably could have gotten in trouble for even mentioning it without special permission. Judging by the intent faces around me as the Mo letters were read, I now began to recognize the sacredness and depth of "Mountain Men."

Moses David lived in London and wrote his instructive letters to COG colonies from his home there. I never asked about him, about his character or physical appearance; no one did. To do so would have revealed an earthly preoccupation rather than the spiritual reverence required of a COG disciple. In the letters Mo usually expounded upon a biblical principle and included several references to Scripture.

Most of his communications dealt with radical, self-sacrificing themes, the kind of extremist principles I'd heard at the COG ranch in Thurber. The life-style that Mo demanded of the Children of God members for the gospel's sake left no room for compromise.

I certainly responded to Mo's leadership. In fact, the COG's radical message was a vehicle for the deep-seated rebellion that had evolved in my heart during my spiritual trials. My anger and bitterness toward the church could now be vented. The rebel in me that had lain dormant was reawakened by the COG's revolution for Jesus.

What I found most fascinating about the COG in those first few days was its great cross section of young people, from the extremely gifted to the simpleminded, from the formerly rich to the chronically destitute. The COG seemed to take no account of a person's background, color, or education. All it required, from what I could see, was one's heart—all of it.

Curiously, none of the Children of God ever spoke about their lives prior to joining the COG; most only told about how they joined the group. Issachar occasionally pointed out disciples and told me things about them, but I didn't get to know anyone very intimately. Since we were in groups for most of the day's activities, what the COG lacked in close personal relationships was made up for in group camaraderie. Unfortunately, there seemed to be no room for individualism.

The COG's usual practice with "babes" was to immediately send them to a distant colony where they couldn't be reached by relatives or friends. There they received three months of intense "babes' training." This consisted of everything we had seen at our compound: strict Scripture memorization, the constant blaring of verses over loudspeakers, changing one's name, dogged accompaniment by a more "mature" COG member, and a rigid morning-till-night schedule that kept babes occupied. There wasn't even a moment for private meditation. "An idle mind is the devil's workshop," the COG leaders insisted.

The thought of having to go through babes' training hurt my pride. I'd been a Christian for two years, and I already knew most of the Scripture passages and biblical principles that the babes had to learn. Also, I had already learned most of Moses David's "Revolutionary Rules" for new converts in the COG's afternoon classes.

Though many of these rules were based on biblical principles, they also demanded strict unquestioning obedience to the COG leaders, because as Mo pointed out from Hebrews 13:17, "Obey them that have the rule over you, and submit yourselves: for they watch for your souls, as they that must give account, that they may do it with joy, and not with grief: for that is unprofitable for you" (KJV).

This was rule eight of the "Revolutionary Rules," and it also applied to doubting. "You must obey implicitly, quickly, and without question, your officers in the Lord," Mo wrote. Anyone who had doubts about Mo's letters or a leader's directives was considered spiritually weak. Thus, whenever I had questions or doubts, I—like everyone in the COG—considered them to be from the devil, and buried them.

At the time I joined COG the Mo letters were read only by the leaders. His writings were to stand on their own merits as modern-day revelations from the Lord to his prophet. No one was supposed to interpret them; they were only to report their instructions to the disciples.

Oddly, that strict adherence to rules provided COG members with a sense of security: None of us had to make our own judgments, so we weren't responsible for the consequences. Everyone felt safe in the COG's chain of command. This further strengthened the group mentality, making it rare for anyone to voice opposition.

So whatever the COG leaders decided about my status as a new member I had to accept without question. Yet they remained divided on what to do with me. Some felt I should be shipped out to a babes' ranch to be retrained. Others considered that unnecessary and felt my musical talents could be better utilized in Dallas. The leader who supported this option most was a former highway patrolman who had been renamed Barnabas. Barney, as he was dubbed, was revered as one of the top leaders. He also was a gifted singer and musician who often added spiritual lyrics to pop tunes. (These adaptations were known among not only the COG but also the Christian community as sancti-songs or "sanctified" rock songs.) One night Barney overheard me humming a harmony to one of his songs and invited me to sing with him. Since I had not been allowed to play with the music leaders because I was a babe, I was quick to accept his invitation. I picked up his guitar and went through a couple of standards that I'd sung in coffeehouses, and he was visibly pleased by my performance. He also realized that I sang from the heart.

After that, Barney let me sit up at night with him after the official "lights out." We would talk about the Lord and about the COG and sing together. During those sessions he began to take me under his wing—quite a privilege for a lowly babe.

It was Barney who came up with a solution for what to do with me: "Give her a guitar and let her go out with Issachar and the other public relations people. Don't let her gift go to waste."

To be involved in the public relations ministry was a high honor. I accompanied the P.R. team on forays like the one they had made to the college coffeehouse the night I met Issachar and Mary. Those sorts of appearances were not always for proselytizing. They also served as opportunities to present a positive image of the COG to the area communities. One of my first experiences doing this was at a "THANKCOG" meeting. The COG organized these meetings to calm fears about the group. They invited parents and friends of COG members who were not openly hostile to the COG, as well as local civic leaders, merchants, and businesspeople who might be persuaded to provide for the group financially. THANKCOG meetings also were a counter-reaction to a growing parental group called Free Our Children from the Children of God (FREECOG).

In June all of Dallas was preparing for a monumental, historic occasion called Explo '72. Explo was a gathering of more than 75,000 young Christians from across the United States and sixty foreign countries for an International Student Congress on Evangelism sponsored by Campus Crusade for Christ International. Billy Graham, the main speaker of the six-day event, would later call Explo "a religious Woodstock."

The youth assembled on the state fairgrounds near downtown Dallas, where countless Christian groups had set up booths. We gained access to a vacant warehouse, set up sleeping and eating areas, and opened it to the thousands of young people who had come without money or accommodations.

The leaders of our COG colony chose Issachar and me as supervisors of the warehouse during the week. He was put in charge of the young men who stayed there; I, the young women. I felt important, trusted, and respected—and it felt good.

Every day that week, we brought in busloads of young people—mostly hippies, and many non-Christians. We used this opportunity to witness to them and make some converts. I especially enjoyed this time because Issachar was one of the most responsible people I had ever met, and I got to know him a little better while we worked together. He was always neat and was patient with everyone, and I found myself growing very fond of him.

After Explo, one of the leaders asked me to pray about going to Houston to help the colony there. I reluctantly said I would, but I didn't really want to go; it would mean separation from Issachar. It became obvious, however, that if the leadership felt God had spoken to them about my going to Houston, then I had no choice but to go. For the first time in my COG experience I felt the very subtle pressure of being asked to pray about something, then realizing that what I was really being told was, "Do it." Within a few days I was packing. As I said good-bye to Issachar, I sensed his hurt that our friendship seemed to have reached its end.

While in Houston, I was assigned the privilege of looking after the infant daughter of Ahaz, the colony leader. I was left alone with her much of the time, though new disciples were seldom allowed to be without an "older" brother or sister. Ahaz also gave me access to his collection of Mo letters. One of the first that I read on my own was a missive entitled "Faith." I read the letter while holding the baby, and was struck by the parental gentleness and compassion with which Mo instructed his disciples. In the letter, he seemed eager for the COG converts to experience the Fatherhood of God:

> "When I go, you folks have got to remember . . . it's just as easy for you to get things from the Lord. You just have to have faith. . . .
>
> "A baby is such an illustration! When he's crying for his mother, you wouldn't think of refusing him. Hearing from the Lord is our spiritual nourishment—and you've got to be able to hear from the Lord!
>
> "Shutting your eyes helps you to see in the spirit and to become unconscious of the things and people around you and get your mind on the Lord, and in a relaxed position where nothing distracts you, and expect then that whatever you hear or see is something from the Lord."

Mo's writing seemed so forthright, yet caring. *It is easy to see,* I thought, *why so many people are beginning to listen to him. He listens to God.*

As it turned out, I didn't stay in Houston for long that summer. Ahaz, a fantastic musician and songwriter, was asked to take a small team to an international surfing championship in Galveston. It would be fertile witnessing ground for the Children of God. Besides his wife, I was the only female who went from the colony.

While there I received a letter from Issachar. I wasn't prepared for its contents; it said he wanted us to be "betrothed." I wasn't sure what that meant.

"Betrothed?" I said to Ahaz's wife after I read the letter. "What does that mean?"

Her eyes grew wide with astonishment. "Ruth," she began as she started laughing, "it means he wants to marry you."

Marry me? I couldn't believe it! He had never even made any advances toward me. But then, the COG had strict rules about that sort of thing. I remembered rule nine of the "Revolutionary Rules," which stated that there was to be "absolutely no dating without permission." And I had never known anyone who asked permission. The only other time I'd heard of betrothal, it was indicated that it was "only for staff members who were ready, after months of service, to go on their own with Team approval." I felt sure that Issachar had already secured approval for a betrothal, so I waited with anticipation for him to send further instructions. Meanwhile I still had work to do.

COG teams from dozens of colonies around the Southeast region showed up at the surfing championships. One group, a band, particularly interested me. Their repertoire included not only beautiful, reverential songs of praise to the Lord, but upbeat tunes with a contemporary folk-rock sound. When they performed on the beach at Galveston, their music thrilled me. And Reuben, the leader, was unbelievably talented and dynamic.

Reuben was tall, and his shoulder-length, sandy brown hair hung in loose waves. His penetrating blue eyes seemed to see right through me. He was full of life, and when he stepped onto the platform the atmosphere changed; his presence commanded attention.

Reuben was in total control of the band. He captivated crowds with his forthright eloquence on the contemporary relevance of the gospel. People walking by were caught up in his boldness, and then as the band started playing, the crowd became immersed in the music. Most of the songs I'd learned paled next to these. Reuben and his band were simply spellbinding.

A few of Ahaz's group—including me—joined Reuben's band onstage for some COG songs. Later during one of the band's breaks when I was passing out tracts, I felt a hand on my shoulder. It was Ahaz.

"Ruth, here's my guitar."

I looked at him quizzically.

"I want you to get up there and sing while they're on break."

"What?"

"Go on. I want Reuben to hear you sing."

I was nervous, but happy to comply. I took the guitar and stepped up to one of the microphones. I started a hard-driving song I had learned with Barney, closing my eyes as I sang. When I opened them during the second verse, I noticed that most of the people milling about had stopped to listen:

> *"Don't you know I thank God for Jesus*
> *For setting me free,*
> *I'll raise my hands and I'll give him praise*
> *For breaking those traditional chains on*
> *   me . . ."*

When I finished the song I walked over to Ahaz, who wore a satisfied smile, and handed him the guitar.

Not long after the surfing championships, I received word from Reuben that I was invited to come and help record the most popular COG songs—a special request from Mo. Reuben also had asked Issachar to come to his colony for the recording sessions. I, of course, was overjoyed at that news.

The COG had been given permission to use an old abandoned building near one of the colonies for a recording studio. Several of the rooms were being electrically rewired, and a ham radio operation was set up. I discovered that most COG leaders used ham radios to communicate with one another, thus saving on long-distance and overseas telephone calls.

We were to record the COG songs because the "family" of the COG was spreading nationwide. Reuben explained that the leaders wanted to provide a sense of unity by having all disciples use the same songs. One by one, the band members who would help record the songs of the "Revolution for Jesus" began to assemble at the studio.

Issachar, who could play almost any instrument (piano, guitar, mandolin, violin, flute, for example) had been one of the first to arrive. A dark-haired, angel-faced member named Luke was there to play fiddle and saxophone. Amos and Ephraim, brothers who were COG leaders and who once performed professionally, played acoustic and electric guitar. Reuben directed the band and sang most of the lead vocals. I sang some lead vocals and harmonized with other members on backups.

The six of us were the core of the band, and we provided a studio band for the other COG members who came to the studio to sing their songs. Reuben seemed more in control than ever, and I was a little intimidated by him. He was mesmerizing, extremely demanding, and overbearing —but likeable all the same.

From the start of the sessions I hit it off with Reuben's wife, Athaliah. She gave me constant encouragement, especially when Reuben's demands of me seemed overwhelming.

It was August when we started the sessions, and the evenings were hot and sticky. We recorded at night when the others in the colony were asleep and outside sounds were minimal. We slept during the day. The sessions were intense and draining, both physically and emotionally. Sometimes when we took breaks I would stroll around outside or through the halls of the building with my guitar to regain my energy.

One night I wandered by a classroom and saw a light on. I peeked in and saw a dark-haired COG brother crouched in a corner, working on some electrical wiring. "Hi," I said.

He turned around, and said, "Hello. You guys really sound good."

"Thank you. What are you doing?"

"Oh, just working on some of the wiring here."

He looked quite involved in his work, and I could tell he'd been pushing himself hard.

"You want to hear a song?" I asked, thinking he might appreciate a break.

"Sure," he said. He smiled, dropped the wires, and leaned back against the wall.

It felt good to play the guitar for someone who wasn't a musician; I had felt somewhat intimidated by some of the professional band members.

"That was great," he said when I finished. "My name's Adino."

"I'm Ruth," I said and smiled. His grin told me he already knew that.

I saw Adino occasionally during the following weeks of recording and sang for him. He was a gentle, soft-spoken fellow, and we quickly became friends.

At the height of our recording, as we peaked in enthusiasm, Reuben told us that NBC had aired a special on the COG, called "Chronolog," and that their portrayal of us was overwhelmingly negative. The top leadership had seen the program and Reuben relayed their blunt reaction: "Somebody is out to get us."

That put a damper on our enthusiasm, but we tried to keep our momentum going. Then one night before the sessions came to a close, Issachar came into the studio with a worried look. Before I could ask him what was wrong, he took me outside into the hall.

"Rachel confronted me tonight," he said, referring to one of the COG's top leaders from London who had flown in to observe the recording sessions. "She asked me if I loved you."

My heart pounded. "What does that mean?"

He simply continued, "I said yes. Then she asked if I thought I could live without you. I didn't know what to say." He paused, looking downward for a moment. "I told her I probably could."

I felt my heart was breaking because I knew what was coming.

"They want me in England," he said. "They need someone to help run the business office there. Rachel said they could really use me there—if I was willing to go."

Willing, he said. That was my notice. Issachar was telling me that he had to be a good disciple—that he had to choose duty to the COG over his love for me. Even though over the past few days I'd felt that we weren't as close as we'd been before the recording had begun, now the possibility of losing him made me feel rejected. I didn't want to let go.

"Look, Ruth," he said. "I believe that if the Lord wants us together, he can provide a way for it to happen. It's like the notes on a music chart: Music happens when the melody lines cross with the harmony. Like we did here. When you went to Houston, I didn't think I'd see you again, but we both wound up here. Who knows, it could happen if it is really meant to be."

I had to struggle to hold back the tears. I knew I wouldn't be asked to go to London. I was probably still considered a babe in the leaders' eyes, and only those worthy of top security comprised the London staff. You had to be prime stuff, and I wasn't there yet.

"OK," I muttered. I couldn't think of anything more to say. I smiled weakly at him and walked out into the night. By this time tears were coursing down my cheeks. How could Rachel possibly know what the Lord wanted for us? This couldn't be it. I truly didn't think that was God's will, but what could I say? I knew more doubts about the COG leadership had been planted, though I never expressed them. Instead, they joined my other doubts, pushed to the very back of my mind.

When the recording sessions were coming to a close, Reuben gathered the band together to read an "emergency" Mo letter. The urgency of the assembly had us all holding our breath.

Reuben simply started reading. The letter was about a prophecy that Mo had received from the

Lord saying the United States unavoidably would be destroyed by God's wrath. Most of it went over my head; I couldn't piece it all together. But what I did grasp sounded terrifying, yet somehow exciting.

When Reuben finished the letter, there was absolute silence. After a while, we looked at one another and seemed to understand that all of the COG were to flee the country.

I couldn't be sure of what was coming. The situation sounded extremely serious. But it didn't take much time for me to count the cost; I had nothing to lose.

CHAPTER
Eight

In the wake of Mo's letter, "Flee as a Bird to the Mountain," all members of the COG were urgently instructed to write their parents to reassure them that they were healthy, happy, and evangelizing successfully—and could the parents please send a little something to help support the cause? Privately, I resented having to solicit funds from my folks. Hadn't the COG demanded that we forsake all, including former relationships? It just didn't seem right.

Nevertheless, I wrote Mom and Dad to tell them of the group's plan to spread throughout the world. Dad's brief reply included a check for fifty dollars (an amount for which I knew he had to scrounge), but it wasn't the boost of confidence I needed: "What happens if you get overseas and don't cut it with the group?" he wrote.

I took no thought of Dad's concern. His doubts seemed only to confirm what the COG had said about those who were "in the world." They taught that our parents and the people from the older generation didn't live by faith, so they could not understand the leadings of the Spirit.

My only fears concerned the simple act of traveling overseas, something I'd never done. But those fears were allayed by Reuben. He invited me to join the band as the lead female vocalist and head to Puerto Rico with them. He said he would organize everything for our colony, comprised mostly of musicians, and I felt confident with him at the helm. Also, I had the security of a new "family," the band.

We didn't want to draw attention to ourselves in a mass exodus from the U.S. So we split up in teams of twos and threes, traveling first to Miami by car, then on to Puerto Rico. It was decided that I would ride to Florida with Reuben, Athaliah, his wife, and her sister, Shimrith.

Athaliah was gorgeous. She and Reuben had met and married while in a COG colony outside Los Angeles. She was fun-loving and easygoing, always encouraging, and not at all overbearing. She and Reuben seemed to be the COG's ideal couple, openly affectionate and always playfully teasing one another.

I was eager to go with them to Puerto Rico. Everything seemed new again: people, places, music. It was a privilege to be a part of the band, and I felt unworthy of the honor. But, as always, I trusted Reuben's decisions. He wielded great influence over us all, both musically and emotionally, and seemed to be a powerful liaison with the

COG's upper leadership. To be handpicked for his pioneering team made me feel important and wanted.

San Juan, Puerto Rico, was humid, something I thought I'd gotten used to in Dallas. The mountains were beautiful, and the land was lush and green, but most of the people were poor. I felt the Lord's compassion rise within me, and I couldn't wait to begin ministering to the people throughout the island.

The colony there was made up mostly of Puerto Ricans and a few Americans. When we got there, however, Reuben took over. The disciples had been living in a small apartment above a noisy bar. It wasn't long before Reuben set about finding us a bigger place to live and cultivating wealthy, more influential friends. He made plans for us to sing in the plaza in Old San Juan and at the local Navy Base. A new convert was added to the band, a Puerto Rican congo player named Nicky. The rest of the band was intact, except for Issachar, but by now I had virtually forgotten him in the midst of all this adventure.

I developed a friendship with a brother named Manuel. I had felt inexplicably lonely and depressed, perhaps due to being abroad and not speaking the language, and Manuel had offered the support of a caring friend. Sometimes at night we sat talking on the stairs above the bar.

But when Reuben caught wind of our friendship, he pronounced it null and void. It wasn't "of the Lord," he said reprovingly, and that was that. We were forbidden to meet one another alone.

I strongly disagreed with Reuben's rebuke, yet he was responsible for me and I had to trust him. Still, I harbored resentment for his breaking up so innocent a relationship. I didn't think he should have been so hard on me, but that seemed to be his way of dealing with me. It seemed the only time I heard anything encouraging from him was through Athaliah. He often chastised me verbally, but in those moments of reproof there was an unspoken communication between us: he was purging me from my fleshly ways; this was my spiritual refinement.

I never could quite reach the level of spiritual maturity that Reuben demanded of me. Sometimes his criticism was so cruel that Athaliah would mercifully intervene on my behalf, but I still was constantly under Reuben's thumb.

Just as in times past, though, I found relief through my music. Songwriting became an emotional outlet, a way to praise God. The day Reuben rebuked me about Manuel I ran off to the beach alone. This was never allowed of disciples, but I needed to be alone and sort out my thoughts. It was there that I wrote "By Faith Alone," a song from which I drew comfort for many years:

> A castle made of sand;
> The storm comes and it cannot stand.
> But a mountain, a rocky mountain,
> Will hang on to the sun—

It will never be moved.
Like a tree planted by the river,
You'll grow tall . . .
And you can just bend with the wind.

You've got to live by faith alone,
Don't try and do a thing on your own;
If you're still, you'll hear his voice
Calling you on home.
Just forsake what's in your heart,
Lay it on the ground,
Turn around,
Walk away,
And start again.

There's a way which seemeth right to a man
But the end is destruction.
Don't lean to your own understanding
Or you will surely fall;
Follow the Son;
Let his light brighten your day.
Get out of yourself,
Get it all out of the way.

Songs like that came to me during the hard times, and through them I began to realize the power of God's grace. In most of the trials I experienced, it seemed, I received the blessing of a song to comfort me and then to share with others.

The COG soon was bustling with growth and spiritual victory in Puerto Rico, and much of that was due to the success of Reuben and his band. We led scores of people to Jesus. Finally Reuben had conquered the island to his satisfaction, and he decided to take the band to pioneer Venezuela. Situated on the northernmost point of the South American continent, it was one of the more Americanized countries in Latin America. Thus it was considered very receptive to our motley group. When Reuben was given the go-ahead by upper leadership, he began to make preparations for a move.

Finally, one day he called a meeting of what by now had become several colonies throughout the island.

"Everyone has been divided into teams," he declared, waving a piece of paper above his head. "Within a week we'll be going into all the world to preach the gospel, as Jesus commissioned us to do."

The room buzzed with excitement. Not only was one team going to Venezuela as we had expected, but now many of the other islands, including the Virgin Islands, would hear the Children of God's message.

Everyone grew silent as Reuben began to read from the list. The first group of names he mentioned would go to Venezuela—the group that would make up the band. When he came to the end of the list, however, my name hadn't been mentioned.

A hollow feeling settled in my stomach. As Reuben read the names of the other team members, I thought maybe he had accidentally left mine off from the Venezuela group. Then I heard my name: I was to go to St. John's in the Virgin Islands.

I sat in shock. *I'm not with the band.* I didn't know what to think; all the other members of the band were going. It was as if I was being singled out, punished for something I didn't even know I'd done.

I looked around at the other disciples' faces. None revealed the concern that mine must have shown. I smothered my disappointment, telling myself that the Lord had his timing for everything. The other members of my team were Zebulun and Jeshua, who both played guitar, and Amasa, who played the flute.

Our mission was to form our own little spinoff band and pioneer the tiny island where we would be joined by a few new disciples from St. John's. Despite my initial discouragement, I was excited about going on the large ferry that would take us to the island, and it felt good to be unexpectedly out from underneath Reuben's leadership.

When at last we arrived at St. John's, I was instantly taken with the astonishing beauty there. The island looked like the Lord's heaven on earth, and my disappointment over Venezuela quickly diminished.

I had never seen such powdery, silk-white beaches, such endless expanse of crystal-clear sea and bright blue sky. We set up our tiny colony in an abandoned, open-air sandwich shop not far from the beach. *This will be like a vacation,* I thought.

We did the same things there we'd done in

Puerto Rico—witness, sing, make friends. Though I still felt an occasional pang of disappointment over not being with Reuben's band, I loved the COG life and my three brothers there, especially Jeshua, our gentle leader. We slept side by side on our mats on the porch, or sometimes in hammocks.

One afternoon after witnessing along the beach I walked up to the hut and Jeshua was passing out the mail.

"Looks like you got a letter from home, Ruth," he said, handing me an envelope.

I took the envelope and opened it. It was from Mom. "Dear Patti," it began, "I don't know how to tell you this, honey. . . ."

Something had to be wrong. I could sense it. Apprehensively I read on.

"Dad has died. . . ."

No. This couldn't be. My hands shook violently and I could hardly finish the letter. It was true; he'd had a heart attack. *Oh, my God, no. Oh, my God.*

I stuffed the letter in my pocket and started running as fast as I could. I didn't know where I was going, and I didn't care. I didn't want to think.

A few minutes later I found myself in a field beside the hut. I put my hands over my eyes; I couldn't bear to look at the world. It couldn't be real. It just couldn't be. Slowly I lowered my hands and stared at the ground. None of this could be real. It had to be a terrible nightmare.

What am I doing here? I wondered in despair.

What brought me here? Why wasn't I with my father?

I turned around in the field and looked back to the hut. The shock was so profound that I longed for tears but couldn't find the strength to cry. It was as if crying would heighten the reality.

I started back slowly across the field. Jeshua, who had been concerned when I ran out, was walking toward me. When he was close enough I said softly, "My father died." He folded his arms around me as I began to cry. He held me for a long while as I cried. *If only I could make the letter go away, rewind the events.* Zebulun came over and put his arm around me for a moment. Then he went and picked up his guitar and began singing to me. The songs and his gentle, caring voice were a great comfort to me. "Mister Bojangles," a song by Jerry Jeff Walker, was the one song that I'll always remember from that day.

Those were tender moments as we opened up to each other, and I began to feel the Lord's peace again. But still I shut out further thoughts of my dad—and with that denial, life started again. Even though I still hadn't truly acknowledged the reality of Dad being gone, I found myself relieved for him. He had always suffered, it seemed, and life had been hard for him.

I kept telling myself that he was better off now. He wouldn't have to endure the endtime chaos Moses David had predicted.

My survival mechanism had kicked into full gear. I never considered my mother's feelings, that perhaps I should go home to be with her at least for a while. My relationship with my parents had been severed for such a long time that they, along with the people of "the world," had slowly become insignificant to me. In effect, they were only to be used for what they could offer us in the way of financial support. I had shut off my feelings from reality, and that non-caring attitude helped me to further deny the reality of my father's death.

I had been doing the ministry work in the islands—passing out tracts, witnessing, and singing—for about a month when I got a telegram. It was from Reuben:

> Come join band. Given clearance to Caracas. Plane reservations made.

I couldn't believe it—I was a member of the band again! Reuben hadn't forgotten me after all! My dreams seemed to be coming true again.

"Jeshua! Jeshua!" I ran out of the sandwich shop and across the field to tell him my good news.

Ten months after I had joined the COG, I arrived at the little colony in Caracas. The house sat on a hill called *Mariposa,* the Spanish word for "butterfly." It was the humble home of a recent Venezuelan convert named David, a towering, sweet fellow who resembled an enormous teddy bear.

When I arrived, I was greeted with hugs by all my friends from the band. I also met a new member, an American named Andrew. He was a sensitive musician and talented songwriter with a ready smile and a quick wit.

Andrew was friendly enough when introduced, but during the afternoon rehearsal session with the band he acted a little standoffish toward me. That got under my skin a little, since I had been an original member of the band.

We both got a little testy during that first session, butting heads over a few minor things. But once Andrew saw that I could hold my own, he warmed up to me a little.

Although Athaliah had only an average singing voice, she sang many of the lead vocals because she was Mexican and spoke fluent Spanish. One of the first songs we learned in Spanish was a song written by Reuben. It referred to Jesus' teachings on having childlike faith (Mark 10:15 and Luke 18:17). Over the next few days our excitement grew as we saw a solid band and enthusiastic ministry emerging.

The band became both my family and the closest friends I'd ever had. Part of our bond was a shared love of music. Another part of it was unity of purpose and love for the Lord. We were sure our bond would always last.

Andrew and I began to enjoy each other's company more, laughing and joking together with the rapport of a comedy team. He was one of the funniest people I'd ever known, and I was an appreciative audience. I realized that our initial conflicts had been because, paradoxically, we were so alike—sensitive, temperamental, and romantic. And I was deeply moved by the beautiful songs he wrote. They came from the heart of a man who was a compassionate, socially concerned humanitarian.

When Reuben thought the band was ready, he booked our first gig: a circus. Despite uncertainties about singing to a circus audience in a language most of us still didn't understand, we had a lot of fun. And the people loved us. We passed out literature after we sang, and we were so royally received we felt ready to conquer the country for Jesus.

The colony in Caracas began to grow rapidly. More COG disciples from the U.S. were arriving. Also, we had begun to make our own disciples among the Venezuelans, teaching them Scripture and introducing them to Mo's writings. Many new colonies were being established in the outlying areas of the city and in the mountains.

The COG's hard-core forms of discipleship had been toned down, even though Mo's message was still strong. But while we witnessed we made only veiled references to Mo. Most of our message was from the Bible; Mo's letters were still something for the disciple's ears only. Increasingly, however, his letters dealt less with inspirational or prophetic themes and more with the practicalities of our daily lives in the COG, especially as the group developed in overseas countries. He even instructed us in matters of personal hygiene, politics, and provisioning.

As the Caracas colony grew, I began to do some public relations work with Reuben's ham radio operator, Micaiah. He and I were supposed to develop radio contacts, and sometimes we spent entire days walking down the streets of the city, looking for a house with a radio antenna. Once again I felt important because only the top leaders in each colony knew about the radio bases. I enjoyed being included in the camaraderie of the COG's upper echelon. Finding favor with them meant I had to be doing something right spiritually.

About this time we received a Mo letter entitled "Maryknoll Fathers." It described a dream Mo had had about some radical priests in Latin America whom the Lord had told him would help the COG. Mo directed us to seek out these men. My confidence in Mo's claim of being God's endtime prophet was strengthened the next day when a COG disciple met just such a priest who indeed was sympathetic to our cause.

The priest invited some of our members to live in the unused dormitories behind his church. Reuben decided the band members should live there, and it was wonderful. Reuben and Athaliah had their own room, as I did. The other men stayed in another. The priest took us along to sing whenever he performed mass in the different villages and towns nearby, and the people loved us. Eventually, we started a coffeehouse in the basement of the church.

Soon Catholic churches became targets for recruiting COG support. Most of the congregations were receptive, which was good because the influence of Catholicism is very strong throughout Latin America.

Life remained fast-paced and exhilarating. We gave little thought or time to ourselves, spending instead all energies in the streets spreading Mo's version of the gospel.

All the while, Moses David became more and more prevalent in my thoughts. His letters were exuberant, full of life and God's Word. And some of them included cartoons which depicted Mo as a lion—supposedly the lion of Judah. I wondered what kind of person he was. My curiosity was peaked even more because he was under such tight security that, while he sent his top staff and his family members to our colonies, he declined to come himself.

At the height of our growth in Caracas we received a Mo letter that contained new revelations for the Children of God: Now the world should hear the messages of Moses David. They were "Wonder-Working Words," Mo said, sent directly from the Lord, and we were to duplicate them and get them into the hands of all the spiritually thirsty people of the world. He called this plan for distributing COG literature "litnessing." Each colony would be responsible for reprinting the Mo letters in the native language, litnessing on street corners and in public places, and soliciting donations. All the disciples were overjoyed at this news; it meant not only that the world would know more about Mo, but also that we, his disciples, could read the letters for ourselves and study them the way we did the Bible.

Shortly after the new revelation, Reuben announced that he and Athaliah would go to Brazil,

South America's largest, most influential country, to prepare for the band's arrival. They would travel by land in order to scout out the best possible route for us to follow later, and on arrival find a place for us to live.

That announcement was difficult to accept. Even though Reuben had been hard on me, I looked up to him. He was still my shepherd, and I depended on his leadership. Soon after he left, Amos was called to Europe by upper leadership to be involved in their music ministry there. I would miss him a great deal too.

My life was still exciting, however, in spite of my fears. I was thrilled by the sights, sounds, food, and people throughout Venezuela. There was plenty to do, plenty of souls to be won and disciples to be made. Also, news broke that COG members were infiltrating not only Latin America, but also Europe, Asia, and the Middle East.

In less than two months, Reuben gave us clearance to start coming down to Brazil. This meant traveling west to Colombia, south to Ecuador, then on to Peru and Brazil. We were to leave in pairs, to avoid the attention of Colombian officials, whose government eyed Americans with suspicion. I was disappointed that Andrew and I would not be on the same team.

By the time I arrived in Bogotá, Colombia, Andrew had been there long enough to contact a huge Catholic church where a handful of COG disciples had already begun living. There was no hot water in the bathroom, so we had to heat our baths with boiling water from a kettle. There wasn't any electricity, either, so we used candles for light and slept covered with our heavy ponchos made out of llama wool to get through the cold mountain nights.

All day long for the next few days we passed out literature and asked for donations. Andrew often stationed himself with the guitar at the front of a bus, where the people crowded on with their chickens and animals, and I stood at the back passing out the Mo letters. But most of the Colombians to whom we sang were unreceptive to our message. Perhaps they were weary of hearing about new movements in their politically volatile country. Undaunted, Andrew and I ventured out each morning with a song of praise on our lips, happy to minister the Word.

In our travels throughout the city we encountered many of the same people Jesus must have seen in his day: the poor, the blind, the lame.

Less than a month after our arrival in Bogotá, we all were summoned to the local police station and told to bring our passports. Once there we were informed that our distribution of literature was considered subversive by several political leaders and we were to leave the country within a week. With that he stamped "canceled" on our visas.

So much for Colombia, I thought. I didn't know whether to be upset because the Lord's work had not been fulfilled in that country or happy to move one step closer to Brazil. Andrew had the answer for me.

"Ruth," he said outside the station door, with a look of hope and resolve, "let's just shake the dust off our feet and get moving."

As we walked back to the church, I sighed and hoped Ecuador would be a little more friendly.

The bus from Bogotá was rickety, like the buses you see in the movies. It was crowded with people and animals and decorated with bright colors. It offered a gaudy contrast to the wondrous, misty mountain landscape as we crossed the border into Ecuador. We saw Indian communities in which the men, women, and children all wore black derby hats and the women wore row upon row of beads around their necks. Their ribboned braids were pulled behind their heads, and they wore big, full peasant skirts and blouses.

"Watch your step, you're in Quito," the bus driver mumbled as he stopped the bus. No sooner had I stepped off and begun to stretch my cramped, weary body than I heard a shout of warning from Andrew.

"Ruth, look out!"

I spun around to find a short, thin boy crouched on the sidewalk behind me, poised to steal my purse, which I had set down between my feet. Before I could move he snatched it and took off, but I caught the shoulder strap. "*¡Para!* Stop!"

The yank of my grip on the strap almost flipped the boy. He fell to his knees, let go quickly, and took off on a dead run. I shook my head in wonder. We'd been warned about beggars and thieves, but not even that incident could diminish the beauty I had seen thus far.

As we walked down the street, we saw detached businessmen in pressed suits walk past poor Indians who wore their mountain dress and begged for food. It was the first Latin city I'd seen in which numbers of Indians lived in the urban area. In Venezuela and Colombia they had remained primarily in the mountains.

The contrast between wealth and poverty loomed even larger as we sought out nearby Catholic churches to help support us. No matter how destitute the people of the community, it seemed, the churches were always huge structures laden with gold from ceiling to floor inside.

"How could this be?" Andrew wondered aloud. "How can the churches be so rich when they're not providing for the needs of the people?" He wrote a song about that experience full of the anguish we all felt at living among those poor people and being unable to do much to help them. Reuben had tried to prepare us for the heartbreak of seeing the extreme poverty in Quito, but I had no idea of what it was really like. The streets were full of poor people living with their children on mats, huddled in doorways with tiny infants, or sitting and begging for food.

We were poor ourselves, but I didn't live with the hopelessness these people had to face daily. I had the Lord's assurance that he would provide for my every need, and I never worried about food, clothing, or other necessities. That attitude was second nature to most COG disciples. We never had any money, but we didn't lack anything. We were the "Lord's good guys," and we had given our all for him.

It never bothered me that my life might have been endangered by the nature of the work I was doing—we could easily have been jailed and tortured in Colombia—or that we never knew where we would live or find our next meal. In fact, there was an excitement in anticipating what God would do from day to day.

Our new colony, which stood unobtrusively in a middle-class neighborhood, was owned by a friendly woman whom we affectionately called "Mama." She cooked meals for us and had two daughters who eventually became COG disciples, though they were allowed to keep their secular jobs. The girls had a bedroom upstairs, which they shared with me. Andrew slept in an apartment over the garage with two other disciples, Harim and Aaron.

Our first few weeks were spent making contacts, mostly for financial donors to help support the colony. But our best connection turned out to be Padre Tomás, a gray-haired, fatherly priest. He was so overjoyed at our ministry that he did all he could to book singing engagements for us at masses, schools, and any place he could think of.

The country was ruled by dictatorship at the time, and we weren't allowed to distribute the Mo letters. That cut off our main means of support, so any assistance we could get was crucial to our survival. Because Padre Tomás endeared our cause both to the people of his parish and to adjoining ones, he was principally responsible for our acceptance in Ecuador.

Because we couldn't pass out Mo letters, our witnessing was mostly personal. Still, we had to be careful. There were antigovernment uprisings in the streets almost every day. Our message could easily be considered subversive, like those of the groups who marched outside the dictator's mansion. (On our trip to Ecuador, the bus had been stopped in the middle of nowhere by the military police. I could still remember how my heart raced as we had filed off the bus and stood on the roadside, being eyed suspiciously. Eventually everyone had been allowed back on the bus. The police had been searching for subversives and undesirables.)

Even with—or perhaps because of—such official resistance, witnessing was a joy to me. I never tired of telling people about Jesus, that one must forsake all to follow him. I had picked up enough Spanish to talk to Ecuadorians in their own language, but it broke my heart that I couldn't communicate with the Indians, who had more difficult dialects.

By now COG disciples were allowed to study, read, and meditate over the Mo letters in the same way they did the Bible. But with singing engagements and constant efforts to evangelize and win support, I—like most other disciples—had little time to truly ingest the philosophy behind our work. I simply read the letters, accepted them, and believed them.

I loved Quito more than any other place I'd

ever been. I had attended the big neighborhood night festivals, where people danced in long, snakelike chains around table after table of food and drink. Those celebrations were everywhere in the city, in every neighborhood.

One day I stood on the back porch of Mama's house, leaning against the waist-high cement wash basin, scrubbing clothes while listening to Andrew and Aaron strumming and singing from the garage. Suddenly, above the din of their noise, I heard a voice that seemed familiar.

"Hi."

I turned and smiled at the young man who had spoken. His face was familiar as well. "Praise the Lord," he said. His dark hair was short and neat, and he had warm, friendly eyes. He wore a suit, which was not usual COG garb unless you were in P.R. The day was hot, and he loosened his tie and slung his coat over his shoulder.

"Hi," I said, smiling to show that I knew him, but trying to recall from where. Suddenly it hit me: "Adino?"

"Yes. You're Ruth, right?" He smiled when I nodded. "I've missed your singing."

"Oh, I've missed you too," I said, though I hadn't given him a thought since I had left Texas. Still it *was* good to see him. We gave each other a hug, and I wondered what had brought him to Quito.

CHAPTER
Nine

Adino and I walked back to his car to get his trunks unloaded. "What are you doing in Quito?" I asked him.

"I'm heading with you and Andrew to Rio. Reuben needs a radio man, and I'm it."

We reached his car and soon had the trunks out and ready to be unpacked. Adino unsnapped one of his trunks and began to sort through his radio equipment. The mass of wires and boxes and buttons fascinated me.

"I saw you at the Rock House, you know," he said, "before you went to the recording studio."

"Really?" I didn't remember his being there, but I was suddenly thrilled that he noticed me.

"I don't think you were in the 'family' then," he said. "I was with a few other brothers living in a condemned building near the leadership colony." He chuckled. "We didn't even have running water. It was worse than any place I'd ever seen.

We lived there, but we came to the Rock House for 'Inspiration' and meals. We were members of the first class of 'David's Mighty Men Radio Training School.' Micaiah was there too. One of the leaders finally came by to see what we were doing, and when he saw how bad the place was he moved us out."

I grinned. He was jovial about it all. In fact, he seemed easygoing about everything. "How did you end up at the recording studio?" I asked him.

"Barney and another leader sent for me. But you know what? You remember Silas? From the Rock House?"

"Mm. I'm not sure."

"Ted Patrick got him. I think everybody was in Galveston then, at the surfing championship."

I looked at him, puzzled. "Who's Ted Patrick?"

"Black Lightning," he said. His eyes turned dark. "He kidnapped Silas and held him in a hotel for about a week, and he convinced him we were satanic. He's back with his family now."

The incident seemed so dramatic that my heart raced as I imagined it.

"You know, Mo actually came to Dallas while I was there," Adino said. "Of course, I never saw him. Just the upper leadership did."

Adino still seemed shy, as he had when I first met him, but he clearly enjoyed telling me all this.

"Just before I left Costa Rica, I heard there were five thousand disciples now." He shook his head. "It's hard to believe what the Lord is doing."

As he spoke, Adino checked through all his

cables and boxes. I was impressed again with his skill and knowledge.

Had anyone seen us at that point and noticed the way I watched Adino as he worked, they'd have seen I was smitten. I found this quiet man extremely interesting. He was bright and friendly, and seemed important—and I was drawn to him.

His radio equipment had been impounded at the airport in Quito when he arrived, and he had to enlist our colony leader to help him convince the customs officials that our use of the equipment would not threaten national security. Transporting radio equipment across Latin American borders during times of political turmoil wasn't something a person did casually. Yet in my mind, Adino's doing just that made him even more intriguing.

A week after Adino's arrival, new regional shepherds came and we moved out of Mama's house and into our own rental facility. Unlike any of the other disciples, Adino had his own room because of his highly secretive radio ministry.

Adino and I sat up talking at night, much the way we had during the recording sessions. Only now he seemed more confident and talkative. He was very opinionated and well informed, and it was stimulating to have subjects other than music or litnessing to discuss. I became increasingly impressed with his work as he told me more about it, explaining how all the equipment worked and what it meant to the ministry. He had a strong sense of responsibility, and I was pleased by that.

More distinct, however, was the fact that he wasn't preoccupied with himself. He had the same quiet, peaceful way about him I'd noticed before.

Staying up late with him was one of the freedoms that came with leadership. Like our colony experiences in Puerto Rico, the Virgin Islands, and Venezuela, the Quito colony had grown rapidly, and I was named tribe leader over the girls. Aside from the Explo experience in Dallas, it was my first position of leadership in the COG. As a member of the band I had enjoyed certain privileges, but never the freedom and authority of leadership.

As we talked I came to learn more and more about Adino's past. I was pleased that he shared so much of himself with me, and—once again—impressed by all he had done and experienced.

Adino was a seeker by nature, though not in the romantic sense. Soft-spoken and somewhat shy, he nevertheless was a tireless questioner who pursued unsolved problems to their end.

As a child, Adino had learned a little about God from his mother, who had a Southern Baptist background. But he dismissed these beliefs when he adopted the atheistic ideals of one of his high school teachers.

Adino had been married for a short time, but when this ended in a painful divorce, he decided to seek answers to his never-ending questions in college.

The questions he wanted answered (in particular, the meaning of truth) were a main focus in his philosophy and psychology classes, and in a special studies class that centered on parapsychology and metaphysics. While he didn't find his answers in philosophy or psychology, he did get glimpses of what he began to think might be truth in his intriguing special studies course.

In one session, the professor brought in a Hindu holy man. Adino sat in the front row of class, skeptical but spellbound. The Hindu, sitting cross-legged, closed his eyes and began to chant. He drew several twelve-inch needles from his bag and, to Adino's astonishment, began to work them into his arm. When the needles' points came through the other side of the arm, Adino could hardly believe what he saw: the holy man wasn't bleeding.

This exposure to spiritual power astonished Adino. He began to believe there was a world entirely separate from yet parallel to what was tangible. He wondered at the possibility of planes of existence.

Several weeks later Adino walked into his psychology class to find that members of some religious group had been invited to come and explain what they were all about.

The group of four young men and women came in and began to play and sing about Jesus. *They sing with real conviction,* Adino thought. More than anyone he knew, these people looked genuinely happy.

After a few songs, the group fielded questions.

The students fired at will, asking why the group followed a doctrine that many people called weird. Adino thought the answer was solid: "We live the way Jesus told us to live."

"What do you call yourselves?" someone else asked.

"The Children of God," one young man responded.

For twenty minutes the group answered questions by quoting the Bible. Adino had never seen such conviction before. They never once tripped up nor contradicted themselves. No other guest speaker that entire term had defended a notion so clearly. Of all the people Adino had heard proclaiming the truth, these people seemed to speak of it with the most confidence and peace.

Finally a student asked one of the young men why he did the things he did. His answer struck Adino forcefully.

"Well," the young man said, "because I love you."

At those words, the room fell silent. Suddenly, Adino felt tears spill down his cheeks. He was overwhelmed by this sincere display of love.

They've really got something, he thought. *They've got something special, and I want it.*

After class, Adino approached one of the group members. "I . . . I don't know what to tell you, but I liked what you said."

The young man smiled and spoke gently. "Why don't you come have dinner with us? There's a lot more to talk about. You can meet some of the other people in our colony."

That night at the dinner table, Adino sat looking at the joyous faces around him. Everyone seemed to be smiling, laughing, and singing. *This is real,* he thought. *I haven't imagined any of it. What these people have is real.*

The dinner ceremony was loud and unusual, with singing and dancing. All the while Adino was welcomed by members of the colony who quoted Bible verses, each of which seemed to directly address the longings deep in his heart. It was the first time anyone had told him that Jesus loved him enough to die for him—and that Jesus was all he needed.

Suddenly he was in tears again. In a single eye-opening moment, Adino knew that he had been wrong, and for years had been living a lie. That night he asked God to forgive him of his sins. Before he hadn't believed sin even existed, except in the tortured psyches of guilt-ridden Christians. Now, miraculously, he knew the full meaning of sin and the full extent of his need for Christ. When he asked for forgiveness, he felt the Holy Spirit filling him. He had found his answer.

"Why don't you stay with us and do what we're doing?" one smiling young man suggested. "We're just telling people about Jesus." And with that, Adino made his decision to become a part of the Children of God.

He never even considered going back to school. He had felt total release from the bondage of his former life, and nothing would get him bogged down in the works of the world again.

Soon after joining the COG, Adino was placed in a coveted "public relations" position. His job included duties as a "provisioner" (one who obtains free food, usually discarded or day-old products from local merchants, for colony meals) and a funds solicitor. Dressed in a coat and tie, he approached local businesses for donations. He had no qualms whatsoever with asking people to support the organization that had given his life meaning. He felt certain Mo had to be anointed of God, and life in the COG was to Adino (as it was to every other COG disciple) the only way a person could serve Jesus fully.

Discovering all of this about Adino only increased my respect for him. I knew he would go far and accomplish wonderful things in whatever he did.

As the country's restrictions on our litnessing lightened, the colony grew and new leaders arrived to take over administrative duties, such as collection of and accounting for litnessing donations. Because of the solid friendship Adino and I had developed in just a couple of weeks, we always tried to stay together when the colony divided up into litnessing teams.

Adino had intensity and clear focus in everything he did. I was constantly amazed at how effortless he made the transition from our light, lively banter while walking the streets to abruptly stopping on a corner to litness. His dark brown eyes lit up when he smiled, but the probing seriousness never left them.

Through our litnessing adventures, I got to

know Adino in a way few others did. Most COG disciples thought he was an introvert, but I saw him in his wildest, most hysterically funny moments. I also discovered in him a fervent yet sensitive reverence for Jesus, and that's what I loved most. I felt so comfortable in his presence that one night, as we walked in the cold on an errand to the corner grocery store, I slipped my arm through his. It wasn't a flirtatious gesture—it just seemed natural. He grinned, not seeming to mind.

A few nights after that, I stole outside and picked a tiny flower from the neighbor's garden. I tiptoed back inside, down the long hallway past the living room full of guys, and taped the flower to Adino's door. Even with the COG's strict rules about dating and hand holding, I wasn't worried that the others might see the flower before Adino rose the next morning. Even if they did, they wouldn't know who it was from.

They weren't blind, though. I'm sure they could tell something was going on, but no one said anything.

Several weeks after Adino arrived, Reuben sent a message calling Andrew, Adino, and me to Brazil. Our work in establishing the Quito colony had been done, and Reuben had prepared everything in Rio de Janeiro to get the band off the ground again. As Christmas neared, the three of us spent most of our time litnessing, trying to raise the money needed to get to Lima, Peru—our next stop before working our way east to Brazil.

One hot afternoon, Adino and I were passing

out literature on a corner near the government palace. Mobs of people surrounded the building, demonstrating against an edict issued regarding restrictions on food distribution. As the noise of the mob increased, I felt an urgent tug on my arm from Adino.

"Come on," he said.

We hoisted our gear and walked quickly up the street away from the palace. As we hurried, we heard a loud rumble approaching. When we stepped out to cross the first intersection, we looked down the street. Coming at us was a throng of angry people that must have numbered in the thousands.

I looked back and saw hundreds of military police frantically surrounding the palace. They had guns and tear-gas launchers.

"Hurry," Adino urged, and we quickened our pace up the block. The roar of the multitude was deafening as they passed the intersection one block from the palace. We thought we were safe until, only moments later, a terrifying noise went up behind us. We turned around and saw masses of frightened people coming in our direction. The police had begun to fire shots at the crowd.

"Ruth!" Adino shouted, clutching my hand, and we ran up the street away from the approaching mob. "Ruth, let's go!" Adino said, pulling me harder. Suddenly my eyes welled with tears, and I could barely see in front of me. The soldiers had shot tear gas canisters at the people and the wind had carried the fumes several blocks away. Adino just kept running, pulling me with him until we were far from the area.

Exhausted and shaken by the experience, we eventually made our way back to the colony. When we got there, we mentioned to the others that downtown wasn't a safe place to be soliciting donations for a while.

A few days before Christmas, Andrew, Adino, and I finally had enough money to purchase bus tickets to Lima.

Before we left I told Adino that I wanted to call my mom. It would be the first time I'd talked to her since I arrived in Caracas from the Virgin Islands a year before. Adino found a ham radio club who let us use their equipment because Adino's was all packed into his trunk.

"Mom?" I shouted.

"Hello?" the voice crackled.

"Mom, it's me. I'm still in South America. I'm talking over a ham radio."

"Oh," she said, startled. "How are you?" Her voice sounded as though she were only a few miles away.

"I'm OK," I said. "I'm in Ecuador now, and I'm leaving for Peru next week. I'll be in Brazil soon."

"Oh, OK," she responded.

"I just wanted to call and say Merry Christmas. Say hello to everybody for me. I've got to go. We don't get to talk long. Merry Christmas, Mom. 'Bye." I struggled not to cry.

"'Bye," she said, and I wondered if I'd ever see her again.

I hated the thought of leaving Ecuador. In my

six months there, I had come to love the tiny country's extraordinary blend of cultures and mystic beauty. One evening before we left, Adino and I were taking our last walk through a park that had become a COG hangout and was also our favorite place to eat. Several Indians cooked over their small fires and sold a delicious blend of miniature wieners and unpeeled, sauteed English potatoes in tomato sauce, spooned onto a square of cellophane.

Just as we crossed the street, Adino took my hand and stopped me. He looked more serious than usual, and at first I thought he was angry with me about something.

"I think we need to pray about what kind of relationship we should have," he said, sounding nervous. "That night you put your arm through mine," he went on, "I realized something about us. . . . Ruth, I want to ask you something, and I'd like you to seek the Lord about this," he said. His eyes penetrated through me. "I want you to consider if our relationship should become more serious."

My feelings for this gentle man had been serious for a long time, but I didn't want him to know it. I didn't want to seem too overanxious now. So I tried to hide how thrilled I was by his words.

"Well, um . . . ," I said, "I'll pray about it."

A week later I told him that I, too, felt the Lord was leading us into a more serious relationship. We were on cloud nine. Jeremoth, our colony leader, wired the regional shepherd in Lima to ask if we could be betrothed. The shepherd wrote back that since Adino and I officially were in route to Brazil, and I was still under Reuben's jurisdiction because of the band, only he could give us permission.

When Adino and I heard that, we beamed. We thought for certain that Reuben wouldn't hesitate to grant us his permission. We became more anxious than ever to get to Rio.

Before we left for Lima, a Mo letter arrived and everyone was instructed to gather in a big field outside the city to hear it. Jeremoth's usually resounding, authoritative voice sounded apprehensive, however, as he led us in prayer. When he finished, he simply opened the letter and read it.

It was a long, complex letter, full of woe and warning, but what I remember most about it was its vivid description of the destruction of the Great Whore: America. According to a prophetic dream that Mo had, the country would be obliterated by the coming Kouhotek Comet. When the letter described the coming destruction, I immediately thought of Mom.

But, Jeremoth went on, the letter was saying that all of Western civilization was to be destroyed. That meant us, too!

Jeremoth read Mo's quotes from several magazines predicting the comet's forthcoming appearance, but, as we all believed, Mo had spiritual insight on the appearance. This time around, he said, it would strike the earth, causing earthquakes, tidal waves, mass destruction—and the deaths of millions.

No one doubted the accuracy of Mo's word; it had always proved good, as far as we knew. Though the teachings and revelations had often been hard on the flesh, they were always good for spiritual growth. But how did this one fit in with the others? What could it mean?

It was signaling the end of the world as we now knew it. It was so literal, this approaching catastrophe. How could it happen to us? And why? We were following the Lord's revelations through his end-time prophet.

When Jeremoth finished the letter, everyone murmured, "Praise the Lord, amen." The meeting was over and we parted in a solemn procession to the colony.

"Adino," I said, "what's going to happen to us?"

"I've been thinking about it," he said. "Before it happens, we need to name a place where we'll meet in case we get separated." We agreed to do so, and chose one place in Lima and another in the U.S.

The next morning my fear was temporarily replaced with enthusiasm about our trip to Peru. Our good-bye to the others in the colony was brief. No parting in the COG was ever prolonged with sentiment; there were farewells too often for that. Besides, when a disciple left one place it was with the joy of facing a new mission in another.

The trip was grueling, miserably hot and dry. We were amazed at the hundreds of people crowding the plaza by the Peruvian border.

"Alto," the guard shouted with raised palms, and the bus came to a stop.

"Pasen, por favor, pasen."

The passengers ahead of us filed off the bus one by one, and we each put on our biggest and bravest smile. We had heard that Peru was more difficult to get into than the other countries where we'd been. The guard wore a rifle over his shoulder. He was tall with a dark, scraggly mustache and fierce eyes.

I immediately put on my P.R. smile and launched into a friendly Spanish banter with him. He loosened up a little, but we weren't safe yet. We were called into an interior office to show our passports. They insisted that all foreigners had to have one hundred American dollars before being permitted to cross the border into Peru. After several minutes of friendly, persuasive conversation, they waived the required money and allowed us to board the bus. In the meantime, the bus had been undergoing a search. For some miraculous reason they didn't open Adino's army trunk full of radio equipment —something that would have been enough for them to detain us.

The guard that we had befriended escorted us to the bus and let Andrew take a picture of him with us. At last we departed, and we all sighed in relief, emotionally exhausted. When the bus jolted to a start and we were headed safely into the Peruvian desert, we hugged each other and rejoiced.

Lima, which sits only a few miles inland from

the beautiful blue Pacific, is a desert city that has required irrigation. Because of this, although the countryside surrounding it was barren and desolate, Lima itself was lush, green, and beautiful.

Once in Lima we started litnessing to raise some money. Since we were officially "in transit" we didn't have to turn in any portion of the donations we received.

I didn't get close to many of the disciples in Lima. One reason was the transient way of life in the COG. The disciples had learned from a Mo letter: "Don't sew your sleeping bag to your mattress." Despite my innate vigor for seeing new places, going to a new colony was mostly a negative experience for me. It meant adapting to different people, different schedules, and different ways of doing things. Yet I had to try to fit in, so I could do the work a disciple had to do.

Another reason I didn't get close to others in Lima was because Adino and I were growing closer and had little free time to spend together. Each day we longed a little more to be married.

My only reservations about marriage concerned getting pregnant because birth control was not an acceptable practice among the COG. I was so in love with Adino by then, however, that my apprehensiveness about having children didn't really matter. And he had already begun to treat me with the care of a husband.

A month after our arrival in Lima, Adino and I received word that our plane fare to Rio had been donated. We could hardly believe our good fortune.

"What about Andrew?" I asked.

"The tickets are just for you," our leader informed us.

We didn't understand why Andrew hadn't been included, but we figured Reuben needed us and he'd gotten word to the overseer in Peru to help us.

On the way home Adino and I didn't even talk about Andrew's exclusion. We could only smile at each other, happy about our own blessings, and thinking as all COG disciples do in such moments that we must be doing something right.

The night before we left Lima, while everyone else was asleep, Adino and I sat upstairs at the leadership colony talking dreamily about Brazil—what it would be like and how long it would be before Reuben married us. Our talk lasted till abut two in the morning.

Adino sat next to me on the bed as I started drifting off to sleep. For a while, neither of us said anything. Suddenly, the window made a rattling noise and Adino jumped up with a start.

"What's going on?" I said.

I heard a low rumble, and the walls began to shake. We bolted off the bed and Adino yelled for me to get in the doorway—it was the safest place to be during an earthquake.

We heard shouts coming from down the hall where the guys slept. Everyone was running around in their underclothes, too frightened to be modest.

The floor and ceiling heaved violently, and I thought the house would collapse on us. We heard screams from downstairs and shouts and desperate prayers from the living room. The walls wouldn't stop shaking. The lights went out, and the noise from the vibration grew louder.

"Jesus! Father!" the yells came from below. I started to look out the window but was overcome with a feeling of horror. I shut my eyes tightly, saying what I thought were my last prayers. Surely this was a part of the destruction Mo had predicted.

Slowly, the noise began to diminish, and the vibration of the floor and walls dwindled. Soon the shaking stopped altogether and there was an eerie silence. I loosened my grip on Adino and realized I had dug my fingernails into his shoulders.

"Thank you, Jesus," echoed down the hall and from downstairs. We rushed down to the living room.

"Is anyone hurt?" Adino asked.

"No, no. We're all OK."

Everyone kept walking around, looking at each other and leaning out the windows to see what had happened outside. I sat on a chair badly shaken but thankful we were alive and still able to carry on in our work until the big destruction really came.

CHAPTER
Ten

Our taxi sped up the cobblestone street, passing a trolley car making its slow ascent. Streets crisscrossed the steep hillside, and hundreds of narrow white houses sat like mushrooms on all sides.

"Santa Teresa." Adino echoed the name of the beautiful hill.

Providing a backdrop to the scene was a lush, green mountain on top of which stood a monument known the world over: the *Cristo,* the Christ. He loomed over the city with arms spread wide, inviting the millions below to embrace him. *His gaze upon the masses,* I thought, *must be out of sorrow at the goings on below.*

Rio was big, bold, and beautiful. And Brazil, the granddaddy of South America, surely was a glorious extension of the city. I felt excitement growing in me as I looked around; if any COG team was destined to conquer this country, it was our band.

For a moment I thought of Andrew and felt sorry for him because I knew he had wanted to get to Rio even more desperately than Adino and I had.

Still, I was no longer bothered that he had been left behind. It was just one of the things that happened in the COG. I realized that he was a nonconformist whose independent spirit often made him a "problem case" in the eyes of some leaders; many of them could not accept his ways. He could be a tremendous asset or a drain, depending on how the leader of the colony reacted to him.

The Portuguese spoken at the airport threw me off guard because it sounded more like French than Spanish. I discovered that my language problems had only begun, though, when we got to the long narrow house that Reuben had rented for the band. "I have a song you need to learn," he said soon after our arrival, hustling us into the living room where I was greeted with joy.

Reuben began singing the Portuguese version of one of our more popular COG songs. *No problem,* I thought at first. But as he sang the words sounded more and more foreign—more nasal than the Spanish I knew. When he was less than halfway through, tears of frustration came to my eyes. After six months of learning Spanish and gaining fluency in it, I couldn't believe I had to start all over again.

Fortunately I had a gift for memorizing music, so I learned the songs with Reuben and the band even though I didn't understand the lyrics. This ultimately aided me in learning to speak the language.

Our first week there Adino and I were escorted by a Brazilian leader who helped us ask for donations, order food, take taxis, and tend to other necessities. We were sent out litnessing every day to become more familiar with our surroundings. And despite my problems with Portuguese, I fell in love with the fun-loving Brazilian people. We were surprised by their friendliness since we had been told the people were embittered by the Americans who they felt exploited the country's natural resources. But we had come to give, not take, and I think it was because of this that they warmed up to us.

Several weeks later, Andrew finally showed up. He looked pitiful. Bearded and bedraggled, he appeared terribly out of place among us. He had traveled across the continent by land—a very hard and dangerous journey. But his arrival was cause for celebration; it meant the reunion of the band.

As Reuben began lining up appearances for the band, the ominous date of Kohoutek's appearance approached—January 31. Every day we went out passing out Mo's "Forty-Day Warning" letter that named the date of the comet's appearance and proclaimed the coming day of destruction.

We waited for that day in awestruck fear. But nothing happened. January 31 came and went with no sign of destruction whatsoever. Needless to say, we were relieved—and confused. Could

God have circumvented his wrath toward the evil kingdom? Or could the inconceivable be true—could Moses David have been wrong?

The latter possibility weighed heavily on the minds of the disciples in Rio. No one voiced their doubts, of course, but it would have been hard to miss the anger and skepticism in the disciples' eyes during the next few days. I myself was enraged. Since we now had the Mo letters at our fingertips, we could review exactly what Mo had said in his Kohoutek letters. When I did so, my anger was refueled.

Almost immediately, though, we got the next Mo letter, entitled "Interpretation." It was written in response to the negative reaction Mo had received about his Kohoutek prophecies from a top leader in England. The letter's contents planted major seeds of doubt about Moses David. He claimed that we all had misinterpreted his prophecies about Kohoutek.

First, he denied having pinpointed the date: "I did not say 'Forty days and America is going to be destroyed'!" He ended with, "Well, that's it. Don't go around peddling on the streets saying, 'Hey, have you heard America's going to fall on January 31st?' Or it could be you'll wind up the biggest fool in town and we'll all be made fools of."

A short time after that he wrote another letter, "The Comet's Tale," claiming that the Children of God were "not the ones that prophesied the actual comet was going to be so tremendous, anyhow."

For the first time I started to believe Moses David was fallible, and I didn't condemn myself for feeling that way. I was angry with him not only for having let us down, but for trying to shift the blame to us for the failing of his prophecy. I found myself feeling betrayed by the leader in whom I had put my full trust—sometimes at great risk. Suddenly, because I could no longer fully trust in the one who had led me to this foreign country, I became aware of the hazards of living the way we were.

Paradoxically, however, my doubts forced me to lean even more heavily on the COG. The unity of the disciples became my crutch. We didn't discuss what had happened—we felt a security in silence—and no matter how I may have felt at the moment, I would have encouraged a doubting disciple. I had been trained by the COG to react by faith, not by sight. We were supposed to be in the process of "renewing our minds," as St. Paul had instructed, and accepting Mo's teachings was part of the renewal process.

And my animosity toward Moses David could not shake the faith I had in the work I was doing. Lives obviously were being changed and souls won for Jesus through the COG ministry.

Then Mo culminated the comet upheaval by "busting" the English leader who had reacted negatively to the false prophecy. (Apparently in the upper levels of the hierarchy, Mo made an example of dissenters.) The leader was stripped of all his authority and sent out litnessing with the lowest disciples.

By that time, an umbrella of organized leadership had developed under Moses David. Archbishops were the leaders directly under Mo; they oversaw COG operations in various regions of the world and reported to the Royal Family. Then in the descending line of command came bishops, regional shepherds, district shepherds, and colony shepherds. This was, we believed, God's spiritual hierarchy, as alluded to in the New Testament—and the leaders were God-ordained.

When leaders did not "bear fruit," however, or when they underwent serious "trials," their positions could be jerked out from under them at any time without warning. Demotions, or being "busted," usually occurred—as with this leader in England —when someone voiced an opinion too strongly, got too proud, or somehow botched a public relations matter.

Adino and I didn't have most of the duties the other disciples had. Our schedule was altogether different, mine with rehearsing and singing engagements and his with his radio work. We were considered to be among the colony elite, and though we went out to litness, we weren't under the pressure of strict quotas. We took direction mostly from Reuben and Athaliah, our regional shepherds.

It was exciting to be under Reuben's guidance again, though he still held the same influence over me as he had before. This was partly because of my deepening commitment to the COG (in spite of my doubts about Mo) and my desire to be an obedient disciple. But it also stemmed from my admiration for Reuben's musical talent and my wonder at his charismatic leadership.

The strong feelings I had for Reuben bordered on idolatry. Yet, while I loved him, in many ways he seemed to be my enemy. He was an emotionally complex person, who chided me about my natural rebellious streak and then scolded me for not asserting myself more. He had me coming and going.

He was ever faithful, however, to encourage me in my music. And, perhaps because of the strange nature of our relationship, I found his praise more meaningful than that of the others.

Several weeks after our arrival in Rio, Reuben made a trip to one of the colonies in Argentina. Upon his return, Adino and I decided to approach him about the possibility of our marrying. During the months since Ecuador, we had spent more time together and had felt we didn't need the remaining mandatory six-month betrothal period.

When we thought the time was right, we walked together to Reuben's office. We prayed outside Reuben's door, and then Adino knocked.

"Yes?"

"Reuben, it's Adino. I'm with Ruth. Can we come in?"

Reuben opened the door and invited us to sit down. When we did, Adino got right to the point.

"Reuben, we've been praying about this—we'd like your permission to get married."

Reuben looked down blankly at a piece of paper on his small desk and folded his hands. He didn't say anything for a moment, then he said, "I'm sorry. I don't think it would be right. I just don't have the faith to marry you."

I was dumbstruck. We had written to him in Argentina about it, so he'd had a lot of time to think it over. I turned to Adino, who looked puzzled. We both wanted to ask why but knew we were expected to just accept what Reuben said. However, Reuben told us his reasons without our asking.

"I really don't think you're ready for marriage," he said. "And, I don't feel you two are right for each other. Since the responsibility is on my shoulders, I just don't think it's God's will at this time. Go pray about it some more."

There was an awkward silence, and I couldn't move my eyes from my lap. After a few moments, Adino and I rose, turned, and walked out as abruptly as we'd walked in.

I didn't want to believe what Reuben had said. How in the world could he think we weren't ready to marry? I could only guess as to Reuben's reasoning. Maybe he thought Adino wasn't good enough for one of his elect because he wasn't a member of the band. Or, Reuben might have felt his authority over my time and commitment was threatened by Adino's influence. He and Adino were as different as night and day. Reuben was gregarious and volatile, a reactionary and a natural performer. Adino, by contrast, had a quiet strength, intelligence, and emotional stability. My hoped-for marriage to him undoubtedly would have affected my stormy relationship with Reuben.

Life didn't stop with Reuben's denial, of course, and Adino and I each tried to deal with our feelings in light of our shepherd's leading. We were determined more than ever to prove ourselves individually and as a team. We dedicated ourselves completely to the colony and the band.

One day we drew a crowd while singing and playing our acoustic instruments in a large park near downtown Rio. About midway through our first set, a Brazilian man in a cream-colored suit emerged from a building nearby. When we took a break, he walked directly to Reuben. The man looked friendly, but his manner was very businesslike.

"Who are you?" he said.

"The Children of God band," Reuben said, smiling confidently.

"Well, how would you like to sing on the radio?"

Within ten minutes we stood before a live radio audience on an upper floor of the building across the street. We glowed with confidence, having sung on the radio in Puerto Rico and Venezuela. The emcee introduced us, and we broke into a song.

The crowd came to their feet when we finished, showing their approval. As we looked at one another, we knew that Brazil would love us and would be won for the cause.

The following week our success snowballed. We were booked to play all over Rio, at clubs, on television, on the radio; Reuben's ambition for the band knew no limits. The man in the cream-colored suit, it turned out, was an agent. He got us an audition at the Rio offices of a major international recording company.

By the end of seven eventful days we were in the recording company's studios, singing our songs for the executives. Within a few days after that we were back at their studios cutting a demo tape. The record producers told us they would listen to it and consider signing us to a contract.

I could hardly believe the news. A record! Me, singing on a record! For years I had dreamed about such an opportunity, and now it was really happening.

One TV appearance led to another, and soon we got calls from all kinds of groups, mostly secular, that asked us to play—orphanages, prisons, a wedding for a government official. Sometimes we were paid well, but usually a fancy meal, transportation, and the great publicity were our rewards.

In mid-March that year Athaliah's mother, who was supportive of her daughter's work with the COG, came from the States to visit for several weeks. She seemed well-to-do and brought clothes and gifts for Athaliah.

I hit it off with Athaliah's mom immediately. She enjoyed the band and our antics, and she seemed to like me especially. When the time came for her return to the United States, her daughters threw a going away party for her at a park near Copacabana. I had hoped to attend, but

I still had a bit of paperwork left to do for Reuben when everyone was leaving for the picnic.

"You coming, Ruth?" Reuben said on his way out to the door.

"I still have some reports to finish for you."

"They can wait."

I looked at him in amazement. Wait? The reports were never to be left unfinished.

"Come on, Ruth, let's go."

Having known I would miss the picnic, I had geared up to do the work. Now I didn't want to leave it for later. Still, I wasn't going to argue; the party would be a lot more fun than the work.

We rushed to catch a bus to the park, and when we arrived, everyone was singing and dancing to the band's rhythmic choruses. The girls had set a long table full of food, with rows of benches all around it. Disciples sat in groups, laughing, eating, and singing. I forgot all about my responsibilities and joined in the fun. The party was a welcome retreat for us during that hectic week.

After a while, Reuben called the group together, as he customarily did, for a word of encouragement or announcements. Athaliah and I sat together on a bench next to the one where Reuben sat talking. I let my mind wander, not listening to what he said, until these unexpected words snapped me to attention: "Is there anybody here who has a burden to get married?"

Of course, the entire colony roared and raised their hands. Almost everyone who wasn't married wanted a spouse.

Reuben looked down in mock seriousness,

tapped a finger on his chin. "Well, is there anyone who wants to get married . . . today?"

I felt Athaliah pushing my arm into the air. Startled, I looked up and saw everyone timidly lowering their hands, except Adino! Then it began to dawn on me what was happening.

I turned bright red. Few people in the colony had known about us, and the other disciples began chuckling in surprise. Most had thought I'd end up marrying a member of the band.

Athaliah was howling by this time, and I turned to look at her mother. She winked at me knowingly.

Suddenly Adino and I were being pushed together by all the disciples to where Reuben stood. It all happened so fast, we were stunned.

The ceremony lasted only a few minutes, and everyone gathered tightly around us to pray. "Bless them, Father." "Give them your love." "Watch over them, Lord." "Keep them strong in you."

"Here," said Reuben. He held out a few cruzeiros, the Brazilian currency. "Don't spend this all in one place," he teased. "Go on, take a few days' honeymoon."

Everyone gave us tearful hugs and kisses as we dashed off.

We decided to head for Petropolis, a tiny mountain village outside Rio that was surrounded by magnificent rivers and waterfalls. Although we knew each other's personalities well enough to know what to expect in marriage, Adino and I had never dated or had much time alone, other than our litnessing outings. So we enjoyed our three days together to the fullest.

When we returned to Rio, we got Reuben's permission to rent a room at a small, cheap rooming house down the street because there was no place at the colony house for another couple to live. We moved our belongings to our room and started our new life together with anticipation.

Immediately after we were married, Adino and I were appointed shepherds of the Rio colony, which was growing steadily. Reuben needed us to oversee the colony's daily management, and I was responsible for the feeding of our household of forty. I did the shopping and planned the meals, but the disciples helped prepare the food. We also set up the litnessing teams, passing out the Mo letters for the day.

As prudish as the COG's mores about dating were, Mo's letters had become increasingly preoccupied with sex. Some letters used illustrations on themes such as seduction and frequency of relations, all presumably to increase sexual satisfaction among marriage partners. Just prior to the appearance of his more sexually oriented missives, though, Mo had written a letter entitled "Old Bottles" that encouraged COG disciples to be flexible with the new revelations he had begun to receive from God. The letter's title was in reference to Jesus' teachings on pouring new wine into old wineskins. That concept was one on which the philosophy of the Children of God still hinged: Being revolutionary pleased God.

One of the most radical of Mo's messages on

sexual matters had come years before in a letter entitled "One Wife." In it Mo declared: "God will have no other gods before him, not even the sanctity of the marriage god! Nevertheless, in order to avoid a lot of problems, it is good for each to have his own—or better: God's own! We don't believe in 'to each his own,' but 'to each according as he has need, of whatever God and his brethren are able to supply'!"

To support his message, Mo quoted Jesus' prophecy concerning those who forsake all to follow God: "A man's enemies will be the members of his own household" (Matt. 10:36). To that Mo added: "He's breaking up private families! We haven't hesitated to break up worldly families by ripping off their kids for God's Family! What is the difference in that and breaking up a husband and wife? Jesus said you're going to have to forsake *all!*"

COG disciples had no trouble with these revolutionary teachings. The group's radical converts from the early days were rapidly becoming leaders of the movement, especially as the group developed in other countries. And Mo's radical dictates and revelations spread as far as the converts would go themselves.

In January the colonies received an unusual Mo letter entitled "The Flirty Little Fishy." In it Moses David told the story of his being out one night with friends when he was struck with a revelation about evangelization. That revelation, he wrote, was confirmed later in the evening by this prophecy: "I have to put to sleep the flesh . . . that I may waken his spirit and revive his soul. . . .

"Show them [potential converts] such unselfish love and concern that they couldn't think more highly of you, and they'll love you more than they ever loved anyone. . . . If you're afraid to give it to them just because of a little pride and regard for convention, you could even lose them because of your God-damned pride and concern about what they think about you. To hell with what they think about you!

"You are just to be concerned about them. . . . If they have to fall in love with you first before they find it's the Lord, it's just God's bait to hook them!

"Fascinate the fish with the lure! . . . Help her to catch him with her fingers of flesh that she might impart unto him thy Spirit, O Lord, for which he hungers . . . be through the flesh the attractive lure, delicious flesh on a steel hook of thy reality, the steel of thy Spirit! . . .

"Art thou willing to kiss many with my kiss of life?"

When we heard the letter read before the colony and later read it together, Adino and I saw its message as merely pointing out parallels to Scripture and past Mo letters that dealt with the crucifixion of the flesh in everyday life. But a similar Mo letter appeared in April entitled "Look of Love." Citing numerous Scripture references in which the eye was called the "window of the soul," Mo described the importance of physical allure to evangelization and encouraged female disciples to dress provocatively.

With that letter, I began to wonder how literally Mo meant for us to interpret his teachings. But I never questioned the matter, not even with Adino, for fear I might disappoint him with my lack of conviction. Even as negative thoughts about "Flirty Fishing" came into my head, I rebuked myself: *We're not supposed to interpret. We're to be faithful servants and unquestioningly obedient.*

CHAPTER
Eleven

One hot Rio morning Adino and I left our room to go to the colony and divide the disciples into litnessing teams. When we walked into the colony house we stopped in shocked silence. The place looked as if it had been torn apart.

There wasn't a soul in sight except for the Brazilian leader, who peeped from behind the dining room door.

"Where is everyone?" I asked.

Her eyes darted with fear. "We were raided."

Adino grabbed my hand. "Who were they?" he asked.

"They had machine guns. They came in through the open doors and windows. They went through everything. Mo's letters, our belongings. We were accused of subversive activities. It was awful. We got dressed at gunpoint, and everyone was led to the secret police van. I didn't have to go because I had the baby." Her face froze with renewed fear. "Do you think they'll come back?"

My eyes met Adino's. He turned to the girl and said, "Don't let anyone know you saw us."

With that, we ran from the house and into the street. We ran toward a crowded trolley and jumped on, mixing in with the passengers, saying nothing. Every person who so much as glanced at us made us nervous; the secret police often dressed in plain clothes. We sat motionless, gripping each other's hand.

After a few blocks, we slid off and ducked into a restaurant. "If we get separated," Adino whispered, "we'll meet by the statue in the plaza. Stay in the doorways of the shops, though. Just watch for me."

I nodded, shuddering at the thought of being separated from him. All that day we stole down alleys, in and out of doorways, glancing over our shoulders to be sure no one was following. Every stare from a stranger renewed our fears of arrest, deportation, or torture. I never allowed myself to think what the other disciples might be enduring. The two intolerable sins in Latin America were political dissension and drug possession; the authorities had no tolerance for violators of either—and we were suspected of both.

Late in the evening, when we finally worked up enough courage, Adino and I crept back to the colony, zigzagging our way across the neighborhood. When we came to the house, we saw several lights on inside. Adino decided to check it out while I waited across the street. A few seconds later he waved me inside.

I was greeted with hugs of relief from several disciples. "We thought maybe they had arrested you, too," said one girl. Other disciples began to join us.

"We were released this afternoon," the girl continued. She said they hadn't been tortured, only interrogated about the Mo letters. But the police had detained one American disciple and one Brazilian leader.

We didn't see those two for days. A Brazilian accompanied me to the police headquarters to ask about them, but the police refused to say where they were being held or even admit that they were in their custody. Finally, the disciples were released without being charged, but it took several threats from the U.S. Embassy for that to happen. Since the government's attitude toward Americans fluctuated constantly, the fear of more raids and even arrests loomed ever before us.

My apprehension was overcome by joy, however, when a few days after the raid I found out I was pregnant. Adino and I were thrilled. And our joy soon doubled as the band began to skyrocket into popularity. Everyone in Rio, it seemed, had heard of the Children of God through the band's television and radio appearances. Everywhere we went they held hands and swayed to our music, sometimes by the thousands, eagerly singing the choruses with us, hungering to know Jesus' love. I never had seen so many people willing to hear the message of eternal life through

God's Son. We preached the gospel endlessly, it seemed, passing out literature and leading dozens at a time to the Lord.

At many of the places where we played, young converts begged to join the COG. In most cases they owned nothing but the clothes on their backs; for them "forsaking all" meant forsaking a hopeless life of poverty among families of numerous children. With the COG they not only had the riches of living full-time for the Lord, but they found a place where their physical needs for food and shelter were met. Our colony's weekly reports on "numbers of souls saved" and "new COG disciples" must have looked impressive when they reached the international office in London. In return we received increasing numbers of the newest Mo letters, which by now were illustrated and bound for litnessing distribution.

Our colony was thriving, but I was troubled about one aspect of COG life: the uneven distribution of belongings. It was easy to see that communal possessions weren't as communal as the COG claimed. The leaders' frugal life-style was much different than that of ordinary disciples.

Yet I was guilty of enjoying the privileges of leadership. In Brazil a young Venezuelan female convert who owned a gold watch relinquished it for my use—I was a leader at the time and felt I needed it more than she. When I asked her for it, she gave it to me gladly; whenever any leader asked for something, a disciple was never in a position to refuse, lest they incur the wrath of their shepherd.

COG colonies multiplied throughout Rio, and the band (including Adino and me) moved to a house in Grajau, a neighborhood twenty minutes from the city. The Brazilian disciples came to us in droves with little to offer except the crucial ability to support the COG through litnessing. As it turned out, their litnessing helped keep the colony afloat.

What the Brazilian converts didn't know was that the upper leaders' children wore nice clothes bought in part with a percentage of tithes that they, the converts, had provided. The disciples had to depend on hand-me-down clothes from colony leaders or buy their own—with their shepherd's approval—with their leftover litnessing money.

Love and shelter were the only material things the Brazilian disciples got from the colony. Thus, Adino and I were disturbed when one leader chided a Brazilian convert for not bringing in enough money and told me not to let him come home until he met the quota. We never enforced these quotas ourselves but had to remain silent if a leader above us made these demands.

Meanwhile, as the band was touring the countryside, Adino put together a sound system for us. He was happy to be able to work closely with me as the band's sound engineer because the mounting number of engagements allowed us very little time together alone.

Touring became our top priority, and our traveling schedule frequently required an absence from the colony for days at a time. Adino was left to handle the responsibilities of daily management when we did TV or radio performances.

I was thrilled by the band's growing prospects. The record company for whom we made the demo tape had signed us to record a single, which would be releasing locally. We decided on a song with a worshipful chorus. Sam led us in and out of the studio in a matter of a few hours, and within weeks we heard our voices over the airwaves in Rio.

Soon thereafter we were booked to play at record stores and on many television and radio programs. We even sang in nightclubs and afterward litnessed to the audiences and talked to them about Jesus. The Brazilians loved our music—we were somewhat of an oddity to them because we were Americans. In addition, the people liked hearing music in tribute to God yet set to a rock beat. Our single became so popular it hit the Brazilian Top Forty, and "Os Meninos de Deus," as the band was known now, was invited to appear on a TV show that showcased performers who had current hits. Suddenly the country's spotlight was on us, and it glowed brightly.

Soon after that, our producer informed us that the band had to be in the studio in four days to cut our album. With a million things to worry about—arranging music and vocals, choosing which songs to record, hoping the female vocalist wouldn't deliver her baby (I was in my ninth month of pregnancy and looked about ready to burst)—we were up against impossible odds.

Amid the rush and confusion, Reuben had

good news for me. "We're going to use one of your songs on the album."

I couldn't contain my joy; I think I even yelped. Then I went down the street to the hotel room to tell Adino. It all was too much to take.

Our first day in the studio was even more harried than our days of preparation, but with the help of our producer—a smiling, curly haired, bespectacled young Brazilian named David—everything came together. A musician himself, David knew how to deal with our disorganization, fatigue, and wandering minds. He helped us overcome all of this by building our confidence.

Once the sessions were underway, David began to get interested in one of our female disciples, a pretty Colombian girl named Melody who helped us with back-up vocals. Everyone got excited at the prospect of David becoming a COG disciple. He was a successful, well-to-do professional, yet he seemed genuinely interested in our mission. He was surprised, he said, that so much musical talent had been culled from a group like the Children of God. David probably was impressed, too, because he had had to handle many temperamental, egocentric musicians in the studio, and we were so easily manageable. Most producers would have thought it beneath them to mingle with the musicians, but David did it casually. As a result, his production of our music became an extremely personal matter to him.

Word came down through Reuben that Moses David had been kept informed about our recording contract and was encouraging and supportive. He was even sending his youngest daughter, Faithy, to Rio as his emissary to observe the sessions. When she arrived, I could hardly believe I was meeting an actual relative of our prophet. Although she held and commanded great authority, I found her to be easy to get along with. She was strongly committed to the COG, and I respected and admired her willingness to take her guitar into the streets to sing and litness like the rest of us.

I got to know her well during the sessions. She liked my music, which pleased me, but her greatest compliment to me was that her father enjoyed hearing me sing—he had heard my voice on the tapes we had recorded at our studios in Texas.

Then in the midst of all the excitement and work I went into labor. Adino and I had prepared for natural childbirth delivery by going through Lamaze training (which had COG approval). After six hours of labor, our son, Isaac, was delivered by a generous and sympathetic doctor who didn't charge us. (This same doctor had provided us with free prenatal services.) Adino's eyes lit up as he gathered Isaac from me and held him closely.

After I got out of the hospital, our colony moved several miles inland to a new house. Prospective converts were urged to come there to enjoy food, drink, music, and skits full of comedy and subtle messages about the COG and the gospel.

At our new location I was surrounded by four

other young moms with newborns. Together we shared the worries, joys, concerns, and hopes of raising a child. I loved the new atmosphere and camaraderie, but in spite of it all, it was obvious that one aspect of COG life wouldn't change as a COG mom: humble living.

The band was still involved in the recording sessions, and I couldn't wait to get back to the studio. Even with the birth of Isaac, singing was all I could think of or talk about. Because our new colony already had leaders, Adino was able to slip away with Isaac to the studio, enabling me to nurse the baby.

At first I relished moments like these, but gradually I began to resent the increasing demands of motherhood. Adino gladly spent the majority of time with Isaac until he began to assume more responsibility in the colony leadership. Then his time with the baby became limited.

Toward the end of the sessions I saw evidence on Adino's face of the strain of trying to be a good leader, a good father, and a substitute mother because I was gone so much. With the tension of trying unsuccessfully to balance singing with motherhood, I was sure he could see the tension reflected on my face as well. I thought the pressure might ease somewhat after the band wrapped up the recording sessions, but instead it only increased. We began promoting the album nonstop, and the following months included more appearances than ever. On many occasions I attended band rehearsals with tiny Isaac strapped on a backpack. Far more often, however, Adino was left to take care of Isaac (and the other disciples at the colony) while I dined in fancy restaurants with the record company executives and influential people in the record industry.

The band's promotions were so hurried and exciting that I gave little thought to my husband during that time. My taste of the high life as a recording artist was a glorious and fulfilling way to follow Mo's orders to use worldly goods. In fact, I enjoyed my time away from home because life there was growing increasingly tense. Far from being the comforting retreat it should have been, home was an emotional letdown. After the excitement of the band's prospects and rubbing elbows with people from the recording industry, Adino's news about the growth of the colony or the personal and spiritual victories of the disciples seemed anticlimactic. I just didn't have the energy to concentrate on anything but my music.

Slowly my pride in my new stature in the band caused me to lose sight of my need for my husband. My pride grew—as did the tension between us. One night I walked in after a promotional event. I had just spent an evening of laughter, song, and fellowship with the musicians who over the months had become my best friends. When I walked into our room at the colony house and saw Adino pacing back and forth with the baby, his hair mussed and the room in disarray, something inside made me shiver with disdain. It must have shown on my face.

He barely glanced at me as I walked in.

"Hi," I said without really looking at him. He

said nothing, but I felt his hard gaze as I walked to where he stood and reached for Isaac. He handed the baby to me, still glaring hard, and I took Isaac and began walking around the room absent-mindedly.

"He's just about asleep," Adino snapped. "You'd better put him to bed."

I reached down for Isaac's blanket and with a sigh I wrapped him in it and laid him in the crib.

"Tired?" Adino said. But it was an accusation, not a show of concern. I didn't respond. "I thought you might be," he said sarcastically.

I wanted very badly to say something to him, but I didn't want an argument. I eased myself into our rocker and began rocking gently.

"Ruth."

I sighed. Why couldn't he leave me alone? "What?" I said in a strained voice.

After a silent moment, I turned to look at him. The dim yellow light from the lamp beside me barely shone across the room to where he sat on the worn sofa, elbows on his knees, hands folded, watching me.

"Let's go to bed," he said, staring straight into my eyes.

His terse words weren't meant as a command, but a challenge. In his anger he wanted a response, to know if I cared. I felt lassoed and reeled in by this man. When he started to talk about the responsibilities of submission in marriage, I had to muster all the strength I could not to be repulsed.

I didn't even look at him, but I felt his anger grow at my silence.

"When is this going to change, Ruth?" he demanded.

I stopped rocking and shut my eyes.

"It's not meant to be like this," he pressed.

I measured my words carefully: "You just . . . don't . . . understand."

"I think I understand," he said. "It's pretty clear what's happening between us."

"What's that?"

"Nothing." Again, an accusation. "Absolutely nothing."

I kept my eyes shut as I spoke. "You can't begin to understand, Adino."

"The only thing I want to understand is how we're going to become husband and wife again with everything that's happening with the band."

"Oh," I said, feigning calm. "The band is a problem for you?"

Without warning he slammed his fist into an endtable, almost toppling it. "No! The band is *your* problem. You're the one who's hurting this family. Is this a marriage, Ruth? Is it? You're not here for Isaac, much less for me—"

I broke in, shouting angrily. "You think you can possess me, when I've been called to minister—to *minister*—with the band? You've got it all screwed up, Adino."

"You want the band more than you want us."

"I want God more than I want anything, and I'm doing what *he* wants."

I felt tears of rage forming, and I stomped to my

feet and stormed outside, slamming the door. Adino began to yell, and the baby started crying. I hurried down the dark street, my hands in my pockets, tears streaming down my face, hoping for a way out of what seemed to be a closing trap.

The band constantly made various promotional appearances as the album grew in popularity. Life at home, however, continued its downward spiral. With each glamorous promotion of the record my respect and feelings for Adino decreased. He was left with Isaac more often as the band's promotional efforts increased, and his consistent willingness to take care of our child in spite of our growing differences had the ironic effect of making him seem even smaller in my eyes. When we were at home together, the tiniest nuance—tone of voice, choice of words—was an invitation to argue. At least once a week one of us stormed out of the house in a rage.

Finally, Brazilian enthusiasm for the record peaked and leveled off, and the band had a short break between appearances. Reuben and Athaliah, whose relationship also had shown hints of strain, decided to fly to the States to visit Athaliah's mother.

The break from promotions allowed me some time at home to enjoy Isaac, but I had little desire to spend the time with Adino. Instead, I spent hours singing, playing, and writing songs with Andrew and the other band members. The pressure of record promotions having eased, the tension with Adino did lessen somewhat.

Finally, Reuben returned to Rio—but he was

alone. I'd never seen him in such a depressed state as when he arrived at the colony. Later that day we heard the incredible news: Athaliah had decided to stay in the United States. She had renounced all ties with the COG, including her marriage. She didn't believe strongly enough in Moses David to follow him anymore—or to stay married to Reuben.

Her renunciation of the cause served only to strengthen my belief in the Children of God. Even though most of us felt sorry for Reuben, we were bolstered in our belief that our chosen life-style was strict and extreme, and was not one to be joined halfheartedly. Athaliah, we thought, must have weakened while at home.

Reuben always had seemed invulnerable, but his wife's desertion visibly affected him. When he first got back into the daily operations in Rio he maintained his usual strong hand, but he wasn't the same. We all prayed for him, asking God to restore his joy and vitality so that he could help sustain the momentum the Lord had established in Brazil through the band.

Gradually Reuben opened up again, and over the next few weeks he seemed to have returned to his old self. Every so often, however, a glint of pain appeared in his eyes, and his thoughts seemed to be elsewhere.

One afternoon I was told by another disciple that Reuben wanted to see me in his room. Immediately I went numb. Being summoned by Reuben was either the best news a disciple could receive or the worst. I always had trouble pleasing Reuben; even when I successfully did what he asked of me, I was nervous about it. Thus my hand trembled as I knocked on the door of his room. I was somewhat relieved, however, when his "Come in!" sounded light, even cheery.

"Hi, Reuben," I said cautiously.

"Hi, Ruth, come on in. Have a seat." He appeared slightly nervous as I sat beside him on the bed.

Folding his hands and wearing a serious expression, he said, "I want you to pray about something."

That seemed simple enough, but joining a leader in prayer could be a privilege or it could be a test of faith, of a disciple's willingness to do what the leader asked.

"Sure," I whispered. "What?"

His voice was soft. "You know what happened with Athaliah. . . ." He hesitated then, as if the hard part was over and he didn't know what else to say. He began talking about his loneliness. "In Mo's letter 'One Wife,' he teaches that we're to have no other gods before our God." He paused, "Not even the 'marriage god.'"

I thought at first he might be relating the passage to his breakup with Athaliah. Then, as he went on, I slowly realized what he was asking.

"You know what I've been going through, Ruth," he said. "If you are willing, and Adino agrees, I'd like you to be with me for a while."

I was shocked but thrilled as well. As I had sat with him, listening to him explain his feelings of loneliness and unhappiness, I had realized how much I really cared for Reuben. I smiled nervously; I didn't want to appear overanxious.

"Of course," I said. "You know I'd do anything for you, and I'm sure Adino will agree under the circumstances." When Reuben looked at me, he must have felt my love for him. This was going to be the perfect answer to all my problems.

He put his hand on mine. "Can I kiss you?"

"Yes," I said, certain the awkwardness I was feeling would soon be displaced by the knowledge that I was giving my all for the revolution.

C H A P T E R
Twelve

The arrangement was that I would live with
Adino as his wife but would go to Reuben whenever he called for me. What I didn't realize was
the turmoil Adino experienced in the midst of
this decision.

When Reuben first mentioned his request to
Adino and asked him to pray about it, Adino un-
derstandably was caught in a whirling, raging
confusion. He wanted to serve and obey, but he
feared he might have heard the death knell of
his marriage. Wasn't that union, too, ordained
of God?

With characteristic reserve he told Reuben he
would pray about the matter. What else could he
have said? COG husbands in those situations
were expected to give their blessings to such relationships. Every fiber of Adino's being
screamed *no,* but he knew that was not the answer Reuben would accept, at least without serious repercussions.

Adino thought his reluctance might be a response from the flesh, that he might be resisting what the Spirit was leading Reuben to do for the good of all. But what if it was a response from his own spirit—something God was trying to tell him?

He would indeed pray.

Moses David's teachings resounded in his head: a true child of God must be able to lay down his life for his brother, to the point of sharing his wife; that much was clear, emphasized and reemphasized throughout many of the Mo letters. But what of the sanctity of marriage? Didn't that mean something? Or was that even a biblical concept?

Adino had accepted Mo's sex doctrines regarding his erotic passages on lovemaking as stories and parables. Now, however, he faced the ultimate test of his belief in Mo's directives: first-hand application.

Adino wanted to know God's direction in the matter. He refused to let personal desires impede the flow of the Lord's workings. Jealousy, no matter how strong, would not influence his decision.

And so he prayed, longing for an answer. If he consented to the arrangement, and that was the wrong answer, the results would be irreversible. He didn't know if he could live with that.

Yet he realized he couldn't face the consequences of his refusal either. He didn't have peace about the arrangement, but if he refused, he knew that somewhere down the line he would pay for his decision. If ever he tripped up on even

the smallest matter, he could lose everything—
including his family—forever. If he denied
Reuben now, he would almost guarantee the
eventual loss of his wife and child.

Reuben would have his own way, Adino knew,
one way or another. For once, the soft-spoken yet
forthright disciple was not able to speak his
mind.

Adino prayed for another day, agonizing over
the decision, but peace never came. Realizing finally that he had been forced into an impossible
situation and that avoiding the decision would
only prolong his agony, he resolved to tell
Reuben he would agree to the arrangement. He
had no choice. However, he determined, he
would not say he felt the Lord's peace about the
decision.

The entire house rattled with the slamming of
the door, and when the baby started crying I
burst into tears. This was the worst fight Adino
and I had had since my relationship with Reuben
had begun.

It was after midnight, and I was sure the other
disciples in the house had heard the worst of it.
As I had indicated to Adino many times, I wasn't
interested in satisfying his sexual needs. Although he hadn't seemed to expect me to want to,
he wore the frustrated expression of one who
was slowly losing everything. However, this time
after our shouting match Adino's face burned
with an unfamiliar fury.

Without warning he balled his fist and smashed

a hole in the wall. The sound of the crash was frightening enough, but the very action—unexpected as it was—shook me deeply. I despised him for it.

As he stormed out, my own anger was released in tears streaming down my face. The more Adino demanded, the less I was willing to give. Now, staring at the huge black hole in our wall, I wanted nothing at all to do with him.

From the beginning of the arrangement, my time with Reuben had been limited. Yet that only made me revel in every moment I had with him. The first time he summoned me to a nearby hotel. Reuben said very little when I walked in—nothing about the Mo letters or his needs—but I felt I was there to fulfill a spiritual duty, and I was even excited about it. Time was suspended for a while in that room until a loud knock on the door made us both jump. It was 4:00 A.M.

The dark-haired hotel manager unabashedly poked his head in. "You must be out," he said abruptly, pointing to his watch. "Time to leave."

We dressed in silence, and I felt dirty and embarrassed. But I thought to myself as I walked out of the hotel ahead of Reuben that I couldn't wait for him to call again.

Now, after two weeks, Reuben had sent word again: we would meet at the colony the next day. I was pleased, of course, but felt sure the news would generate further tension with Adino. And it did, triggering his violent act and leaving a hole in our wall. It wasn't so much the message from Reuben, however, that infuriated Adino late that night; it was my obviously growing disdain for him.

The afternoon with Reuben was much the same as the time before. We tried talking this time, but it was awkward. We were still a shepherd and a disciple, a leader and a follower. I didn't mind; I was with him again, and my thoughts were far away from the turmoil of my marriage.

Then Reuben shocked me back to reality. "How are things with Adino?" he asked. This subject was on par with the awkwardness of our attempted conversation, but it wasn't just more idle small talk and it caught me with sudden indescribable pain. The way Reuben had asked the question told me he wasn't interested in details; he was just slightly curious.

"Oh," I stammered, looking quickly at him, then back downward. "Well, we're having some trials. But not because of this. We've been having them for a while."

That was the end of it. I hoped he would forget I even said it. For some reason I wasn't very glad he asked. He'd issued no response to my answer, and I couldn't tell how heavily he weighed the matter.

Later that evening I realized I ached to be with Reuben all the time. I couldn't keep my mind from wandering to thoughts of him. It was getting late when I wondered where Adino was.

"He told somebody he was going over to Ed's this afternoon," a disciple said. Ed, a young Englishman, was our next-door neighbor. He lived with an Irish artist and owned electronic equipment and tools that Adino frequently borrowed for COG use.

"Did he say when he'd be coming back?"

"No," she said, looking up with little concern. "In fact, he's been gone several hours."

Adino seldom spent much time at Ed's. None of us did. Even though he and his roommate were friendly and enjoyable, we knew they smoked marijuana; obviously, we didn't share the same moral standards.

About that time, another sister walked in. "Hi," she said. "Guess what? I just saw a DOPS [secret police] van pull out of Ed's driveway. Any idea what happened?"

I had to check this out. I walked next door and knocked. No answer. I peered through one of the windows; it was too dark to see. I walked to the side of the house and looked through another window.

In the dim light of a lamp that lay on its side on the floor, broken glass and furniture made hideous shadows against the walls. I gasped and ran back to the colony house.

"Something's happened to them! Something's happened!" I screamed as I burst in.

"What?" The disciples began filing into the living room.

"Ed's house! Something's happened!"

Everyone fell silent, aghast. Someone whispered ominously: "Drug raid."

The news couldn't have been worse. Adino had most likely been caught up in it all, and I felt completely helpless. In the morning we decided to gather some Brazilian disciples from the other colonies and split up into groups, each going to a different police station. I went with a group to the central office downtown. The police there would not admit they were holding Adino, assuring us they had no knowledge of the arrest.

The other groups reported the same story: no cooperation. We knew the police had secret places in the woods where suspected drug and political criminals were taken and tortured. Now my worst fear about Brazil had been realized: the police had taken my husband and were holding him on drug charges. There wasn't a more serious crime, and we couldn't even get to him to prove his innocence.

For three days after Adino's disappearance I hadn't been able to sleep. I looked terrible, and every moment seemed filled with fear for my husband.

Then we got an anonymous call from someone who told a disciple where Adino was being held. Immediately we called the American consulate in Rio and told an official about Adino's arrest and the call we'd just received. The official said he would contact the police and that we should wait until he called back.

A few hours later, he called and said the police had arrested Adino, Ed, and another man in hopes of capturing one of Ed's friends who was a drug trafficker. Adino and the others would be released the next day when the drug pusher returned.

For some reason, Adino and the two Britishers

were forced to sign some sort of confession before being released. Then they were driven back blindfolded and dropped off in downtown Rio. From there they caught the bus to our neighborhood.

When I heard that Adino would be returning that day, I waited for him with Isaac, who was nearly six months old, on the front porch of the house. The sun was setting when I saw Adino walking up the street. I ran to him and threw myself in his arms. For those four days I had felt absolutely empty and helpless without him.

We went inside and Adino told me what had happened. He and the two Britishers had been placed in the three-and-a-half foot high trunk space of the police van. They couldn't see where they were being taken. As the van stopped, they were hauled out of the trunk and taken into a large, dank building, somewhere in the woods. The police confiscated their possessions and escorted them through a courtyard and into a long, dark room. Adino and the two Britishers were pushed into a line of suspects, who stood against the walls.

An officer came in and shouted at the suspects. Then he pointed at Adino, announcing something as he walked toward him. The small, dark man stopped directly in front of Adino. He took hold of Adino's long hair and, slowly curling it around his finger, yanked hard.

A guard noticed a Swiss army knife on the back of Adino's belt that hadn't been confiscated. He jerked the knife from the belt and, opening it, held it to Adino's face, taunting him. Adino said he had understood none of the accusations being leveled at him, but fearful instinct had told him to remain silent.

Ed was detained in the room as Adino was taken through the courtyard to another building and locked in a tiny, filthy cell. Within a few minutes he heard screams: somewhere nearby people were being tortured. Adino began to pray. He listened to the screaming for several hours, wondering if he would leave there alive.

Sometime in the early morning a guard appeared; he was dragging Ed. The guard shoved Ed inside and he fell to the floor, trembling violently. Almost an hour passed before he could speak.

"They had a hand-cranked generator," he whispered, his voice breaking. "They hooked the wires to my index fingers and started cranking. Then they started asking questions, questions about drugs. I didn't know what they were talking about. Then they started cranking harder and harder and I couldn't stand it anymore. . . . I–I admitted to what they were saying, but we didn't do anything! I didn't even know what I was saying yes to."

Neither of them slept that night. In the morning they were fed rice and beans and told they wouldn't be fed again until the next morning. Adino gave one of the passing guards money to buy some decent food for him and Ed. The guard did so, but at a high price. He also allowed Adino to have his small Bible. Then, as day turned to night, Adino feared the torture would begin again. He read passages of Scripture and continued to pray.

Just as they had begun to fall asleep, the cell door was flung open and a young man was thrust inside. He looked naive and afraid. They asked him why he was arrested, and he said he had been arrested on false charges of drug possession. Adino sat up with him that night, comforting him with passages from Scripture and sharing the gospel. Late into the night the young man accepted Jesus as his Savior.

The next morning a guard told the young man that someone had vouched for him, and he was being released. As he waited for the guard to return with his belongings, Adino wrote down the telephone number of the COG colony and gave it to him.

"Please call them to tell them where I am," he said. "Thank you."

The young man had returned Adino's look of gratitude. "Thank *you*, my friend," he said.

I watched Adino's face while he told his story, and felt wonder at the way God had protected him. Once again I gave thanks that he was safe.

The disciples in the colony were shaken by the incident. They continued litnessing, but the fear that they might be picked up by the police at any time was strong. Then our promotion of the album resumed, and Reuben went to São Paulo to set up some appearances for us. In spite of the trauma of Adino's jailing and the relief his release had brought, the tensions between us continued. Knowing Reuben was interested in me, I could not make myself love Adino—and he knew it.

A week after leaving for São Paulo, Reuben called and gave the band the date we should arrive there. Our prospects looked great, he said. He left word also that I was to come down a week prior to the other members.

That news had the expected impact in our home. The resulting fight was just another aggravation in a long string of mutual antagonisms. This time Adino wasn't around on the day I left—and I was glad.

I spent the first day in São Paulo alone with Reuben. He seemed more open to discussing things with me. I thought that perhaps his asking the question about Adino the last time we were together made him feel a bit more at ease with me now. I wished he hadn't seen me worried and distraught during the days Adino was in jail.

The band came down the next week and promotions went into full swing. With our work having been interrupted by Reuben's losing Athaliah and the police scare, it was soothing and healing just to play together again.

Adino didn't come to São Paulo; he hadn't been summoned with the rest of the band. After our quick public relations tour of the city was over, though, Reuben called him to come and make contacts with local merchants for electronic equipment and repairs. We would be staying in São Paulo for a while, it seemed, and Reuben wanted to have the band ready to play.

Adino arrived with Isaac. As expected, he had

little to say to me. We maintained somewhat of a distance during the following weeks, though we did live in the same room. The emotional gap between us was growing again and our arguments resumed. I threw myself deeper and deeper into the work of the band—the music and the expanding promotions. Soon Adino moved out of our room to live across town at another colony.

I was so self-involved by now that I couldn't see the intense hurt Adino suffered from his unrelenting jealousy. No matter how rigorously he fought it with Scripture, conviction, and resolve, every day was a battle; it was utter agony knowing that the one he loved was in love with someone else.

One afternoon Reuben beckoned me to his room. I hurried in, but my anticipation was thwarted by his ill-at-ease manner. He looked slightly worried. "Ruth," he gestured with a pencil from behind his desk, "sit down, please."

I sat on his bed, and he began to make small talk. All my responses, however, seemed to fall flat. Finally, he got to the point.

"You need to go back to Adino. You need to be together," he said quietly.

My head started swimming.

"It's important—for the baby's sake, Ruth."

"But Reuben, I don't love him." By that, I meant for Reuben to understand that I loved *him*.

But he just replied, "Ruth, give it one more try."

The intimacy that had been in Reuben's voice during our visits was absent. His tone was flat, patronizing: he knew I loved him and that I didn't want to go back to Adino. But he obviously was not interested, as I had been, in our relationship becoming deeper and more permanent.

I looked at him in helplessness. I felt betrayed. Dirty. Used. The pride I had felt from being with him was gone. Instead, my face flushed as I realized that our relationship had meant nothing more to Reuben than sexual satisfaction. He had thought of me only as an intermediate solution to his needs.

My dreams of living with Reuben as his wife were gone. I couldn't believe it.

Soon our promotions for the "Children of God" album wound down, and our colony of mostly band members and their families was invited for a weekend retreat at a ranch house just outside São Paulo. Everyone welcomed a mini-vacation from the recent exertions.

If anyone required a break from the regular COG activities, it was I. A couple of days after my split with Reuben, a COG leader named Tamar left her husband, Peter, and volunteered herself to Reuben as my replacement. Naturally, I resented her. But I soon realized her personality was better suited to Reuben's than mine. Even so I couldn't get over the fact that I was only Reuben's interim lover until a more permanent replacement for Athaliah was found.

Adino was already at the ranch when I arrived with Isaac and the band members. I wasn't too excited about that. But Tamar's constant closeness and catering to Reuben throughout the weekend was much more difficult to deal with. Neither situation, however, was enough to keep me from horseback riding, enjoying the expensive food, and trying to relax.

One night toward the end of the retreat, as most of us were lounging around on the front porch of the house, singing and enjoying the beautiful sunset, Adino walked out onto the porch and signaled to me. He wanted to talk.

We walked around to the backyard. Adino wanted to talk about us. I shot him a look that told him it was the wrong time. He had no idea what Reuben had told me or that Tamar was Reuben's new mistress. He only knew that he was at the end of his rope. I thought I was, too.

In a short time our conversation turned into another argument. As I raged, Adino's entire countenance changed. Slowly, his expression grew blank. The care had grown into bitterness, the patience had grown into hardness, the steadfastness had grown into rage—all traces of love for me vanished without even a whisper. And with that subtle transformation, I knew my life with him was over.

He turned and left me standing alone. He must have seen the sudden fear in my face—but he didn't seem able to care. It was gone. Everything. Soon he would be, too.

Even before he turned to walk away his eyes told me what was happening: he was leaving, for good. I followed him, my heart pounding. When we reached his room, I began to shout at him as he stuffed his bag with his belongings.

"You coward! You can't even face yourself! Go on, leave!"

He never even looked at me. As he leaned over the bed and purposefully tied his bedroll, his eyes held a distant look. It was as though he didn't even hear me.

"Get out! Leave your son! Leave me and everything else!"

He slung the pack over his shoulder and went downstairs. I was on his heels.

"Turn around!" I screamed. "Tell me you're leaving! You can't even say it!"

He strode through the spacious living room and out the door.

I choked on the curses I wanted to hurl after him as he walked straight down the long gravel drive, never breaking stride. I stopped in the yard and screamed at the top of my lungs.

"Leave me! Go! Leave me—"

He never looked back.

Suddenly I burst into sobs. Adino was a tiny figure now, still walking away from me down the long road. For an instant I lost sight of him. I thought he was just being melodramatic and would certainly turn around and come back any minute. But he didn't. And when I realized it was for real—that he was, indeed, leaving me—I ran down the driveway after him.

"No! No!"

He walked on. I was afraid he would disappear, and I scrambled to keep my footing in the driveway's loose gravel—I had to catch him. "A-di-nooo!"

He kept going. He turned onto the country road, walking farther and farther away from me.

"A-di-nooo!"

I cried harder, stumbling past the gatepost at the end of the drive and into the road. My tears blinded me, but I didn't stop.

"Nooo!"

He kept walking.

With what I felt would be my last breath, I screamed as long and as loudly as I could. "Nooo!"

I sank to the ground, unbelieving. He was gone. And everything I'd hoped for and wanted was gone with him. I had driven away the truest love I'd ever known.

I looked to the sky and cried silently to God. *Help me*. . . . When I lowered my eyes to look after Adino, I caught my breath.

He had stopped. He stood still, watching me. I stared at him, but still he didn't move.

I gathered my strength, got up, and walked toward him. *God, don't let him go. Keep him there.* I could see his eyes. They were staring hard at me, and they were alive again.

With what little strength I had left I fell at his feet onto the hard gravel and clutched his legs.

"No . . . no . . . no . . . ," I said.

He stood there without moving. I looked up into his face. He didn't look as though he loved me. But he was here; he hadn't left me. And I began to hope that there might be a tiny fragment of love remaining between us that could be salvaged. Above all else, I knew now that this was what I wanted.

CHAPTER
Thirteen

Something ended for me on the dirt road that night—an inexplicable longing that gnawed at my spirit. Even as I knelt on the gravel, before Adino gathered me up and took me back to the ranch house, I had felt release. It was the end of something terrible within me.

The next morning we dressed and went to breakfast together. We were each still recovering from a private battle and on the verge of something unknown. We sat at one end of the long table, eating in silence. My new-felt freedom was countered by an uncertainty about the future of my marriage—more specifically, about the uneasiness in Adino's eyes.

"Ruth." His voice startled me. His expression was serious but calm, and his eyes did not move from mine. "I've been thinking about this and praying about it. And I think the Lord has an answer for us." He placed his Bible on the table and opened it. "Let me read you something," he said. "Listen."

His finger marked a place on the page, and he looked down and read from Genesis 2:21-24: "So the Lord God caused the man to fall into a deep sleep; and while he was sleeping, he took one of the man's ribs and closed up the place with flesh. Then the Lord God made a woman from the rib he had taken out of the man, and he brought her to the man. The man said, 'This is now bone of my bones and flesh of my flesh; she shall be called "woman," for she was taken out of man.' For this reason a man will leave his father and mother and be united to his wife, and they will become one flesh."

His finger pointed downward, tapping the page. "One flesh, Ruth."

Suddenly, I began to understand how deeply he had suffered. The words from Scripture rang in my ears and in my heart with new meaning. I was overwhelmed by the tolerance and love Adino had shown, in spite of—and even through —our constant fighting. In that moment I became aware of his commitment to me, to our marriage, and to our family. No person had ever loved me in such a way.

I realized, too, that he had been given a strength that surpassed his own with which to love me; he had been given the love he needed by God. Now we both knew our marriage was God-ordained.

That evening, as the time neared for us to leave the ranch, Reuben decided that instead of making the long trip back to Rio we all would break into teams of two and three and go into the outlying areas of the city to litness. Adino and I became a team, along with Isaac, of course. The next morning we went down the long, dusty road to wherever it was the Lord would have us take his message, depending on him to guide our steps.

Only a short time into our renewed relationship, I became pregnant again. We rejoiced that God had blessed our restored union with yet another young life and that Isaac, now nearing his first birthday, would soon have a playmate. It would be a new beginning for us.

As Isaac learned to take his first steps, Adino and I were learning to walk together in the faith of renewed love. Because of the constant adversity we faced—the uncertainty of shelter and food—we grew even more dependent on each other for spiritual strength. We came to tiny villages of poor yet seemingly content people and passed out the Mo letters to those who would accept them.

In one village, we met the padre of a local church. He agreed to let us stay in the vacant maid's quarters in the basement of his home. The room was typically barren. It contained a narrow bed and one crude wooden dresser. At the back of the tiny room was a small bathroom containing a shower stall, a sink, and a commode. We felt fortunate to have a roof over our heads. Isaac slept on coats and his baby blanket piled on the floor; Adino and I laughed as we hung onto each other to keep from falling off the tiny bed.

About the tenth day there, I awoke with an unusual rash covering my entire upper torso. We didn't have a thermometer, but I knew I had a high fever. When neither the rash nor the fever had subsided after the whole day had passed, Adino insisted we walk down to the all-night clinic. The doctor took my temperature and blood pressure and looked in my throat. After a few questions, he deduced that I most likely was having an allergic reaction to chocolate! I informed the doctor that I had been eating chocolate all my life, and I walked out the door laughing in unbelief.

When we got back home, I pulled out my *Better Homes and Gardens Baby Book* and turned to the section about illnesses and their symptoms. After about twenty minutes of thorough reading, I decided I must have contracted German measles. The worst part of the information was the conclusive evidence of deformity of the fetus in a mother who had German measles during the first trimester of her pregnancy. I was numb. I had to be wrong. *O, God, how can I cope with the fear, the uncertainty?* I wondered. I was reluctant to voice my concerns to Adino. I felt he expected better of me than that, and I didn't want to let him down now after all we'd just gone through. But soon my fears became strong enough that I couldn't keep them to myself.

At the end of that week we reported back to Reuben and were relieved to hear the instructions to come back to São Paulo. Once back at the colony, Adino and I gripped hands and prayed fervently that our child would be normal. Andrew and his new wife, Hope, prayed with us, and though we agreed that our faith in the Lord and his love for us were sufficient, I lived in dread that our baby would be handicapped in some way. With the COG's seemingly limited resources, I would never be able to give a deformed child the love and care and attention he would need; surely it would take a dozen of us, litnessing day and night, to raise that kind of money—and who would care for Isaac and the baby while we were out?

Even as our prayers grew more fervent, I grew more fearful. Then one hot day I became nauseated and had severe cramps. I knew something was wrong when I saw I was losing blood. The next morning I miscarried. I began to moan softly. Hope, Andrew's wife, held me and tried to comfort me, but the shock, the grief, and the guilt I felt for the child could not be quenched. I found a measure of peace as Adino and I clung together, finding the Lord's comfort in one another.

In the aftermath of the miscarriage, I began to become more aware of Adino's strengths. I realized that when I had first met Adino, I had been fascinated by his electronic expertise and impressed by his apparent maturity. He had been someone to look up to—but that isn't the best reason to love someone. Now I knew that what was truly impressive about Adino was his unswerving quest for truth. It was this that ultimately empowered him to love me in a way that could overcome the hurt, the jealousy, even the justifiable anger at what I had done to him. His was a deeper understanding that kept him hanging on—an understanding I hadn't possessed—and a determination that his family would not come to ruin at anyone's hands. His love was a love from God, and when he withdrew that love, though only for a moment in the driveway of Juan Mendías's ranch, my very foundations had been shaken into a vital realization: This love was real.

Not long after I miscarried, we were called back to Rio to begin work on a second album. Though life seemed to resume normally, Adino found himself beginning to question one aspect of Mo's ministry: he wondered just how much money was being brought in by the disciples. Using some simple arithmetic and a conservative estimate at how much each colony must be making from litnessing, Adino came up with some astounding numbers.

When he figured Moses David's cut from it all, his jaw dropped. "What in the world could they be doing with all that money?"

He kept his astonishment to himself, but even so he couldn't help wondering how the money was being spent, especially in light of how humbly COG disciples were living.

Our constant financial worries soon intensified when I found I was pregnant again. With one baby to care for already, and now another on the way, we would be scrounging even more desperately just to survive. I was trying to use the Montessori method to teach Isaac, and I became resentful when I discovered that the upper leadership owned sophisticated materials for teaching their children. Adino and I had to litness constantly for funds to buy crude facsimiles at the dime store. Also, Isaac had to wear whatever clothes I could find for him, but most of the leaders' children's clothes came from the United States and Europe.

The distinction was clear: Some of us had to struggle while others had it easy. That wasn't the message I had been given when I joined the COG, and it certainly wasn't something new converts were being told.

In the meantime, Mo's letters seemed to focus more and more on sex. Adino and I read the letters together each morning, but because of our training, we never discussed them or what we thought might be possible errors in them.

The letters carried both subtle and direct messages. "Revolutionary Women" told women how and why they should appear as alluring as possible to their husbands: "On the whole, a woman should wear as little clothing as possible, so as to both partially reveal and yet at the same time partially and provocatively conceal her beauty and charm." A letter entitled "Revolutionary Sex" explained a few of the COG's unorthodox doctrines on sexual matters: "There are many biblical exceptions to so-called incest, or the marriage of certain near relatives. In fact, there would have been no human race if Adam and Eve's two sons, Cain and Seth, had not married their sisters."

Every time I had a doubt about Mo's authority

on these matters I suppressed it. I thought my natural repulsion was "caused by society's and ignorant parents' repressiveness," as Mo put it. In one letter he wrote, "May God damn every self-righteous, sex-condemning, truth-hiding hypocrite who would hide the truth and beauties of God's creation from his holy pure-minded children!"

As I read and accepted Mo's writings, it became easier for me to accept each subsequent letter. Whenever I found myself dwelling on doubts about them, I turned my thoughts to all my friends in the COG who followed them, all the worldly people and ways I had forsaken, and how for almost five years I had lived what I believed to be the only true way. To break from that now would be unimaginable.

A few disciples, however, had begun to leave the COG because their consciences were bothered by these writings. The rest of us viewed these deserters with disdain. We had been taught that to leave the COG was to forsake God. If you did so, you left his protection. When disciples wanted to leave the COG, Moses said, the best thing to do was simply to let them go.

The influence of the Mo letters truly affected every aspect of life in the COG. Our unquestioning acceptance of them held true on every count, including the increasingly prominent Flirty Fishing policy. When the letters became more direct and explicit, Adino and I dealt with them just as we did the others—without discussion. The implications of these letters, however, were a different matter altogether. After the ordeal with Reuben, neither of us was eager to become involved in another sexual entanglement.

Even though I outwardly accepted Flirty Fishing as a legitimate COG method of evangelism, I was cautious to avoid discussing the subject with other COG members. Deep down it disturbed me, and by not talking about it, I was able to ignore its reality.

Flirty Fishing was considered a great fleshly sacrifice for the saving of souls, and the women who did it, whether married or single, were respected for their commitment. The married womens' husbands never complained publicly, but Adino and I could often see the pain in their eyes.

The COG parties of the early days, with "Inspiration Singing" and hugs all around, soon gave way to parties held for the distinct purpose of Flirty Fishing. Potential converts were presented with huge spreads of food and drink, and we sang our less evangelical songs about love and acted in skits.

For the most part, the parties were a lot of fun because they provided outlets for all the zany personalities in our group. But I was always tense since many Brazilian men came expressly for the purpose of meeting young COG women. Still, I knew the parties were a part of my ministry in the COG, and for that reason I attended them faithfully.

Then one day something unexpected happened. I was visiting David, our producer, at the leadership apartment. He revealed that Mo had written him a personal letter. When he said he didn't want to make a big deal about it by sharing the news with the rest of the family, I light-heartedly implied that he was being selfish by withholding such a precious document. Somehow I must have used the wrong Portuguese words because he suddenly became distant.

I felt awkward and embarrassed and tried to explain what I meant. Hoping I'd sufficiently bailed myself out, I left for home. But the word got out: David was offended.

The ensuing ostracism was the hardest trial I'd had to endure as a COG member. Soon our overseer arrived and, without giving me a chance to explain or apologize again to David, he demoted us.

Losing our position of leadership wasn't half as painful as losing my friendship with David. I loved him and cherished our special relationship. I cried and wrote a long letter of apology to him, insisting that the entire matter had been a misunderstanding. But by that time the damage was irreparable. I thought my leaders easily could have circumvented the trouble by explaining that I had meant no harm. But the incident was allowed to be blown out of proportion. Now Adino and I had to accept a humiliating position under Andrew's and Hope's leadership.

In spite of our woes, the band's work continued. And, as before, we went to the recording studios when I was toward the end of my pregnancy. It was a hot August night after a huge gathering of all the local colonies that I went into labor. I was riding home in the back of Reuben's Volkswagen Beetle, bouncing up and down along a stretch of bumpy road. I experienced some discomfort, so the next morning I went to get a routine examination from our doctor friend who informed me I was in the intermediate stage of labor! This time Adino, donned in sterile garb, aided in the birth of our second child, a beautiful daughter whom we named Aurora. (We had chosen that name just the day before when we read it in the Portuguese Bible—it means "dawn.")

A few days later, our joy in our newborn was interrupted when we heard the shocking news that Reuben had been busted. We didn't know what had happened, only that because of some failure on his part Reuben was being sent back to Argentina to oversee some colonies he had helped pioneer years before. That was truly a demotion considering the tremendous influence and power Reuben had wielded while in Brazil.

By this time my respect for Reuben—and his peculiar power over me—had already dwindled. So, though saddened somewhat by the news, it just served to emphasize that he was no longer the powerful leader or the domineering factor in my life that he had been. He was just another disciple who had been put in his place.

The band had mixed feelings about Reuben's departure, but the real grief began when his replacement arrived. Zechariah (or Zach, as he was called) was a short, dark-haired converted Jew who was proud and demanding. He was commissioned by upper leadership to bring order to the Rio colonies in the wake of Reuben's demotion. But order was the last thing Zach would bring.

Up to than point the band members had been treated like royalty, but all that changed with Zach's arrival. Suddenly Reuben was accorded martyr status as Zach embarked on a reign that changed our privileged status to that of ordinary workers who were to be examples for the rest. The band tried to continue despite the fact that Zach was not at all musically inclined, but we lost our momentum.

Finally, I reached my limit. With two small children to care for and the band in apparent decline under a minor dictator, I decided I didn't need the aggravation. I was through. Adino supported my decision, and even encouraged it. The worst part, though, of leaving the band was having to say good-bye to Andrew and my other friends and all the wonderful moments we shared in music.

Then, a few weeks later while Zach was in São Paulo, he summoned Adino and me to see him. "You're needed . . . ," he began bluntly as we entered his room, and when he unrolled a map of Brazil on his desk, we knew it was all over for us. Because of my untimely departure from the band, we were being exiled to a struggling colony.

Zach pointed to a dot on the map. It was a tiny village several miles northeast of São Paulo. "I need you to pray about going," he said. "The colony there needs some help."

If we hadn't been so discouraged, we might have laughed outright. He knew full well what our answer would be, just as we did: "If that's where the Lord wants us, we'll go."

Buoyed by our growing need and love for each other, Adino and I decided to make the best of the situation. My disappointment in the COG was shared by Adino, and our struggle together in that obscure village made us closer than we'd ever been. But being there just didn't hold the challenge and adventure of ministering in a city like Rio or São Paulo.

Several weeks after we arrived in the village we received an urgent phone call from Zach instructing us to get back to São Paulo immediately. We took the next train, and when we arrived at the colony, Zach was suspiciously friendly toward us.

"Ruth," he said, "we've got to talk to Juan Mendías. He's upset about some article he's read about us."

"Really? What article?"

"It's in *Christianity Today*. You're one of his favorites, so you need to go over there with me to translate it and to let him know everything's OK."

Juan Mendías welcomed us uneasily that night. We sat down in his living room, and he read the article aloud to us. It was about a girl who had left the COG in Ohio and was fighting for custody of her two sons, who were being held by members of her colony. She said her decision to leave the COG was influenced by Mo's instructions for female COG members to "sacrifice" their bodies. She told how Flirty Fishing (which she explained as girls in the COG being "hookers for Jesus") had been practiced at the leadership level for several years. She went on to say that "religious prostitution" had been a way of life for the COG's disciples for just the last few years.

Juan's expression pleaded with us for an explanation. "Tell me, what does this mean? Is this prostitution occurring? Why don't I know about this?"

Zach smiled and said that obviously *Christianity Today* was out to get us, the way all organized Christianity was. As he launched into a speech intended to smooth everything over with Juan, I had to sort out the article in my own mind as well. The part about Flirty Fishing was true . . . in fact it all seemed to be true. How could I deny the article when it was all true?

The trusting expression on Juan's face pierced me with regret throughout the six-hour train ride back to the village. I had come face to face with the implications of our practices in the COG, and they went round and round in my head in accusation. No matter how hard I tried to figure it out, I knew I couldn't explain the benefit of such practices to anyone other than a COG member.

Shortly after our return to the village, I discovered I was pregnant with our third child. This motivated us to pursue a new challenge—to get out of the village and back to civilization! We felt our talents could be better utilized by God in another place. After a couple weeks of prayer, we finally came to a decision: we had to leave Brazil.

COG members had been pioneering Mexico for years, and the leadership there wanted to enlarge their music ministry. Adino and I knew our talents were needed in Mexico and that going there would help us get away from Zach. We had done as much as we could in the tiny village, and we were hungry to prove our leadership elsewhere. The hardest part would be leaving the country we had grown to love in spite of our hardships and trials there. We both hoped the Lord would someday allow us to return to this beautiful, spiritually fertile country.

We wrote to get clearance from the leadership in Mexico, and after it arrived we made our plans known to Zach, who was shocked at the news. We became disciples "in transit" and went about the task of raising the necessary funds to go to Mexico.

Adino and I knew that a long trip by land to Central America would be hard and possibly dangerous for the children, so we decided to try and procure passage on a freighter or cargo plane. When one of the disciples found out we needed help getting to Mexico, he gave us the phone number of a retired Brazilian Air Force officer. I called him and set up an appointment to see him. When Adino and I finished packing and were on our way through São Paulo to Rio, we went to meet the man at his downtown office. We decided we might get better results if I were to go upstairs and talk to "the colonel" alone, playing the "fair damsel in distress" game. Though Adino was apprehensive about this, we knew it was probably our best option. So I went into the building while Adino went to a nearby cafe to wait for me.

As I entered the room, the colonel's gaze traveled from my hair to my shoulders and then downward. I tried to keep my pleasant smile in place and remember Adino's encouragement: "You've got natural charm, and Mo says in his letters to use it. You'll be able to do it for us, honey, I know you will." I had thought it would be easy, too, but this man would have made anyone nervous. He had said very little, but his eyes hadn't left my body since I'd come in.

He looked the way you'd expect a retired military officer to look: gray hair, distinguished features, thick hands and forearms. As I told him about our request, he pursed his lips and nodded, typically noncommittal.

"Well, sir?" I pressed, hoping for a positive response.

He continued staring, as though sizing up the situation.

"Sir," I repeated, "do you think it can be arranged?"

He tapped his fingers on the desk. "Oh, I think something can be arranged. But I can't be sure." He smiled at me.

I smiled back cheerfully. "We appreciate your help. We need to get there desperately."

He pushed back his chair from the desk and stood up. "Can we, mmm, sit over here?" He gestured to a love seat near the door.

"Sure," I said, reminding myself, *Cheerful—not inviting.*

I sat down first, and as I was afraid would happen, he sat next to me.

"I—you should come to our party this weekend," I said nervously. I was afraid the situation was getting out of control. And suddenly my fears were proven when his stare intensified and I felt him move one hand to the back of my neck and the other onto my knee. I couldn't believe this was happening.

"There are some beautiful, young Brazilian sisters at the colony that I'd like you to meet," I said, trying to sound calm. But my mind was screaming, *God, no.*

He fingered my hair, then slowly put both arms around me and pulled me toward him. Fear immobilized me as he leaned to kiss me, and when I felt his hand on my blouse I knew I was in serious trouble. I pushed him away with what I prayed was a playful laugh.

"Stop it," I squealed with ferocious good nature, still trying to keep the good will. *The plane,* I told myself. *You need him for the plane.*

He still smiled but was clearly disappointed. I trembled, hoping he wouldn't notice. I didn't know what to do next other than keep up the act. It took every bit of my will to playfully slap his sleeve. "Please come visit us, though," I said, lifting my shoulder bag as I rose. Forcing a smile took all the strength I could muster. "We'd like to see you there."

He smiled, stood, and pivoted, walking around

to the other side of his desk. I stood at the door awkwardly, until finally, as if surprised, he turned his head and looked at me quizzically. I couldn't tell whether his expression said a polite "Good day" or a "Are you still here?"

"'Bye," I said, still trying to keep a friendly tone. Then I turned and walked out, my hand shaking as I pulled the door closed behind me.

I leaned against the door for a moment, fighting a feeling of weakness. The corridor stretched long and narrow before me, and suddenly I was running as fast as I could, brushing by people in a fury. I began to cry, overwhelmed by the awareness of what had almost happened.

As I approached the cafe, my eyes frantically searched for Adino. Where was he? I dodged cars and finally, almost stopping in the middle of the street, I saw him standing in front of the post office.

I dashed across between two cars and threw myself against him. I was breathing hard and crying. "Honey," I said weakly, "I almost got raped by that crazy man. . . ." I dissolved into tears.

All those years of indoctrination into Flirty Fishing should have prepared me for this experience. And, according to what I had learned through the Mo letters, I should not have resisted the man's advances. But when the time had actually come, I couldn't go through with it—and this realization became a major turning point in my life. For the first time in many years, my conscience had spoken too loudly for me to ignore. Mo's letters and admonitions could not drown out the inner conviction that had told me to resist the colonel.

Adino and I felt it best not to linger in São Paulo waiting for the colonel's response, so we decided to head for Rio. Once there we would stay at the colony while we raised the money we needed for the trip to Mexico.

CHAPTER

Fourteen

When we arrived in Rio, we were given the only room available at the colony, which was a storage room in back of the house. I knew there wasn't room for the children in there, let alone our whole family.

"Can't we stay in the maid's quarters?" Adino said.

The leader shook his head. "Got to keep the room open for the regional shepherd, who'll be arriving soon."

Reluctantly, we took our few belongings out to the small, cement storage room, and while Adino went out to litness in the hot sun, I washed clothes by hand over the porch sink. The room had one small window at the top but no ventilation other than the open door. Once again my resentment stirred and tears of frustration began to form. How could I allow my children to suffer this way in a stifling, cramped room where there was no relief from the heat?

No! I stopped my thoughts in midstream. I wouldn't allow myself to harbor thoughts that undermined what I knew was right. I'd proven before that I had what it took to live the COG life. If I doubted that the Lord would make a way for me and my family, I would only make life more difficult for all of us. Besides that, my faith had to come before my family.

Adino and I both felt downcast much of the time. Our friends thought it was because we'd been busted and couldn't seem to get on our feet again. But that didn't bother me as much as the feeling that I was trapped—and I didn't know why I felt that way. Some days I felt pressure for no apparent reason. It didn't help matters when we heard rumors that several disciples had been deported because the police had accused them of distributing pornographic materials (illustrations on the Mo letters were frequently sexually explicit). In Argentina one disciple had been threatened at gunpoint while being held in solitary confinement. Subsequent to a military coup, the government was cracking down on communist sympathizers, and hundreds of people disappeared without a trace. A priest in northern Brazil reportedly had been tortured and then expelled from the country for his association with socialist priests, but officials denied the allegations. Adino's experience in jail, however, was undeniable.

My imagination often ran wild upon hearing these horror stories, and I wondered how I could ever endure torture or imprisonment if jailed for my religious beliefs.

Meanwhile the pressures Adino faced were becoming increasingly intense. Every day he would stand for a few moments as the sun began to cut through the haze, deciding which area of the city he should canvass with the Mo letters. Every morning I saw the troubled expression on his face and the long breath he took before leaving. I wondered what was going through his mind, but I didn't ask. I thought he was just experiencing some trials, and sooner or later he would tell me about them.

Another reason I didn't dig too deeply into Adino's troubles was that I had trouble of my own. I worried about my children, about my coming child, and about Adino soliciting donations on the streets of Rio, constantly at the mercy of the Mo letters' appeal.

About two weeks after we'd arrived in Rio, Adino was witnessing downtown at a large, cobblestone plaza when suddenly a young Brazilian disciple came running up to him.

"Adi-noo! Adi-noo!" he said in excitement. The short teenager's eyes were wild, his entire face smiling. He triumphantly held up a rolled-up magazine as though it contained news on the order of another Kohoutek.

"Adino!"

"What is it?" Adino asked as the boy stopped beside him.

He stopped, bending over for breath. "Have you seen it?" he gasped furiously. "Have you seen it?"

"Seen what?"

"The picture!" He jumped up and down, unable to contain his excitement as he unrolled the magazine. It was the new issue of *Time*. "The picture of Dad!"

Adino started at him. "A picture of Mo?"

"Yes! A picture of him and others. Here." He opened to an article under the heading of "Religion," and poked the page frantically.

Adino hesitated momentarily, then looked.

The headline read: "Tracking the Children of God." Under it was a small mug shot of a woman named Rachel. And under that photo was a picture of Moses David.

He was sitting on a sofa with two females on each side, one of whom was Rachel. Mo wore a black robe, and a silver medallion hung around his neck. He had a long, gray beard, and his eyebrows arched over round, dark eyes. Standing directly behind the sofa was a bevy of ten females, all wearing low-cut blouses and dresses. The caption read: "Elusive cult leader Moses David and friends during Canary Islands sojourn: 'Be Happy Hookers for Jesus,' the prophet told female followers."

Adino was stunned. Seeing Mo at all was shocking enough, but it was even more shocking to see how weird Mo's appearance was. Adino sat down on a bench and read the article. It said Mo was fifty-eight. It also said he had recently written a letter entitled "God Bless You—and Good-Bye," in which he confessed to be a fraud and ended the Children of God movement, but leaders now denied its authenticity. In fact, the article stated *Time* had received a taped message from Mo saying the letter was fraudulent.

As Adino read, he became fascinated not just by the article's chronicling of COG practices but by its overall accuracy. The article quoted information from *Stern,* a mass-circulation German magazine, recounting that the estate of the Italian Duke (whom Rachel had married) had "a school where the Children train good-looking disciples in the arts of seduction." The article went on to explain that "such allegations are amply corroborated by the Mo letters, which advocate not only Mo's version of the *Playboy* philosophy, but the ancient practice of religious prostitution. . . . *Stern* and Spain's *Interviu* also reported that Berg resided in the Canary Islands until recently and appeared every night at a bar in Puerto de la Cruz with a harem of girls looking for pickups. . . . Asked about all this, the Duchess [Rachel] denied the magazines' reports but said: 'There is nothing wrong with a sexy conversion. We believe sex is a human necessity, and in certain cases we may go to bed with someone to show people God's love.' But 'this is the exception rather than the rule,' she added."

Adino was shaken. The article was written both rationally and objectively. Its content was far from the "hatchet job" full of lies and distortions that he'd expected. Instead, it was simply informative and true.

That aspect disturbed Adino most. From an objective viewpoint—even from a rational

Christian viewpoint—the Children of God were a way-out group of sexual deviates. And worse, the COG practices as described in the article appeared to be indefensible.

Adino closed the cover of the magazine and noted its date: August 22, 1977. He had a feeling he would remember the date for a long time. He rolled up the magazine and carried it with his stack of Mo letters as he walked down the busy boulevard toward the bus stop. He knew he couldn't do any more litnessing that day.

Adino kept the magazine tucked in his shoulder bag and didn't mention it to anyone as he entered the colony. He went straight to our storage room, where I was resting with the kids.

When he walked in, I noticed he had a peculiar look on his face. He handed me the magazine and directed me to the article—and I soon understood why he had looked so troubled. In the picture, Moses David looked like some sort of sorcerer or wizard, and the women around him looked cheap. I didn't know what to make of it.

This is my leader? I thought. All the feelings I'd had about Mo—the respect, dedication, love—abandoned me as I stared at that picture. And suddenly I was filled with fear. Fear that we, the Children of God, perhaps were not holy; that possibly I'd given my life and energy and time to something that wasn't the truth after all. I looked again at the picture and couldn't find in it what I desperately needed to see: a trace of the beauty that I'd known in the COG.

I began reading the article aloud, and I imag-

ined reacting to it as I thought "normal" people—
people of the world—would react to it. When I
finished, two questions pounded in my brain: *If I
died at this moment, would I be able to face God
with a clear conscience about following Moses
David? And if I were to be persecuted for following him, would I be able to endure the suffering
because of my belief in him?*

The reports of torture and persecution came
rushing back into my mind. *Yes,* I told myself,
*I'm willing to suffer for Jesus; but no, I am not
willing to do so for this man.*

The question of commitment tormented me.
When I looked at Adino, I ached to tell him of the
turmoil I was in—but I knew I couldn't. I was
afraid my admission of doubts about Mo would
almost surely cost me my husband's respect and
love. At the very least, he would feel obligated to
tell a leader about my problems because if it
should ever be revealed that he'd covered it up,
we both could become suspect and probably be
separated. That, in fact, had happened with
Deborah, Mo's eldest daughter, after she tried to
run away from the Royal Family colony in London. When she came back, she was exiled to a se-
cluded home in Paris, and her husband, Bill, was
sent to a tiny, isolated outpost in southern Africa.
I couldn't let that happen with Adino and me, not
after everything we'd been through together.

Almost immediately after the *Time* article appeared, Mo issued a letter of response denying its
allegations and reiterating his frequent denunci-
ations of the press. He also said the article in

Stern about the COG's actions in the Canary Islands was a pack of lies. Several of Mo's denials, however, conflicted with what he had written earlier in letters describing those events. Remembering Kohoutek, I was disgusted by his defensiveness.

It became more difficult each day to be a good revolutionary. I prayed with Adino and together we read the Bible and the Mo letters. Despite our good intentions in doing things, it became nothing more than ritual to me because now I didn't know if I believed what I was reading. The prayers for Adino's prosperity in litnessing, for our children, for the trip to Mexico, all lost significance amid the war being waged for my soul.

I had nowhere to go to escape the confusion. I had to take care of the children, and as I entered the fourth month of my pregnancy I had little hope of relief from my growing distress. Some days the only reason I got out of bed in the morning was to keep Isaac from wandering outside. Finally, as I realized that the children could end up victimized by my plight, I knew something had to give. I couldn't go on any longer with the conflict of not knowing the truth about Mo, about the COG, about the decision I had made years ago to sacrifice my life for it. I had to know the real truth; and I had to tell Adino.

My frustration had only been compounded with guilt when Adino came home at the end of each day dog tired. He was faithfully caring for his family—and I wondered if I was about to destroy it all.

He had shown perseverance, faith, and unusual strength during the ordeal with Reuben, and I had grown to love him for those things. Now—in a foreign country, pregnant, and friendless apart from the COG—losing Adino would be like dying. Yet I knew I had no choice.

Moses David was not the prophet of God I'd thought him to be. He wasn't the savior of America's youth. He wasn't the end-time prophet, crying as a voice in the wilderness. He wasn't the voice of God, calling down upon America the destruction of Kohoutek. He wasn't the strong yet gentle voice that had spoken to me seven years before with peace and calm as I rose from the depths of the freezing Columbia River. He wasn't the bond of love that welded my spirit to Andrew, Isaiah, and others whose friendship and closeness ran deeper than that of even a brother or sister. He wasn't the spirit of courage and humility and faithfulness that saved my marriage and ultimately taught me that imperfect love, like imperfect humans, could be redeemed. No, Moses David was none of these things.

I sat on the bed in our room and heard Adino walk slowly toward the door. He opened it and walked in. I looked down quickly to control myself, then looked up at Adino. *This is it,* I thought.

My smile must have looked like a grimace because Adino looked at me in surprise. His expression calmed quickly, though. "Hello," he said cautiously, gently dropping his pouch to the floor. He sat next to me on the bed, folded his hands, and leaned forward toward me with his elbows on his knees.

I looked at him again as I began to speak hesitantly. It was a struggle trying to find the right words.

"Honey," I started. *Keep going,* I told myself. "I've got to talk to you about something that's been bothering me."

His eyebrows arched at this, but he didn't move otherwise. "I've been afraid to tell you," I went on, choosing my words carefully. My hands were locked together in a vise-like grip, and I looked at the floor again. "I'm afraid if I tell you ..." The floor began to blur. I shut my eyes and the tears fell down my cheeks as I finished, "... you might not love me."

Adino was still calm, leaning forward, his hands folded. "Tell me, Ruth."

"You can't ... I ... I just don't want you to misunderstand me."

The reservations had left Adino's face. He seemed to want to hear what I had to say. "Just say it," he urged me gently. "Don't worry."

"It's different, what the Mo letters are saying," I said slowly. "I don't know how much I believe anymore. It's hard for me, living like this and not believing the way I used to. Some of the things he says don't seem scriptural, and I can't help how I feel."

My voice cracked at the realization of what I was saying. Adino was silent. Then his eyes met mine as he said, "You know, Ruth, it's really something you should say this because I've been having doubts of my own."

My heart began to race as he went on. "In fact, I've been feeling the same way for a long time, and I didn't think I should tell you."

The tears started to form again, only now they were tears of relief. In one moment we both had been set free. All the fears of the weeks before dissolved as we embraced, relieved, free—and conspirators. We knew we couldn't go on living something we didn't believe in. Almost immediately we decided: "We're going to have to leave."

That seemed impossible. How could we leave something that had been our sole source of friendship, love, and material needs for most of our adult life? We had no one to help us, nowhere to go, no jobs, no bank accounts, and little money. But what we did have was purpose. In the days following, Adino litnessed with renewed fervor to raise enough funds to last us after our escape. It didn't matter how much he doubted the authority of the letters. Adino knew he was responsible for his family's well-being, and he would do what he could to get us out of what we now knew to be a lie.

He called a friendly German family that we'd met while in São Paulo. They had loved Adino and me, and they said we could stay with them as long as we wanted while Adino looked for work.

Adino advised them not to tell anyone what we were doing. He explained our reasons for leaving the COG, and they seemed to understand. We knew they would be loyal to us.

We also knew that if someone in the colony found out we were leaving, we'd be reported immediately and, if not dissuaded, at the very least we would have our Mo letters confiscated. Adino was adamant about keeping the letters. Though he disagreed with some of Mo's teachings, he still wasn't sure Mo was a false prophet. He wanted to be able to scrutinize the letters outside the confines and influence of the COG community to find out for himself whether or not our suspicions were unfounded. I agreed.

We decided we would make our move on a weekend while the vast majority of colony members were at the beach or litnessing. Thus, during the next two weeks we made sure we both stayed busy, trying to appear as if we were hustling to prepare for our trip to Mexico so we wouldn't arouse suspicion.

After a while, Adino stopped litnessing and began selling the few items that had come into our possession over the years: a camera, radio equipment, etc. The next Saturday we slipped away to a nearby park and talked. Adino pointed out how some of Mo's teachings deviated from scriptural authority.

We spent the next several days in prayer, feeling the pressure of the constant fear of being found out. As our funds grew, however, and the day approached for our escape, we trusted God more and more. I had grown increasingly buoyant with the sense of freedom I had begun to feel.

Finally the day of our departure arrived. I rose that morning feeling a strange mixture of fear and excitement. We prayed that our fears would be hidden from the others and that we wouldn't be seen as we left.

I stood at the window, watching until everyone left for the beach. When the last disciple had run down the street after the others, Adino lifted Aurora in his arms, and I took Isaac by the hand. We walked briskly up the street, constantly looking over our shoulders. We headed for the van we had rented to go to the bus depot. From there we would catch a bus to São Paulo.

When we arrived at the depot downtown, I hurried toward the long line of buses with Isaac in tow, while Adino held Aurora and carried the baggage. Isaac and I found our bus and took a seat next to the window, watching Adino as he waited for the porter to load our suitcases in the baggage area below. We had perhaps another twenty minutes to wait before leaving, and I was thinking we might have time to go to the cafe for food. Then I saw them.

Less than fifty yards away, three COG members from another colony were walking toward our bus. I quickly tried to lower the shade. The latch wouldn't come loose. Frantically I knocked on the bus window. Adino didn't look up.

The group was getting closer. Finally they stopped next to us. They inspected their tickets for a moment, then one of them looked up and pointed toward our bus.

God, no!

Finally, Adino looked up at me, and I pointed to the COG members behind him. He turned quickly, swung Aurora onto his hip, and pushed his way through the other people. He jumped hurriedly onto the bus and sat down beside me.

The COG members stood just beyond the people with baggage, looking from our bus to the one in front of it. The member who had pointed at our bus was now pointing at the other one. Laughing, the group walked away toward it.

Adino and I sat there breathing hard, both of us silent. After a long while, I reached out and grabbed his hand.

The bus motor started, and in a few minutes we were moving out of the depot. We passed through the city onto winding roads, then up the mountain range leading to São Paulo. Isaac stood up on my lap and pressed his hands against the windows—and I began to cry with unspeakable joy.

CHAPTER
Fifteen

After two weeks of gathering our thoughts at the German family's home in the country, it became evident that Adino would not be able to find work very easily with us living so far out of the city. We had the equivalent of about fifty dollars and knew our only chance for survival was for him to find a job quickly.

We contacted a Brazilian family that Adino and I had befriended while still in the COG. They lived in town, and they opened their home to us after we explained our dilemma. They had a furnished basement apartment, and they said we could move in right away and pay rent whenever we got on our feet financially.

The apartment was like a heavenly sanctuary: a haven, safe from the outside world—safe from the Children of God. Although we had never considered ourselves to be in any physical danger, the emotional repercussions of a confrontation with a COG member at this time could have proved devastating.

We needed time alone, time to heal, time to recover. It was hard adapting to our new life outside the security of a colony. Adino hadn't worked at a "regular" job for over six years, and we weren't sure if he'd be able to find someone willing to hire him and give him a chance to prove himself.

But God was gracious far beyond what we could ask or think, and only a couple of days after we settled into the apartment Adino was hired as a consultant for a sound and lighting company. He'd met the owner on one of his trips to São Paulo to repair the band's equipment, and the man had just relocated his office three blocks away from where we were staying. In a sprawling city with a population of over 11 million people, this was obviously not a coincidence.

We were thrilled because Adino could walk to work instead of taking two or three buses to get to his destination. I wouldn't have to be alone for such a long period of a time because he could have lunch at home with the kids and me. It was ideal.

While Adino worked, I had the children to look after, but I felt very lonely. For six years we had led an existence in which we were surrounded constantly by COG brothers and sisters, sharing the common bond of the aspirations and joys of our life-style.

Now I had nothing to keep me occupied, encouraged, and growing, other than the children

. . . and the Mo letters. As odd as it sounds, even though we knew that indeed we would never consider going back to the COG, Adino and I hadn't entirely given up reading the letters. We still prayed every morning and read a few of the letters for encouragement, revelation, or enlightenment. We used them just as a Christian would read Scripture. Adino was fairly convinced by the time we left Rio that Mo was a fraud, but I still wanted to weigh the evidence concerning his claim to be a prophet of God.

During those first weeks my loneliness and my uncertainties about the future were unrelenting. Since I still didn't talk about such things, I turned to another source of comfort: liquor. Before long, I was drinking most of the gallon jugs of wine that Adino brought home in the evenings, hoping to dull those oppressive feelings. During the days I pumped coffee into my system; at night I offset the coffee with the wine. Soon the rough mix of alcohol and caffeine began to take its toll.

I awoke so often in the middle of the night with my heart palpitating and my body shaking uncontrollably that I began to fear going to sleep. One night when I awoke, my attack was so bad that Adino, who until then hadn't noticed what I was doing to myself, had to drive me to the hospital. The doctor told me that I wasn't having a heart attack, as I'd suspected, but that I was under extreme duress. He told me to stop drinking wine and coffee and to take Valium instead, or my condition would worsen. I followed his advice about the wine and coffee but not the Valium. (I was very leery of taking any kind of drug, even prescription.) As a result, my health improved dramatically.

About a week later we decided to call the colony because we didn't want anyone to worry about us. We made sure to tell them, however, that we had no intention of returning. Before the week concluded we had an unannounced visit from Zach and Gehazi, a COG brother to whom we had been especially close. Needless to say, we were shocked to see them.

"Praise the Lord," they chanted in unison. They stayed for an hour or so making small talk before really opening up about their purpose in coming to see us. Adino and I exchanged suspicious glances as they began asking, in a superficially friendly manner, why we left. They tried to talk us into coming back to the COG, but we gently yet firmly let them know we had left for good. After another hour or so, they gave up and left somewhat deflated. It would have been a real feather in their cap if they could have redeemed us from "backsliding."

As we shut the door behind them, we sighed in relief. We hadn't been sure how we would hold up if a confrontation like this occurred. So until now we had still been running. At last we knew we were safe—once and for all. Our decision to leave the Children of God was irrevocable.

The end of 1977 was approaching, and this would be our first Christmas as a single family unit—our first Christmas in freedom. We experienced feelings of loneliness and nostalgia, but they were mixed with wonderful anticipation and hope for the new year ahead.

Exchanging gifts was not a custom the COG had practiced, other than for the children. So when Adino presented me with a brand new set of luxurious velour towels and a new watch, I was ecstatic. I marveled that such beautiful things could really be mine after we had lived in such squalor. I even felt a twinge of guilt for having such pretty things.

The best surprise of the season, though, was when Juan Mendías accepted a proposal from Adino to develop a light-dimming system for television studios. This eventually led to their co-partnership in a new company, which afforded us quite a substantial raise in income and an increase in security. This also meant we could rent our own place and start making a life for ourselves and the children.

By February I was a very round, eight-months pregnant lady with two toddlers. We had moved into a nice row house that Adino found only a few miles from the laboratory Juan Mendías was providing for his work. Our materially destitute state became even more apparent when we arrived at the unfurnished house with only two pieces of furniture: a couch and an armoire that our Brazilian friends had sold us.

The house had no refrigerator, built-in kitchen cabinets, carpets, or central air or heat. There were no bathtubs, drawers, or light fixtures. And we didn't own any silverware, pots and pans, dishes, or sheets. So our first order of business was to get some mattresses to sleep on. Adino had to buy these on credit because our cash flow was still almost nonexistent.

Several kind neighbors offered to let us store our perishable food in their refrigerators; the rest we kept in empty fruit crates. These crude wooden boxes also came in handy as our dining room table. I'm sure I was a real sight, sitting on a bare tile floor, hardly able to get up and down in my condition. But I truly was content. This was the first place where we were completely on our own, not depending on the hospitality of others —and it felt good.

When the time came for the baby's birth, Adino and I requested that no anesthetics or drugs be used because we were still using the La-Maze method of natural childbirth. As Adino sat by my side, helping me with my breathing techniques, everything went well. After several hours of labor, our second son, Nicky, was born.

Several weeks later when I returned home from the hospital, I met some neighbors, an older American couple, who had moved in across the street. They introduced themselves as Peter and Alice Sawatsky, missionaries to Brazil for over twenty years.

Alice was a kind, soft-spoken, motherly type who sincerely cared about people. She constantly reminded me by her example that people were more important than activity. She would promptly drop her work whenever I came to visit and spend time paying attention to me.

I was a little apprehensive about the possibility of them trying to shove their religion down our throats, but that never happened. Even though they invited us to the English-speaking evangelical church they attended (when not ministering to one of the Brazilian churches they had started), they didn't badger us about it. And, while Adino and I craved the fellowship and camaraderie of other believers, our misconceptions from our COG teachings about Christians held us back.

Finally, after several months went by and the Sawatskys had earned our trust and respect through their love and concern for us, we agreed to attend a service with them. But we did so just to please them, not to gain any benefit ourselves.

When the scheduled Sunday arrived, I wished we hadn't agreed to go. But we were already dressed and it was time to leave. Suddenly the Sawatskys ran over to us and announced they couldn't go with us after all—something urgent had come up and they wondered if we would mind going by ourselves. Not wanting to disappoint them, we agreed.

The small evangelical church was made up almost entirely of Americans, some of whom were missionaries. We went to a Sunday school class, and although I wanted desperately to like it and to fit in, I couldn't help seeing what I felt were flaws; I had learned to be very critical during my years in the COG. I could tell Adino felt the same, but I fought the rising judgments and apprehensions desperately, hoping the worship service would be better.

Dr. Russell Shedd was preaching that morning. We expected the message to be some watered-down version of the gospel, but instead we were overwhelmed not only by Dr. Shedd's knowledge of the Bible but by his mastery in conveying its truth. Throughout his sermon Adino and I stole amazed glances at each other. When Dr. Shedd finished his message, we both were convicted enough by what he'd said that we resolved to come back the next week. We were sure this church would indeed challenge us.

We began attending that church regularly, and over a period of time Adino and I found ourselves being purged of our prejudices against the church—not just for that particular congregation, but for the church at large. When we first decided to go to the Sunday school class on a regular basis, Adino thought that perhaps they would ask him to teach because of his knowledge of the Bible. After the first few months, however, he could see why they didn't. Many of the Scriptures we'd learned in the COG, most of them learned directly from Mo's writing, had been taken out of the context of the Bible passages where they appeared. Their meaning had been distorted to support Mo's own ideas about prophecy, discipleship, sex, and so on. In fact, after surveying the Scripture on our own, we finally were able to see the depravity of the COG's sex practices. And, with that important barrier removed, we were able to see the light of God's Word as it shone on the Mo letters. It revealed a strong-minded but errant interpretation of Scripture that had increasingly degenerated into rantings on unbridled lust. Finally, we packed the Mo letters away.

Our thinking concerning the authority of Scripture proved to be one of our most difficult adjustments to life outside the COG. The passages and doctrines we'd read, learned, memorized, and embraced from the Mo letters constantly came to our minds in the same way Bible verses come to the minds of other Christians. It was essential that we make conscious efforts to stop ourselves from using Mo's passages in prayer, in conversation, even in thought—but that was no easy task. We had lived by their content for the vast majority of our adult lives.

During our first year in the church, we took advantage of the Bible teaching and discussions to clean our minds of COG's erroneous doctrines. The messages from the pulpit at that church were always strong, and Adino and I devoured them. God revealed himself to us through both his Word and his people in that place, and as we got involved we felt that we truly belonged. We didn't realize how vital that would be to our returning to a normal life. We only knew that, week by week, our former enemies—the world outside of COG and the people out in the system —were becoming our friends.

Several months after our initial visit to the church, I began to experience a strange, spiritual oppression. The first manifestation came in the middle of the night in the form of a horrible, frightening dream. In it I was overcome by a feeling of evil and darkness. I was enveloped in fear, and though I knew I was asleep, I couldn't wake up. Finally I began repeating the phrase "the blood of Jesus" over and over, and I was able to awaken. Immediately I shook Adino from sleep and told him what I'd just experienced.

"I'm afraid to go back to sleep," I said as I finished describing the dream. He held me close and prayed for me, but though I stopped shaking, I didn't go back to sleep.

This type of dream occurred several times, and I decided to seek help from Bill and Mary Fawcett, another missionary couple from the church. After listening to my description of the dreams, Bill shook his head.

"That may have been an innocent dream," he said, "but from the other things you've told me, I think you're being oppressed by Satan. We need to examine your past and pray for the Lord to deliver you from any area in your life where the devil has taken a foothold."

As we prayed for my deliverance from the sins I'd committed through the COG, I felt the Lord release me from bondage. We also prayed for the healing of my emotions. As the Holy Spirit brought past hurts to my mind, we prayed for the Lord's healing and freedom from demonic oppression. When we finished praying, I knew I'd been released from a spiritual bondage to the past—and I never again experienced difficulty in this area.

After the freeing experience of praying for my emotional healing, I knew it was time to reestablish contact with my mother, so I began writing to her. She was happy to hear I'd gotten out of the COG, she said. My brother Barry, especially, had been worried about me all along, no matter what I'd said to try to comfort him.

Though I felt I was making some progress in my relationship with my family, my concern for my friends who were still in the COG was still causing me some intense battles. One of the most difficult and trying aspects of having left the Family was knowing that I would be considered spiritually "lost" by Andrew, Reuben, and the others. I had gone through most of my twenties in the COG; now all my adult friends from those years had been left far behind. Chances were I would never have friendships like those again, even with our new friends at the church. It hadn't been easy being uprooted from the people with whom I'd witnessed about the love of Jesus and watched countless people come to know Jesus. Yet, though I missed them terribly, I could not make myself write them.

All in all, however, life seemed only to get better for us. By the end of our first year out of the COG, we were doing relatively well. But the day I discovered I was pregnant again, I thought my world had come to an end. We had tried every natural means of contraception, and they all had failed. How could we afford another child? My depression over this lifted somewhat when we received news from Adino's mom that she would be coming from Alabama to visit us. His father had promised his mother that if she quit smoking, she could take a month's vacation to see us. Isaac and Aurora, at ages five and three, were old enough to be excited about having a grandmother come to visit them. And sure enough, when she arrived she was instantly adored; her stay was very special to us all.

About a month after she returned to the United States, however, we got a letter from her saying she was concerned for our safety. It hadn't occurred to us how different our lives must have appeared to her. But at the mention of our safety, Adino and I found ourselves facing each other. We were both struck by the same thought: This was something neither of us had seriously considered.

"Honey, do you think we'll ever go back to the States?" I asked Adino.

He looked reluctant even to talk about it. "I don't know. How could we? We've spent so many years here."

"But . . . do you ever think about going back?"

"Yes, I think about it. Then I start thinking about social security numbers, credit, job experience. Do you realize what we did for seven years, Ruth? We peddled literature on the streets. That's what we did for a living. And what American employer is going to call somebody in Brazil for a reference on me? Besides, I don't think we should make any major decisions like that unless God really guides us to do so."

I let the subject drop because it seemed to me,

too, there was no way we'd ever make it back. Latin America—the people, the cities, the country—had been our home. We had found each other here, gotten married here. We had lived like Brazilians over the past seven years. Adino was already thirty-six and I was soon to be thirty. With three growing children we still lived humbly, as we always had. I caught buses to the market with a child on one hip, another by the hand, and my eyes glued to yet another as he grew restless and weary of my warnings about drifting too far away. But Isaac was almost five now, and as the time approached for him to enter school, my preoccupation with the United States grew.

The winter of 1979 found me going to the hospital to give birth, by caesarean section, to our fourth baby. At the same time, though with much reluctance, I decided to have a tubal ligation—no more children. Adino had reservations about that because we both had been against artificial birth control since our COG days. But we also knew childbearing was becoming more difficult for me each time.

After we took Jeremy, our dark-haired, handsome baby boy, home to meet his excited brothers and sister, we realized our talks around the house about the United States were becoming more frequent. Adino and I now agonized over what had developed from a nebulous idea to a serious possibility. We watched Isaac and Aurora playing with the neighborhood children, listening to them yelp out their delights in Portuguese, which they had learned from the maid and their friends.

As the days passed, Adino and I discussed another reason for staying in Brazil. We didn't know what the United States held in store for two spiritual expatriates and their children. And we didn't know if we could ever tear ourselves from our memories—good and bad—of Brazil.

America was home. And we knew the day was coming when we would respond to the inner call we both were feeling to return there.

CHAPTER
Sixteen

On October 28, 1980, we flew into the Miami airport. As we walked off the plane we received our first taste of culture shock. Everything seemed ultramodern—the long, silver escalators, the sleek cars . . . We felt as though we'd stepped into a future-world. After living in South America for eight years it all seemed incredibly luxurious.

As we retrieved our bags I realized I had missed nearly all of the seventies. The country had witnessed the fall of Saigon and the end of the Vietnam War; the fall of a president and the end of the presidency as we knew it; the fall of hemlines—and the end of an unusual decade. The big news at the time was that a number of hostages had been held in Iran for more than a year, and this was a threat to the presidency of Jimmy Carter, a man about whom I had heard little.

As we walked through the airport gazing at the

people and their fashions, the automated tellers, and push-button phones, we felt as though we'd stepped out of a time capsule. Adino had been right about the problems we would face in trying to adjust to American life. Everything happened quickly around us, and everyone seemed to be in a great hurry. That would change, Adino assured me, when we got to his parents' farm in Alabama. For now, though, we were a family with four young children, three hundred dollars in cash, and nothing else to speak of.

Our first disappointment came when Adino was unable to rent a car without a credit card and we had to spend almost all the rest of our dwindling funds on a flight to Birmingham. We must have looked like refugees because the management of one of the airlines offered us a back room in which to rest until our scheduled departure. When Adino's parents, two sisters, and their families met us at the airport, I felt like a stranger.

We first stayed with Adino's folks on their seventeen-acre farm, and all we could think about was recuperating from the strenuous twenty-hour journey. The soft, thick carpet on their floors made the place seem like a Park Avenue penthouse. The kids sat spellbound in front of the color TV (as did I), and Adino talked to his brother-in-law about finding work in Birmingham, some seventy miles south, where they lived. Suddenly something exciting came on the TV program we were watching, and Adino's mother yelled into the next room, "Mark! Come look at this!" Adino ran into the room, and I suddenly realized I wasn't married to Adino Eznite anymore. He was Mark Gordon, and I was Ruth Gordon.

We spent a couple of weeks at the farm, then moved in with his sister in Birmingham. I tried to help my sister-in-law with the household chores to ease the burden of her family's generosity toward us. What was left of our three hundred dollars was disappearing rapidly, and I wanted to do what I could.

The first time I went to the grocery store with her, I was astonished by all the brightly colored packages and food items, some of which I'd never seen before. That trip to the store was like walking into a giant treasure chest. I saw familiar items I hadn't thought about for years—and I craved them all. I crisscrossed the aisles ahead of her, ecstatic. "Hey! Look at this! Take a look at these! I can't believe it! Look!" I said gleefully. She just smiled.

Because all that was normal to society seemed foreign to me, I was paranoid about people staring at me when I went to the grocery store, the laundromat, the drugstore, wherever. I was sure they thought I was different in some way. I didn't know what to say to people, what to talk about. Unable to cope with the stress, I often crept into the kitchen after Mark was asleep at night and drank any wine that might be in the refrigerator. I also found myself eating more than usual—not from hunger, but from nervousness. In almost no time, I had gained twenty pounds.

My self-esteem began to plummet and the stress

began to build as the weeks passed and Mark couldn't find work. It was the end of the year and no one was even interviewing, let alone hiring.

Finally, just a couple of weeks before Christmas, he was offered a sales position at Radio Shack. Many men with Mark's varied technical background and training would have felt it beneath their dignity to accept a job like this. But Mark was thankful to find a job that enabled him to fulfill what he considered his God-ordained responsibility as a provider for his family.

When we got Mark's first paycheck we moved into an unfurnished apartment about twenty miles from downtown Birmingham. Although we seemed to be back to square one—in an empty house with no belongings to speak of—we felt wonderful about not having to be a burden on Mark's sister and her family any longer.

One Saturday afternoon we received a visit from a couple of youths from the Baptist church down the street. They tried to hide their embarrassment at our humble living conditions as I apologetically led them into the living room.

Mark and I had wanted to find a church quickly, but there were so many in the area that we didn't know where to begin. When the young people invited us to the service at their church, we gratefully accepted, anticipating the spiritual fellowship we so desperately longed for.

The afternoon after our first visit to the church, we were stunned as a dozen or so people from the congregation marched into our apartment with a truckload of supplies for us. They brought linens, dishes, clothing, a crib, a double bed and mattress, and several sackloads of food. We tearfully thanked them for their kindness and concern for us, and the beginning of hope took seed in our hearts.

Whenever people asked me about our background, I remained elusive. We had come to recognize that the COG was a cult, and the word *cult* carried connotations that I didn't want associated with us at our new church home. I didn't want anyone in our family to be treated differently or ostracized because of our past.

After a few months Mark landed a full-time engineering job with a major U.S. corporation, and we rented a house back in town, closer to his work location. Isaac enrolled in first grade, and I packed him off to school every day with a bag lunch. Everything about us appeared normal on the surface, and that was just as I wanted it to be. We were determined that our children would not suffer for our sins.

After some time, I started to think about Julie Reese, the woman I had lived with in Dallas before I joined the COG, and I decided to call her. I realized that her daughter, Heather, was now twenty-one, a year older than I'd been when I'd known their family. I could hardly believe that the child I knew as a skinny teenager was now capable of making the same decisions I'd made at her age. (Lord forbid!)

The sound of Julie's voice was wonderful. At first it sounded a bit distant, as if I were just a memory speaking to her. But she soon warmed up and we talked like old friends. The news that I had four children astonished her; the news that we had left the COG relieved her.

"You know," she said after we'd been talking a while, "our daughter still has the guitar you left behind when you joined the Children of God."

"You're kidding! I forgot all about that!" I told her I had sold my two guitars to help pay for our plane fare home, and she offered to send the guitar her daughter had back to me. I was overwhelmed with her unchanged sensitivity.

We couldn't afford for me to make many calls like that one, so I started a letter-writing campaign to my friends to let them know where I was and that I had broken all ties with the COG. The first letter went to someone I'd thought about for four years: Ken Parks, a missionary whose daughter, Nancy, I had helped win over to the COG. Mark and I learned that many of the COG disciples abroad had begun to return to the United States after the Jonestown tragedy. COG members' parents had become worried that their children would suffer a similar fate, and apparently Moses David had thought it wise to send many of them home (a decision that was, of course, contrary to all his prophecies about "America the Whore"). Nancy Parks, we learned from her father's sad letter, was one of those sent home:

Dearest Ruth and Mark,
    Greetings in the purest name of our wonderful Lord and Savior, Jesus Christ, whose

we are and whom we serve with glad hearts daily. Your letter arrived today, and we hastened to answer it.

Your names came to my attention last year when I was visiting Brazil. Phil and Bonnie Grath told me of your having left the COG. . . . We never got in touch with you. . . . We have been fooled so much by the group that I may have felt that more time was needed before I could contact you and see if your deliverance was real or not.

We know that some have left the group from time to time for convenience' sake only and have gone back into it later. We understand too that some are presently infiltrating American institutions for COG's purposes. Frankly, we wonder if anyone can ever be really delivered from the negative influences of the COG. Undoubtedly an ultimate deliverance can be had through the forgiveness of God and the blood of Christ, but the scars must remain throughout a lifetime. Even for us, we have scars inflicted by [COG].

We had a nice visit with our daughter. After our visit, we got a letter from her advising us not to try . . . to influence her. We had invited her for Thanksgiving, but I don't think she will come . . . the ties are not at all strong, it seems, unless there is a chance of getting more money out of us.

Still, hope lives eternally and we continue to pray for her deliverance. Many

thanks for your letter, and we look forward
to hearing from you again.

Be assured of continued prayers,
Ken and Joan Parks

My heart nearly broke when I read the letter.
Now, though I knew I could never fully compre-
hend it, I better understood what parents of COG
members went through in losing their children to
the cult.

During the next few years I was only able to
maintain sporadic communication with selected
members still in the Family. This was partly due
to our radical change in life-style—we just didn't
have anything in common anymore. Still, I
wanted to make sure they had our stateside address. I didn't want to lose contact with my COG
friends forever. My love for them had remained
strong despite all that had transpired.

But I had no idea how they would react to my
letters. In fact, I had no idea what to say to them; I
only knew that I should—that I had to—tell them
what I now knew was true. I didn't know if they
would want or even be able to hear what I had to
say; but I knew that if anyone could reach them
with the truth about Moses David and the COG
doctrines, it was someone who had lived as they
were living and experienced all they were
experiencing.

First I wrote friendly letters to Andrew and
Reuben, reassuring them of our friendship and
prayers for them. I asked about the music ministry, their children, and all our friends in Rio—

then I told them about the change in our lives. Knowing their position and beliefs, I had to restrain myself from lashing out against the way Moses David had led us astray, in some instances causing irreparable damage in our lives.

I prayed over the letters for days. Finally I sent them off, and I had the peace of knowing I'd acted as the Holy Spirit had prompted me. Nevertheless, I cried inside because I realized I could alienate my friends from perhaps the only voice outside the COG they would ever listen to—the voice of one of their own. I worried for days after the letters were gone until I realized I had to release my concerns to the Comforter, the Holy Spirit. He would do the work that needed to be done.

As the months in Birmingham passed, our children seemed to grow visibly. Isaac suddenly wore the sophistication and experience of a second grader, and Aurora made her kindergarten debut. Three-year-old Nicky began to relish his role as guardian over Jeremy, the youngest. Time was relentless in its progress, never stopping as I wanted it to. And, as I reflected on the never-ending march of time, I realized I could no longer deprive my children of knowing their maternal grandmother.

I had talked to Mom only briefly while in the COG, but I hadn't seen her in ten years. I wondered how she looked, if she'd changed since Dad had died. The letters between us had been few since then, and that bothered me, as did the "lost" years of being separated from her, not only geographically, but spiritually and emotionally. Now she had four beautiful grandchildren she'd never seen. The time had come to do something about that.

I went to the phone and called her, uncertain of how she'd react. But the Lord must have prepared both our hearts because we talked in a way we never had. As I hung up the phone, I started thinking of ways to save pennies for a trip to Santa Barbara. It didn't matter how long it would take—someday I would go home to see my mother.

I started writing more letters, this time to people I had known in the COG who had left the group and settled somewhere in the United States. They wrote back, and over the months we corresponded whenever we could, encouraging and updating each other on our progress since leaving the COG.

One day we got a letter back from an address in Houston: it was from Tamar, the girl who had moved in with Reuben after he had ended our relationship. She wrote to tell us that she and Reuben had married, had a son together, and had left the COG some time after we did. They had settled in Houston during the oil boom, and Reuben had tried unsuccessfully to break into the music business there. Later he had felt the pull of the COG life again and had left Tamar, their son, and her four children by a previous marriage. He returned to a COG colony in Puerto Rico where they had promised him any girl he wanted and leverage in the music ministry there.

I was shocked. Reuben had wanted to have children for years, and finally, with Tamar, he'd had a son. Yet even his only child wasn't enough to make him break from the COG.

The next letter we got was from Andrew, who sounded as if he'd been glad to hear from me. He said the COG were now calling themselves the "Family of Love," for various reasons. He was working in a "system" job in Mexico City as a producer, playing low-key COG songs for one of their programs. He wanted to use some of my songs on the show but knew he should check with me first. He said he gathered from my letter that I had "differences" with some of the COG teachings, and he didn't know if that would be a factor in my decision about the songs.

At first I was furious at the thought of those songs being played to benefit the COG. They had been written with a love for Jesus to be used to bring others to the Lord. The COG would not see one penny from them! Then I became furious with myself: I hadn't been strong enough in my letter to Andrew—I hadn't let him know my true feelings about the COG. This time I would make it clear.

I wrote him another letter, but only after I had calmed somewhat. Again I reassured him of my friendship, but I told him I didn't want him to use the songs and explained why. I didn't hear from him for months, but when I did, he had a strong message for me.

He started out by telling me that my letter hadn't really surprised him, but he had been sad to hear I felt the way I did about the COG. He said he could understand my differences with the Family and with Mo's doctrines about sex and other things, but those weren't really the most important issues (though Christians throughout the world were speaking out against them). He felt I was going too far by saying "Dad" was wrong and that the Family was not of God. He reminded me of the number of souls that had been won in the COG's short history, and then asked how many people I had lead to the Lord since I'd been out of the Family.

He admitted that he hadn't really been litnessing actively lately because his "system" job at the radio station took up his time. But he emphasized that his music program was of the Lord, and that it was bearing fruit and winning souls. He was using the basic Mo letters on his show, and he stressed again that he didn't feel I was being reasonable in disagreeing with them.

Then he wrote something that struck me deeply. He told me that through his music show I had a chance to use my songs to reach the world. While I could decide, he wrote, to keep my songs and talent buried, he warned that if I didn't give these things to be used by people who appreciated them, the Lord could take them away and give them to someone else.

He responded to my assertion that Mo was a false prophet by stating that he himself was a follower of Jesus Christ and believed in Moses David as God's prophet. He then asked me to reconsider my stand, to look at the Family's history and Mo's goals, which were, he said, to teach people how to hear from and follow God and to give his "message of love" to the world. He ended by urging me to forget my differences over doctrines and to consider working with him in reaching the world for Jesus.

I put down the letter and cried. The last thing I wanted was to lose contact with Andrew and the others. But I also knew that I had to say to them what the Holy Spirit led me to say—it was in his hands now.

That afternoon I thought about Andrew's assertions that Mark and I didn't witness anymore and win souls to the Lord. In a way he was right, and that bothered me. I wanted to witness—I had never known greater joy than when leading someone into the saving acceptance of Jesus— but our circumstances now just didn't seem to allow it.

What bothered me most, however, was my music. All the beautiful songs that I knew the Lord had given to me to sing to his glory lay dormant and unused. The COG wouldn't be able to use them, and I realized then that I never would, either. That frightened me.

Also, I wondered if the Lord would really revoke my gift of music, as Andrew had written. Had he already? I hadn't so much as opened my mouth to sing in the two years and I didn't know if I ever would again.

I knew we had made the right decision to follow the Lord out of the COG; but had it cost us the gifts he had given us with such promise years before?

I didn't want even to think about it. I started supper as usual, but when Mark came home I couldn't hold anything back, and the tears started flowing.

"Ruth," he said, wrapping me in his arms. "Listen, listen."

We walked out on the front porch and sat on the steps. The sky reddened as the children ran across the lawn.

"You've got to remember," he said, "those are the people we're praying for. They're not the ones you're supposed to be listening to. We've done too much of that already."

I thought about that for a minute. "Don't you miss witnessing and winning souls?" I asked him.

"Yes, but when we are ready, we'll be able to do it again . . . soon."

In the following days, my faith and my prayer life increased, and I realized that for now, instead of witnessing, I had to pray for those who had gone astray—the Children of God. The COG was indeed battling for people's souls, but now I knew their battle was based on a lie. Their case was polluted by doctrines influenced by Satan through Moses David, and they couldn't see that. So now I fought in prayer for *their* souls.

Still, I worried about the emptiness I felt. Even with the joys and activity of raising the children, I held a longing deep inside to praise God as I once had in music. I talked with Mark about it, but he didn't share my feelings. His work helped channel his energies, and he took comfort and pleasure in providing for his family. He had discovered that, contrary to the negative COG credo about the "system," there were great freedoms in an eight-to-five job. Being able to provide for a family was only one of them. But I wanted to be able to praise the God I loved through my music.

One particularly hectic day after I had rushed all over town hauling the kids with me on my errands, I made my final stop at the post office. We had received notice that there was a package there that was too heavy to be delivered to our home.

The post office doors were closing as I rushed in, red-faced from the humid heat. Gasping for breath, I slapped the yellow package-claim paper on the counter. The crew-cut, fiftyish mail clerk picked it up and looked down the bridge of his nose through his reading glasses. "Oooh," he said, pivoting toward the back room. "You're the one."

Curious, I tapped my fingers on the counter while I waited for him to return. I didn't know what it could be; we weren't expecting anything from anyone.

The clerk came back around the corner, his arms straining to carry the well-taped, oblong cardboard box with "Fragile" marked in bold red letters on each side.

What on earth?

He lifted it with a grunt and placed it on the

counter. There was no return address, but it was postmarked "Dallas, Texas."

"Hope you know what to do with that thing, whatever it is," the clerk said with a sigh. My curiosity proved too strong to wait. I picked up a letter opener from the counter and cut the tape down the front of the box. The top came open and white styrofoam popcorn fell out.

I reached in and gripped something round and hard. I pulled it upward. It was the neck of a guitar; my old nylon-string guitar.

There was a note folded between the strings. I opened it and read:

> Dear Ruth,
>   Mom said you called and she told me what had happened with you. Sorry I've had your guitar so long, but I think you should have it back. You need it more than I do.
>   Thank you for leaving it with me.
>
> Love,
Heather Reese

I brushed away all the white Styrofoam curlicues and felt the excitement build inside. It was a beautiful instrument. I recounted all the old bruises and scratches and noted a few new ones. But I didn't mind—the marks were part of its beauty.

I strummed it. It was out of tune and the strings were old, but it was beautiful music to my ears. I wiped away the tears as I picked the guitar up—my only link to the pre-COG past. It held a lot of tender memories.

"Like I say," chuckled the clerk, "I hope you know what to do with that."

Of course I did; I knew exactly what to do with it. And I knew, once more, that God had heard and responded to the longings of my heart. No, he wasn't taking the gifts he'd given me away. Instead, he'd given me a new life in which to use those gifts—and I would do so, gladly.

EPILOGUE

How does a person readjust to life after coming out of a cult?

I have had anxiety attacks ever since I left the COG. They don't occur as often as they used to, but I believe these attacks were partly a result of the many years of bottling up my emotions. The years in the COG had been especially bad because I suppressed every bit of natural curiosity, doubt, or questioning I had. I constantly denied my conscience, living one way when deep down I believed another.

By neutralizing my conscience, I also suppressed the voice of the Holy Spirit. The doubts I harbored about so many of Mo's teachings were actually the urgings of God's counseling Spirit— *not* simply the result of a misguided upbringing, as the COG inferred. If I could have realized that, I would have spared myself many wasted years and heartaches under Mo's ungodly influence.

It's a tragedy that I couldn't accept the truth many years before I did. But to do so I would have had to face up to the knowledge that I was living a lie—living in darkness rather than in the light of God's truth—and I didn't have the courage to do that. As a result, I sinned by indulging the flesh, following the perverted directives of Moses David and reading of his sexual encounters, which were the basis of many letters, with vicarious enjoyment. Of course we believed, as COG followers always have, that the letters were spiritually edifying.

Though I accepted Mo's teachings and was accountable to my "spiritually appointed" leaders for living by those directives, I was ultimately accountable to the Lord for my actions. Granted, I had been duped by a charismatic, powerfully persuasive man; Mo's knowledge of the Bible and seemingly pure intentions would have appeared honorable to any young zealot whose immature faith wasn't ready to challenge his teachings. The fact remains, however, that the voice of the Holy Spirit did speak to me; I just didn't allow myself to accept it as the Spirit of truth.

Finally God provided the means for me to recognize the error of my ways and to turn from it—and for that reason, I became responsible for my sin. We know from Scripture that the Lord will not tolerate humankind's sin forever (Genesis 6:3), and I thank him that he helped me recognize his voice before I had hardened my heart to it completely.

Now I live with the knowledge that my friends

in the COG are living a lie and continue to suffer (in ways they do not realize) because they accept a lie as truth. I don't allow myself to dwell on that beyond intercessory prayer for them because prayer is the only way I'll be able to reach them. Just as the background and religious training of devout Jews makes it almost impossible for them to accept Christ as the Son of God, the training of a COG disciple makes it almost impossible for an outside force to interfere with his "orthodox" beliefs.

What was once orthodox in the COG, however, has changed several times. In his writings, Moses David has shifted positions on countless issues. They were subject to change with the influence of spirits that he claims speak to him (some with whom he also claims to have had sexual relations): the Dancer, the Pied Piper, Abrahim the Gypsy King, Madame-M, the Abominable Snowman, Grandfather, Heidi, Ivan Ivanovitch, and others. It's hard to believe that anyone could accept such "revelations" as true prophecy from God, but I and thousands of others are testimony to the fact that what begins as one man's delusion can ultimately lead multitudes astray.

Deborah Davis, the elder daughter of David Berg and ex-COG member, has written a book *(The Children of God,* Zondervan, 1983) that chronicles her life with her father and the history of the COG from its origins as Teens for Christ in Huntington Beach in the late 1960s. After the group's migration from southern California in the early 1970s, its name changed to the Revolution for Jesus and ultimately the Children of God. Today it operates under a number of pseudonyms, including the Family of Love, Music with Meaning, and Heavenly Magic.

Many members of the Children of God moved back to the United States under David Berg's direction following the Jonestown tragedy in 1979. Deborah confirms Ken Parks's assertion that most of these disciples returned to make money in "system" jobs that they could take back to their foreign outposts or to gain influence among Americans who might become financial supporters of the COG. Some, however, were "deprogrammed" by professionals like Ted Patrick while living at home with their parents.

Many members of the COG remain abroad, and although observers say the number of COG members has dipped since 1980, their operation still flourishes. The total number of disciples worldwide is estimated by some at close to 10,000 (although David Berg reports considerably higher figures).

I believe that by now Moses David is not even capable of realizing the depths of the lie he has perpetrated or the extent of the damage he has done to countless people, including not only COG members but their families and friends as well. There are no "coming out" programs for COG members, and the vast majority aren't as fortunate as Mark and I were in readjusting to society. At the time of this writing, Deborah Davis's family has two ex-COG members living with them.

One left the COG in 1973 and still hasn't been able to find a job.

The majority of ex-COG members do not follow the Lord Jesus after leaving the group. In most cases, they adopt one of three basic attitudes: (1) the pursuit of materialism, (2) confusion and guilt, or (3) the desire to find a balanced life outside the COG. Most fall into the first category. When the average COG member leaves the group, he's usually in a rebellious state. He thinks he's been "taken" by the COG and its severe lifestyle. He has lived without luxuries of any kind for a long period of time, so his natural tendency is to do exactly what the COG had told him not to do: to gain material possessions, or, for many COG members, to return to their former bondage of drugs or alcohol.

A COG member's life is occupied with constant activities and accountability for his actions, works, words, and thoughts. When a member leaves, he's as free as a bird—there is no one to answer to, no motivation to find Christian fellowship. And there are huge spiritual, social, and emotional voids to fill.

The COG member who leaves the group because he's disillusioned by its practices and beliefs is likely to find himself in a state of confusion. Having disassociated himself from those with whom he identified spiritually for years, he is suddenly in the midst of the people his group condemned for being hypocrites and "spiritually retarded Christians." He probably will suffer doubts about having abandoned the "only true way" to follow Jesus, especially if he encounters Christians who he perceives to be uncommitted or weak. Even if he meets dedicated Christians, he may still be caught by the trap of the COG-mandated prejudices he's built up over the years.

The COG member who leaves, as Mark and I did, because he believes the evil within the group is greater than without, finds himself faced with both the temptation of materialism and confusion regarding God's perfect will. Of course, Mark and I had each other, and we were fortunate for that. But even then we both had trouble adjusting. I leaned for a while on alcohol and food, but they couldn't satisfy the hunger for the moment-to-moment faith in and service to God that life in the COG had seemed to provide. But when anything, even service to God, becomes all-consuming to the point of distortion, it has the power to destroy.

Some ex-COG members never find a way to fill the void in their lives, and they abandon all hope. Having left the COG, they eventually come to believe, as the COG taught them to believe, that they have failed God. And when one has failed God, they reason, what else is there to live for? Because of this, suicide has been the chosen "solution" for some ex-COG members.

Sadly, no one is immune to the lure of cults like the Children of God. But there are danger signs to watch for.

On the surface, many cults appear to operate just as churches do, claiming to feed the spiritual needs of their followers. But cults always deviate in some way from the gospel. Tragically, the hunger for love and acceptance can become so desperate that the false teaching is overlooked and people become sidetracked from the pure and holy message of the gospel. It's actually easy for groups like the Children of God to recruit disciples because they actively seek people who hunger for spiritual purpose. Most of their converts, not surprisingly, are people who are looking for God but who have little knowledge of Scripture and no understanding of the gospel or spiritual maturity.

Once a person joins the group it becomes almost impossible to leave. He sees other disciples promoted and demoted according to their "spiritual" standing. If he produces "good fruit," he is rewarded; if not, he needs spiritual "pruning." What he doesn't realize is that this is nothing more than a judgment of works.

Scriptures are used out of context to justify the cult's beliefs and practices and to give the cult leader unquestioned authority. This, of course, undermines the biblical safeguard that "the anointing you received from him [Christ] remains in you, and you do not need anyone to teach you. But as his anointing teaches you about all things and as that anointing is real, not counterfeit—just as it has taught you, remain in him" (1 John 2:27).

Even though Mark was brought to Christ under the COG's influence, he was so overwhelmed by the experience of accepting Jesus that he kept Jesus' words hidden in his heart. Though he was heavily influenced by the COG and their garbled use of Scripture, Mark had a clear desire to follow the God who had led him to peace and fulfillment. He knew that no man, not even the seemingly infallible Moses David, could provide the kind of peace he found at his conversion. In that sense, he avoided succumbing to the blind trust expected of COG members and of disciples of other cult leaders. Mark's case testifies to the long-suffering and perseverance of the Holy Spirit, who can reach anyone, even those of us involved in cults.

Mark and I realize we are two fortunate and blessed ex-members of the Children of God. At home, we make a point to be affectionate toward one another in front of our children; we want them to know we love each other and will always love them. We cherish our church family. They have nourished us with their unadulterated teaching of God's Word and with the fellowship of other believers whose sole desire is to love God and serve him forever. Mark and I are growing in the Lord's peace each day. We are coming into the full awareness of Romans 8:28: "And we know that in all things God works for the good of those who love him, who have been called according to his purpose."

Because of the many blessings we have received, we realize we now have a duty to warn others of the dangers of cults like the COG. And we shall pray every day for the rest of our lives for those who are still involved.

A FINAL WORD

There are many important issues facing the church today. One of the most profound is that of the cults. The activity of cults and other false religious systems has been steadily escalating and will continue in these last days.

Even though every book in the New Testament has something explicit to say concerning the dangers of false teachers and heresies, the majority of Christians continue to be oblivious to all the implications of cult growth and the real destruction cults cause.

The result is that cults have become the largest unevangelized mission field in our country and beyond. Conservative figures demonstrate that at least 30 million people are involved in cults, with estimates of 80 percent of their converts coming from the pews of mainline denominational churches.

The typical responses of the church have been

either to retreat from the phenomena or merely to critique the cults by way of books or pamphlets. I appreciate the contribution of Ruth Gordon's *Children of Darkness* because it provides for us a personal dimension rather than allowing us to treat the cults merely academically or abstractly. This book gives us some key insights.

One of the first steps in motivating Christians to respond appropriately to the problem of cults is to dispel the notion (or excuse) that people in cults are the enemy. They are not the enemy; they are victims of the enemy. We need to understand that no one is too intelligent, too sophisticated, too spiritual to be deceived by the cults. We need to understand that cults' "doctrines of demons" will cause real personal and family destruction and inevitably leave emotional and spiritual scars.

Cults have been called "the unpaid bills of the church." Indeed, they can be viewed as a thermometer to reveal to us as Christians symptoms of our own weaknesses. Until the body of Christ awakens to the radical nature of Christian commitment, our identity with Christ, and our responsibility and provision to be salt and light, the massive involvement with alternative false religions will continue.

Unless the church is involved in regular Bible study, personal discipleship, evangelism, and missions—unless we are active in ministering love in the body and in the outside community, in developing a comprehensive biblical world—and life-view—people will look elsewhere for answers and reality. For us as individuals and families, Christ must be a daily reality in prayer, decisions, and ministry.

Too often it is the cult groups who reach out to the lonely, hurting, and disenfranchised people. Individually and collectively, the body of Christ needs to reflect the reality of the presence of Christ, otherwise it will become merely an academic, unreal failure.

Finally, the church needs to develop an educational program and an aggressive ministry specifically geared to the cults. Cult awareness and evangelism will serve as a constant reminder for the body of Christ that they must be involved in the solution. Listed below are several good ministries, churches, and individuals to contact for assistance. I agree with Gordon Lewis's words in his forward to *Unmasking the New Age:* "God forbid that in this 'new age' of unparalleled opportunity and challenge, evangelicals will respond with too little too late!"

Craig Branch
Alabama Director, Watchman Fellowship, Inc.

American Family Foundation
P.O. Box 336
Weston, MA 02193

Cult Awareness Network
P.O. Box 608370
Chicago, IL 60626

Personal Freedom Outreach
P.O. Box 26062
St. Louis, MO 63136

Spiritual Counterfeits Project
P.O. Box 4308
Berkley, CA 94704

Watchman Fellowship—
Personal Freedom Outreach:
  P.O. Box 7681
  Columbus, GA 31908

  P.O. Box 13251
  Arlington, TX 76013

  P.O. Box 26062
  St. Louis, MO 63136

  P.O. Box 74091
  Birmingham, AL 35253

Other Living Books Best-sellers

THE ANGEL OF HIS PRESENCE by Grace Livingston Hill. This book captures the romance of John Wentworth Stanley and a beautiful young woman whose influence causes John to reevaluate his well-laid plans for the future. 07-0047 $2.95.

ANSWERS by Josh McDowell and Don Stewart. In a question-and-answer format, the authors tackle sixty-five of the most-asked questions about the Bible, God, Jesus Christ, miracles, other religions, and creation. 07-0021 $3.95.

THE BEST CHRISTMAS PAGEANT EVER by Barbara Robinson. A delightfully wild and funny story about what happens to a Christmas program when the "Horrible Herdman" brothers and sisters are miscast in the roles of the biblical Christmas story characters. 07-0137 $2.50.

BUILDING YOUR SELF-IMAGE by Josh McDowell. Here are practical answers to help you overcome your fears, anxieties, and lack of self-confidence. Learn how God's higher image of who you are can take root in your heart and mind. 07-1395 $3.95.

THE CHILD WITHIN by Mari Hanes. The author shares insights she gained from God's Word during her own pregnancy. She identifies areas of stress, offers concrete data about the birth process, and points to God's sure promises that he will "gently lead those that are with young." 07-0219 $2.95.

COME BEFORE WINTER AND SHARE MY HOPE by Charles R. Swindoll. A collection of brief vignettes offering hope and the assurance that adversity and despair are temporary setbacks we can overcome! 07-0477 $5.95.

DARE TO DISCIPLINE by James Dobson. A straightforward, plainly written discussion about building and maintaining parent/child relationships based upon love, respect, authority, and ultimate loyalty to God. 07-0522 $3.50.

DAVID AND BATHSHEBA by Roberta Kells Dorr. This novel combines solid biblical and historical research with suspenseful storytelling about men and women locked in the eternal struggle for power, governed by appetites they wrestle to control. 07-0618 $4.95.

FOR MEN ONLY edited by J. Allan Petersen. This book deals with topics of concern to every man: the business world, marriage, fathering, spiritual goals, and problems of living as a Christian in a secular world. 07-0892 $3.95.

FOR WOMEN ONLY by Evelyn and J. Allan Petersen. Balanced, entertaining, diversified treatment of all the aspects of womanhood. 07-0897 $4.95.

400 WAYS TO SAY I LOVE YOU by Alice Chapin. Perhaps the flame of love has almost died in your marriage. Maybe you have a good marriage that just needs a little "spark." Here is a book especially for the woman who wants to rekindle the flame of romance in her marriage; who wants creative, practical, useful ideas to show the man in her life that she cares. 07-0919 $2.95.

Other Living Books Best-sellers

GIVERS, TAKERS, AND OTHER KINDS OF LOVERS by Josh McDowell and Paul Lewis. This book bypasses vague generalities about love and sex and gets right to the basic questions: Whatever happened to sexual freedom? What's true love like? Do men respond differently than women? If you're looking for straight answers about God's plan for love and sexuality, this book was written for you. 07-1031 $2.95.

HINDS' FEET ON HIGH PLACES by Hannah Hurnard. A classic allegory of a journey toward faith that has sold more than a million copies! 07-1429 $3.95.

HOW TO BE HAPPY THOUGH MARRIED by Tim LaHaye. One of America's most successful marriage counselors gives practical, proven advice for marital happiness. 07-1499 $3.50.

JOHN, SON OF THUNDER by Ellen Gunderson Traylor. In this saga of adventure, romance, and discovery, travel with John—the disciple whom Jesus loved—down desert paths, through the courts of the Holy City, to the foot of the cross. Journey with him from his luxury as a privileged son of Israel to the bitter hardship of his exile on Patmos. 07-1903 $4.95.

LIFE IS TREMENDOUS! by Charlie "Tremendous" Jones. Believing that enthusiasm makes the difference, Jones shows how anyone can be happy, involved, relevant, productive, healthy, and secure in the midst of a high-pressure, commercialized society. 07-2184 $2.95.

LOOKING FOR LOVE IN ALL THE WRONG PLACES by Joe White. Using wisdom gained from many talks with young people, White steers teens in the right direction to find love and fulfillment in a personal relationship with God. 07-3825 $3.95.

LORD, COULD YOU HURRY A LITTLE? by Ruth Harms Calkin. These prayer-poems from the heart of a godly woman trace the inner workings of the heart, following the rhythms of the day and the seasons of the year with expectation and love. 07-3816 $2.95.

LORD, I KEEP RUNNING BACK TO YOU by Ruth Harms Calkin. In prayer-poems tinged with wonder, joy, humanness, and questioning, the author speaks for all of us who are groping and learning together what it means to be God's child. 07-3819 $3.50.

MORE THAN A CARPENTER by Josh McDowell. A hard-hitting book for people who are skeptical about Jesus' deity, his resurrection, and his claims on their lives. 07-4552 $2.95.

MOUNTAINS OF SPICES by Hannah Hurnard. Here is an allegory comparing the nine spices mentioned in the Song of Solomon to the nine fruits of the Spirit. A story of the glory of surrender by the author of *HINDS' FEET ON HIGH PLACES.* 07-4611 $3.95.

NOW IS YOUR TIME TO WIN by Dave Dean. In this true-life story, Dean shares how he locked into seven principles that enabled him to bounce back from failure to success. Read about successful men and women—from sports and entertainment celebrities to the ordinary people next door—and discover how you too can bounce back from failure to success! 07-4727 $2.95.

Other Living Books Best-sellers

THE POSITIVE POWER OF JESUS CHRIST by Norman Vincent Peale. All his life the author has been leading men and women to Jesus Christ. In this book he tells of his boyhood encounters with Jesus and of his spiritual growth as he attended seminary and began his world-renowned ministry. 07-4914 $4.50.

REASONS by Josh McDowell and Don Stewart. In a convenient question-and-answer format, the authors address many of the commonly asked questions about the Bible and evolution. 07-5287 $3.95.

ROCK by Bob Larson. A well-researched and penetrating look at today's rock music and rock performers, their lyrics, and their life-styles. 07-5686 $3.50.

THE STORY FROM THE BOOK. The full sweep of *The Book*'s content in abridged, chronological form, giving the reader the "big picture" of the Bible. 07-6677 $4.95.

SUCCESS: THE GLENN BLAND METHOD by Glenn Bland. The author shows how to set goals and make plans that really work. His ingredients of success include spiritual, financial, educational, and recreational balances. 07-6689 $3.50.

TELL ME AGAIN, LORD, I FORGET by Ruth Harms Calkin. You will easily identify with the author in this collection of prayer-poems about the challenges, peaks, and quiet moments of each day. 07-6990 $3.50.

THROUGH GATES OF SPLENDOR by Elisabeth Elliot. This unforgettable story of five men who braved the Auca Indians has become one of the most famous missionary books of all times. 07-7151 $3.95.

WAY BACK IN THE HILLS by James C. Hefley. The story of Hefley's colorful childhood in the Ozarks makes reflective reading for those who like a nostalgic journey into the past. 07-7821 $4.50.

WHAT WIVES WISH THEIR HUSBANDS KNEW ABOUT WOMEN by James Dobson. The best-selling author of *DARE TO DISCIPLINE* and *THE STRONG-WILLED CHILD* brings us this vital book that speaks to the unique emotional needs and aspirations of today's woman. An immensely practical, interesting guide. 07-7896 $3.50.

The books listed are available at your bookstore. If unavailable, send check with order to cover retail price plus $1.00 per book for postage and handling to:

Tyndale DMS
Box 80
Wheaton, Illinois 60189

Prices and availability subject to change without notice. Allow 4–6 weeks for delivery.